Praise for *The Te*

'*T* ... n... ...ease retur... ...ath prob... ...therine, the protagonist o... ...novel, aims to solve. In this novel – the scope of whi... ...ggering – Chung has crafted a story that is moving, elegant and richly written. Her prose, as it unfolds, becomes an elusive equation readers will yearn to solve'
Roxane Gray

'An elegantly constructed puzzle of a novel ... what had seemed to be a *Hidden Figures*-style female-genius-in-a-male-world narrative turns into a thrilling back-to-my-roots mystery'
Daily Telegraph

'A most memorable heroine, a sympathetic, mesmerising voice who tells a deceptively simple story centred on identity and a never-ending quest for knowledge and truth'
Irish Times

'Two great enigmas form the centre of this elegant novel, in which a brilliant mathematician attempts to solve the impenetrable Riemann hypothesis and learn the truth of her family history'
New Yorker

'*The Tenth Muse* is keenly aware of how easily the past can be rewritten, achievements and lives subtracted ... A panegyric to women who blaze their own paths, and tell their own stories'
New Scientist

'If you like puzzles, then this mesmerising novel has them all: human, historical and gloriously mathematical. It charts the life of a woman who seeks to conquer the Riemann hypothesis, a quest that could reveal the truth about her own identity and hidden deeds from the Second World War'
Herald

'Ambitious, mesmerising and immersive, *The Tenth Muse* gives us a character we'd follow anywhere, and journeys well worth following her on. This novel dazzles'
Rebecca Makkai

'A page-turning intellectual thriller, a family romance, an alternative history of twentieth-century math – I couldn't put it down'
Elif Batuman

'Catherine Chung has written a deft, spellbinding emotional puzzle-box of a book, rich and intricately layered. *The Tenth Muse* slowly, carefully builds to turn your every expectation on its head, and reading it feels like a glimpse of what mathematics might be in the eyes of its ablest practitioners – both secret and sublime'
Téa Obreht

'Not only is the writing dazzling, this intelligent novel about a woman ahead of her time is also a proper page-turner'
Good Housekeeping

'A truly spellbinding read'
Woman & Home, Book of the Month

'Chung's impressive, poignant second novel explores the intersections between intellectual and familial legacies'
Publishers Weekly

'Arresting in scope and its treatment of time, its prose at turns crystalline and richly balletic, this story pulls puzzle from puzzle – human, historical and all too contemporary'
Helen Oyeyemi

Catherine Chung is the author of *The Tenth Muse* and *Forgotten Country*, for which she won an Honorable Mention for the PEN/Hemingway Award. She has been a National Endowment for the Arts Fellow, a *Granta* New Voice and a Director's Visitor at the Institute for Advanced Study in Princeton, and was the recipient of a Dorothy Sargent Rosenberg Prize in poetry. She has a degree in mathematics from the University of Chicago, and worked at a think tank in Santa Monica before receiving her MFA from Cornell University. She has published work in the *New York Times* and *Granta*, and is a fiction editor at *Guernica Magazine*. She lives in New York City.

CATHERINE CHUNG

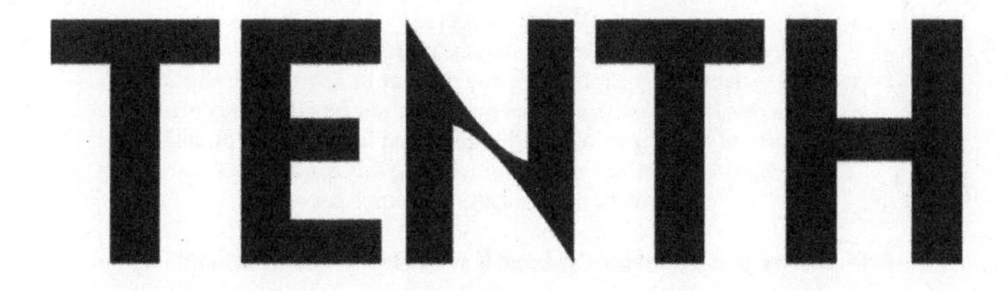

ABACUS

First published in the United States in 2019 by Ecco, an imprint of HarperCollins Publishers
First published in Great Britain in 2019 by Little, Brown
This paperback edition published in 2020 by Abacus

1 3 5 7 9 10 8 6 4 2

A CIP catalogue record for this book is available from the British Library.

ISBN 978-0-349-14280-7

Designed by Suet Yee Chong
Printed and bound in Great Britain by Clays Ltd, Elcograf S.p.A

Papers used by Abacus are from well-managed forests and other responsible sources.

Abacus
An imprint of
Little, Brown Book Group
Carmelite House
50 Victoria Embankment
London EC4Y 0DZ

An Hachette UK Company
www.hachette.co.uk

www.littlebrown.co.uk

For the women who light the way forward,
and for David—here, there, and everywhere

An Invocation

Everyone knows that once upon a time there were nine muses. They were known as the daughters of Zeus, and wise men loved them, for they bestowed the gift of genius. *Sing in me O Muse!* cried Homer, and the muses answered: filling his voice and spinning out his mortal talents to make immortal tales.

What not everyone knows is that once there existed another sister, who chose a different path. She was the youngest of them, and the most reckless, and when she came of age and it was time to claim an art, she shook her head, and she refused. She said she did not wish to sing in the voices of men, telling only the stories they wished to tell. She preferred to sing her songs herself.

Her sisters were shocked at this rebellion from their most beloved sister and ordered her to push these dreams aside. "Don't you know the rule," they said, "that the price of your dearest wish is always everything you have?" But her dreams were her dreams and she was stubborn, and when she refused to turn from them, her sisters offered her their own gifts to choose from, in the hopes that one of them might tempt her. "You may have the epic poem," said Calliope, the most powerful among them. "Just put away this notion, and you may have anything you wish."

But the tenth muse would not be commanded thus, nor tempted, and in the end her sisters bowed their heads and, weeping, prepared to bid their youngest one good-bye. Their tears turned to stars that they hung in her hair, and formed a shimmering veil down her back. The sisters called the birds to sing to her, and the crickets and centaurs—all the sweet-voiced animals in the world. They gave her everything they could in that kingdom of immortals, hoping she would stay, knowing if she left she could take nothing with her.

But she would go.

And so the tenth muse was stripped of her title and her gifts, and immortality. I say stripped, though she was the one who shrugged them off, as lightly as a dress, and laid them quietly aside. What she received in turn was no more, no less than exactly what she'd asked for: a voice to sing with what she would. But of course her voice was now a woman's voice, in a mortal woman's body, and could bring her death, or worse. Still, she never once looked back, choosing to walk among us mortals to the end. She made her fate a human matter, and this is why of all the muses, I cannot help but love her best.

Since then she has told a thousand stories, she has lived a hundred million lives. She is born again in every generation: Sappho. Hypatia. Scheherazade. Woolf. And all the rest unhailed, unnamed, erased. Returning and returning, she is the tale embodied. Long may she live, again.

Chapter 1

There is nothing as intriguing as a locked door. Which is why in 1900 when David Hilbert presented the first of his twenty-three unsolved mathematical problems in his address to the Second International Congress of Mathematicians in Paris, he changed the course of scientific inquiry, and thereby the course of the world. Twenty-three locked doors to beguile the foremost minds of his time: twenty-three locked doors to stand in front of and circle throughout the century. To this day, twelve of these problems remain unsolved. In my youth, I dreamed of scaling the heights myself and drawing forth a solution—as gleaming and perfect as Excalibur. One day, I told myself, I would open one of Hilbert's fabled doors—join the honors class of mathematicians who have conquered one of those twenty-three problems, whose names will be known throughout time.

I've lived long enough to know now that no matter what one's contributions, one falls in and out of favor. Even Hilbert, even Einstein. For now, I am in the amusing, slightly awkward position of finding that while my reputation is on the rise—my actual presence, my opinion, my thoughts, are less relevant than ever. I'm invited less and less to participate in things that involve actual math. Nobody asks me to advise or work with them anymore.

I suppose everyone is waiting for me to die. Certainly no one expects me to be on the cusp of a new discovery. But here's a secret: I've recently found a key to a door that has long been hidden, a mystery I feel I was born to unravel. And not just any mystery, but a door that could lead to the solution of part of the eighth and most famous of Hilbert's problems—the Riemann hypothesis, which predicts a meaningful pattern hidden deep within the seemingly chaotic distribution of prime numbers.

I've told no one yet because I know that until I have all the evidence in order, I'll be laughed at—the same as if I suddenly announced I'd fallen in love. At my age, all passions look foolish to outside eyes. If I were a man, it'd be different. I don't mean that as an admission of envy, but as a statement of fact. Because who has time for envy anymore? The days speed by so quickly, gaining momentum with each passing month. The fear that I'll die before I get to the end fuels my work, and I wake with an urgency that feels like an echo from youth—a reflection of the desperation I felt in my early years when I feared I'd miss my chance.

Perhaps this is why I dream more and more of people from my grad school days, my old competitors and colleagues, my professors, and especially Peter. In my dreams, everyone is dying. They lie down one by one in perfectly ordered graves that proceed along a straight line, head to toe, forming a road that points at the horizon. I ask them where this road leads, and each time I ask my question, they smile and reach up to close their own coffins, shut their eyes, and die.

Good-bye and good riddance, I'd say, if the dream ended there, but then I notice that the closed coffins have numbers and symbols on them, and the string of them forms an equation strangely familiar to me—one that I know the solution to. So I walk up and down, trying to figure it out—whether I should be walking in the direction of the heads or the toes, whether what I need to find is the beginning or the end, until I realize that no matter what, in the line of infinite coffins that stretches out to the ends of the earth, one coffin is missing, and it is mine. And then I know that the missing piece of the formula, the key, is my death, and that I will lose the answer in completing it, and I wake up furious, and cursing, and filled with a terrible grief.

All my life I've been told to let go as gracefully as possible. What's worse, after all, than a hungry woman, greedy for all that isn't meant to be hers? Still, I resist. In the end we relinquish everything: I think I'll hold on, while I can.

MY RECENT DISCOVERY is rooted in the work and time of another mathematician, named Emmy Noether, and those who orbited around her. It was during her time that we began to anticipate how complex things might get without yet being entrenched in that complexity—like standing on the brink of chaos. And what company she stood with, on that very brink! It was the time of Bohr, of Heisenberg, Wittgenstein, Gödel, Einstein, and Turing. Quantum mechanics was being born, as was modern atomic theory, relativity, the computer, the uncertainty principle, the black hole, and the nuclear bomb.

It was an exciting time, but everything was in disarray—there was the rubble of creation, the rubble of destruction. We were at the heights, from which we imagined we could see everything—not just what we knew, but all the possibilities as well—a theory explaining everything, and its inverse: the collapse of science, of language itself. We were on the brink of understanding God, or killing him forever, we didn't know which. Exhilaration and dread came together, and the knowledge that no great discovery can come without bringing an equivalent terror.

It was around that time that Schieling and Meisenbach exploded onto the scene with a brand-new theorem that dazzled everyone who read it and seemed to sketch a possible opening to the Riemann hypothesis—a hypothesis some mathematicians say is too beautiful not to be true, and others say would be akin to proving the existence of God.

This theorem captured the attention of every major mathematician who mattered then and was quickly labeled a triumph for the side of order and beauty: an attempt to knit together the chaos. And even after the proof was reviewed, and tested, after a public cheer went up, even after Einstein himself made it known that he would like to shake their hands, neither Schieling nor Meisenbach stepped forward. It eventually became known that Meisenbach had been a student of Noether's at the University of Göttingen before she was exiled by the Nazis. Though he'd remained there in Göttingen through the war and afterward, his partner Schieling had disappeared shortly before publication of their paper.

In deference to his partner, in silent vigil, Meisenbach refused to appear for any of the honors offered to him, and he never spoke of the man who'd coauthored what would be his greatest contribution to the field. Instead, he waited for word or news of Schieling's whereabouts. Word never came. And so Schieling, vanished, and

Meisenbach, silent, were both forgotten, lost to the turmoil of their times. It would be shocking how quickly this happened, given their contribution, but they were working during one of the most exciting times for science, and also the most dangerous. The world order was changing on every level: to quote Newton, for every action there is an equal and opposite reaction, and the earnest idealism that had briefly ignited the hearts of students all over the continent of Europe in the aftermath of the First World War had been overtaken by fury and nationalism.

The sky was opening. The gods had fallen. Fascism had gained its foothold: Mussolini was leader in Italy; Hitler was on the rise in Germany. The mood of the times was turning murderous. And so the war came, and bombs were dropped and schools were closed and the Jews and homosexuals, the dissidents and handicapped were led away as their neighbors watched on, and so many, so many were killed.

Emmy Noether was the first of the mathematicians in Göttingen to lose her job, and she went to America to live and work, where she died very soon after. Göttingen, that haven, that bastion of mathematics and science, was overtaken by Nazis. Courant was gone. Klein was gone. Everyone who could escaped to England or America. When asked what would happen to the famed mathematics department, now gutted, Hilbert responded, "What mathematics? There is no mathematics in Göttingen anymore." And such was the loss in the realm of mathematics and science, and such was the loss in the world, that no one noticed too much when both Schieling and Meisenbach were forgotten.

Until me.

I entered their story decades after they were lost to anonymity—their beautiful theorem referenced and used, but old enough that no one asked anymore what had happened to its authors, no one

Chapter 2

I SUPPOSE I SHOULD WARN YOU THAT I TELL A STORY LIKE A woman: looping into myself, interrupting. Things have never seemed straightforward to me, the path has never been clear. When I was a child, first discovering numbers, the secrets they yielded, the power they held, I imagined I would live my life unchecked, knocking down problem after problem that was set before me. And in the beginning, because I outstripped my classmates, my parents, and even my teachers, it seemed possible that it would be so. That was pure hubris. I would have been better off reading Greek tragedies.

The first thing I remember being said of me with any consistency was that I was intelligent, or quick—and I recognized even then that it was a comment leveled at me with disapproval as much as admiration. Still, I never tried to hide or suppress my mind as some girls do, and thank God, because that would have been the beginning of the end.

I GREW UP in the 1940s and 1950s in the small town of New Umbria, Michigan. The women there were mothers or grandmothers, a handful of elementary-school teachers and maids, the town librarian, and the school nurse. Back then, we were expected to get married and settle down, not go to college or have careers. But my family and I were newcomers where most residents went back multiple generations, and so while I never really fit in—or perhaps because of it—I also never felt that such rules applied to me. Before, we had lived in Virginia, but we had moved when I was young enough that I had no memories of this. When anyone asked me where I was from, I didn't know how to answer. All I knew was the answer was not New Umbria or Virginia, because whenever I gave those as answers, I was always met with more questions. "No, where are you really from?" Or, "Where are your parents originally from?"

When I asked my parents, "Where am I really from?" they would change the topic, or look sad, or tell me not to be bothersome. "You were born in Virginia," my father said, "as was I. And that's the end of it."

My mother had been born in China, but when I asked her anything about it, she always said, "I don't know." And I believed she didn't know in the way I didn't know. I thought perhaps China had been for her like New Umbria was for me, a place she didn't belong, which had never felt like home, and that was how she ended up in America, with us.

Neither of my parents had any living relatives, so there was no one else I could ask. To some degree I accepted this uncertainty as part of who I was in the context of our town, but also in the larger context of life and history. I felt as if I lived outside of time and place, like in a fairy story.

Many of the things I believed to be true would turn out to be wrong, but this is what I was sure of back then: my father was a war hero with a medal to prove it, and he had been hired as the lead machine engineer at the New Umbria Glass Company, so he was treated with respect wherever he went. As his wife, my mother was usually afforded some modicum of courtesy, but she was Chinese by birth, and so we were never very sure what response she—or I—would provoke, wherever we went, where we were always the only ones of our kind. I heard her called a dirty Jap once, and China Doll, and Red China, and while I flushed red with shame, my mother never so much as flinched at the slurs, so that I was never sure that she heard them. In any case, she was also very young and beautiful, and drew looks and comments wherever we went.

These facts alone made her extraordinary, but she was different for other reasons as well: she was happiest, it seemed, lying in our backyard on her stomach, watching lines of ants file by, or the grass wave in the breeze. She was always dressed as if for winter—in long sleeves and thick stockings—and did not do typical mother things; it was my father who took care of us, the one who cooked and bought our groceries and clothes. My mother's attention drifted elsewhere—to the seeds spiraling down in the wind, or the distant wingbeats of birds, or the passing shadows of clouds. For the most part she was quiet, often subdued, and prone to periods of sadness. She touched me very rarely, and even those instances were less and less as I grew older, though I longed for them.

Between my mother and father there was kindness, and I think respect—but there was also an unbreachable distance. They never touched each other, and in fact rarely spoke, though it seemed to me my father was always trying to make her happy—bringing home pretty scarves that he draped over her chair, or leaving heart-shaped rocks on the kitchen counter, which she tucked into her pocket with a smile. She spoke with an accent and told me stories about brave princesses and angry kings, and the story of the tenth muse. Everything she told me felt like a secret, with a message hidden inside.

I told her secrets, too—about the spiral I saw twirling out from the cut side of a cabbage when she sliced it in half, and how it echoed the spiral I'd once seen on the shell of a snail. The way one half of a leaf was a perfect mirror of the other half. I told her about the games I played with numbers, how I'd noticed that two odd numbers added together always made an even one, or how an odd number and an even always made an odd. And my mother listened, and nodded, and told me there were patterns everywhere in nature, and that numbers held their own hidden stories that unspooled if you followed them far enough along—stories that once you knew the beginning ran on and on. Even back then, I realized the power of what my mother was telling me: that numbers underlay the mysteries of nature. That if you could unlock their secrets, you could catch a glimpse of the order within.

I did quite well in school until third grade, when I was assigned to the class of a teacher who took an instant dislike to me. Mrs. Linen was a stiff, lean woman with little patience, and was in the habit of giving us busywork, which we were supposed to complete in silence. I had gotten in trouble more than once for completing this work too quickly, but it came to a head one day when she asked us to solve 1 + 2 + 3 + 4 + 5 + 6 + 7 + 8 + 9 and went back to her desk.

I raised my hand immediately, and when she sat down at her desk and took out a folder, and seemed likely not to notice my outstretched arm, I waved it around, stretching forward in my chair.

She looked up. "Yes?"

"Forty-five," I said.

"Forty-five?"

"That's the answer."

Mrs. Linen sighed. "How many times do I have to tell you, guessing does not count?"

She had, in fact, said this to me many times, and each time it had wounded me. "I'm not guessing," I said. "I never guess."

She stood up then and strode to my desk. She picked up my paper, and when she saw it was blank, she cried, "You didn't even write the problem down! If you don't show your work, you get no credit. Now stop wasting my time."

Back then this idea of showing work was one of the most difficult concepts for me to understand. What did it mean to show your work? Why did I have to write something down if I understood it perfectly? And when was it necessary, and when was it not? For instance, if I didn't have to show my work to say $1 + 2 = 3$, why did I have to show my work for $1 + 2 + 3 + 4 + 5 + 6 + 7 + 8 + 9 = 45$? How were they different? This was a far more complicated idea for me than that of simple sums because it involved tracking the movements of my own mind, which was a skill that took me much longer to learn.

Now I would be able to tell you that I had solved the problem so quickly because I'd realized a simple pattern: that if you took the numbers on the opposite ends of the sum, 1 and 9, and added them together, they equaled 10. So did the next two numbers moving inward: 2 and 8. As did 3 and 7, and 4 and 6, with only 5 left over. So four tens and a five. Almost two centuries ago Carl Gauss had presented his teacher with the formula to solve a similar problem, but that explanation took more sophistication than I was capable of back then: for me, math and its attendant pattern-making was purely intuitive.

Perhaps this is what frustrated Mrs. Linen about me—the inner workings of my mind were inaccessible to myself, and thus, to her.

After standing over my desk sternly for a moment, she said, "Very well, add 1 + 2 + 3 + 4 + 5 + 6 + 7 + 8 + 9 + 10 + 11 + 12 + 13 + 14 + 15 + 16 + 17 + 18 + 19."

"One hundred ninety," I answered at once. (This I was able to deduce because of course it was the same as the first answer added to itself plus 10 tens.)

"Nonsense," she said.

"One hundred ninety," I said.

Mrs. Linen went to her desk and began writing. After her hand stopped moving, she looked down for a long moment. Then she looked up, met my eye, and said, "You don't know everything."

"I know," I said. Of course I didn't—that was the unmet goal, wasn't it, toward which I was hurtling as fast as I could, headlong?

She stood up and went to the front of the blackboard. "Katherine, please come here to the front of the room," she said.

I obeyed.

She took a piece of chalk and drew a small circle on the blackboard. "Put your nose inside the circle and do not move at all until class is over," she said. This was a punishment she reserved for the worst infractions in our class: when boys fought or said bad words, they were often made to stand in front of the classroom like this. I was the first—and it would turn out, only—girl to be punished this way.

When I hesitated, Mrs. Linen put her hand on the back of my head and pressed it against the blackboard until my nose was firmly squashed in the center of the circle she'd drawn.

The other children had only ever been made to stand like this for half an hour, but I stood for over two hours with my face pressed against the blackboard. My knees grew stiff and my back started to ache. I kept waiting for Mrs. Linen to release me, but even after the last bell had rung to announce the end of school, and I turned away from the board to leave, Mrs. Linen said, "I did not give you leave to move, Katherine."

I knew I would miss the bus if I didn't go with the rest of my classmates, but I pushed my nose against the board again and felt as if anything could happen.

I heard Mrs. Linen leave the room. Still, I did not move. I heard her return and sit down at her desk. I heard her shuffle through some papers. I heard the scratch of her pen. And then after some very long minutes, she said, "You may take a seat, Katherine."

So I went to sit at my desk, my legs trembling.

"I called your mother," Mrs. Linen said. "She's on her way."

MY PARENTS ARRIVED TOGETHER, tense and unsmiling. They greeted Mrs. Linen and sat beside me in the small student-size chairs.

Our classroom was decorated with maps and giant-size letters and drawings, and my teacher stood in front of them. She struck an imposing figure, and it was only then that I noticed how out of place my parents looked, squeezed into child-size furniture. My mother, especially, looked ill at ease, and this frightened me. Until that moment, my parents had been the ultimate authorities in my world. And now I felt as if I had gotten them into trouble, as if they had to answer to Mrs. Linen as well.

"Your daughter refuses to follow instructions," Mrs. Linen said. "She won't show her work, and she skips ahead without waiting for instructions."

"I'm not sure I understand what you mean," my father said. "Is she in trouble for being advanced?"

"No," said Mrs. Linen. "She reads ahead and interrupts. She doesn't listen, and she shows off. It disrupts my lessons and makes the other children feel bad. I won't have it in my classroom."

"That's not true," I gasped. "I listen."

"This is what I'm talking about with the outbursts," Mrs. Linen said. She shook her head. "No self-discipline, I'm afraid."

"I have self-discipline," I interjected, but my father held up his hand to silence me and nodded at the teacher. "We'll talk to her," he said. "We'll see to it that she behaves."

"Please be sure that she does," Mrs. Linen said. And then she motioned at the door, to say she was done with us. My parents stood up quickly, my mother took me by the hand, and we left.

AT HOME my father sat me down and said, "Tone it down."

"I didn't do anything wrong," I said. "I answered her questions."

"Then do it without showing off," my father said.

I flinched. The problem was I enjoyed answering questions. Numbers were predictable and knowable, and I liked getting them right. Why was it bad to take pleasure in this? Why was it necessary to pretend otherwise, when the thing I loved most about numbers was their very straightforwardness? Other children were praised when they answered—only I was punished. Tears sprang from my eyes. I choked them back.

My mother, sitting silently next to me, unexpectedly reached over and took my hand. I sidled up to her, eager for comfort. "Katherine," she said, and her voice was kind. "Do your best. No matter what anyone says. Next year you'll have a different teacher, and things may change then. Life is long, and nothing lasts forever. So don't worry, and maybe for now, don't draw attention to yourself." My mother often said things like this that seemed both wise and wrong at the same time: my best could not help but draw attention—that was the problem.

"Why do I have to do as she says?" I asked. "What if she's wrong?"

"She's your teacher," my father said. "She's in charge, and you have to treat her with respect, not think that you know better than her."

The injustice of this choked me. But I told my parents I would do as they said. And I did. I stopped talking in class, and soon I stopped listening, too. I read my textbooks and ransacked the school and public libraries for more. Because it was impossible to please my teacher, I learned to please myself. I stopped trying to follow her guidance and followed my own interests instead.

The following year my new teacher immediately skipped me forward a grade, and for the most part things were much better. Still, I have always thought of my confrontation with Mrs. Linen as a defining moment from school. It was how I became a freethinker, the moment I learned to distrust authority and question whether grown-ups had my best interests in mind. For that, I am grateful, because without this early preparation, I would never have made it in life. Still, I wonder now why it had to be necessary, and why my teacher disliked me so much—whether it was because I was a girl, or my family wasn't from New Umbria, or because I was half Chinese. But it occurs to me now that even if those were not the reasons she treated me badly, they were the conditions that made it possible to do so.

Chapter 3

THE FIRST THING I EVER OWNED WAS A NOTEBOOK that my father gave me before I can even remember. My father had brought it back from the war as a souvenir, he told me—he liked the look of it. It was made of soft brown leather, with a cord that wrapped around it. Inside, the whole book was stuffed with writing. It filled the pages and looped around the margins—words in German I couldn't read, as well as formulas and symbols, and incredibly precise, small graphs and drawings, all in a handwriting that was nearly impossible to decipher. On the front page were the initials S. M., and beneath that, Universität Göttingen, 1935.

When I asked my father where he'd gotten this book, how he'd acquired it, he would never answer—only say that it seemed like something I might want someday. He refused, as a general rule, to talk about the war or his experience in it. I knew he'd shattered his right arm and been sent home, that he'd been told he'd never regain full use of it again, except that against all expectations, he had.

The one time I pressed him for more information about what he had done as a soldier and what the war had been like—I must have been seven or eight at the time—he dropped his head in his hands and wept. I had never seen him cry before, and the suddenness of his grief and his inability to overcome it terrified me so much that I didn't ask again. It made a deep impression on me—that even the memory of war, years later, was too terrible to discuss.

As I grew older I couldn't help but wonder about all the things my father wouldn't tell me. I wondered if he had killed anyone. I knew he probably had, of course—that's what soldiers did. It was their job. But my mother wouldn't tell me either. Her past was even more a mystery than his. Sometimes I heard her cry out at night, and when I ran to my parents' bedroom to see what was wrong, the door was locked against me. When I pounded, she or my father would respond from the other side, "Don't worry, Katherine, it was just a nightmare," but their voices were strained and they never let me in.

Sometimes I had nightmares, too, that I woke up crying from. They were always the same—I came upon my mother's body in the creek that ran through our town, her body caught by a branch, being pushed back and forth by the water. My father stood over her with a gun. After these dreams, I crawled to the door of my parents' bedroom in the dark and curled up against their door. When my parents found me in the morning and asked me why I did this, I couldn't answer, couldn't tell them I was afraid that they would die and leave me utterly alone. I had learned the silence of my parents well. I knew all my grandparents were dead, but neither my mother nor father discussed them, much less how they'd died or when. That topic was off-limits, but I felt the proximity of those losses, the enormity of them, and was afraid that if I voiced my fears, they would come true.

One day I begged my parents to promise they would never die.

And when they promised, I protested. "But that's impossible. Everybody dies."

My father laughed and said I was too clever, but my mother sat down on the floor next to me and said she would tell me a story.

The Story of the Wise Princess Kwan-Yin

Once upon a time, there was a king who had three daughters, and of the three he loved Kwan-Yin best. She was kind to everyone, especially the suffering and the poor. The king had no sons and declared that whomever she married would be heir to his throne, and she would be queen. Kwan-Yin did not wish to marry, or to rule a kingdom, and begged her father to reconsider.

"I do not want to live in wealth or power when others are sick and in pain," she said. "Instead, let me join a convent, where I could study and devote my life to serving those in need."

Her father the king was angered by her request, but because he loved her, he reminded her with gentleness that of all the virtues, filial duty was the most important. He would not grant her wish. Instead, he would choose a husband for her and in one month hence, they would marry, and she would rule as queen.

When Kwan-Yin saw she could not change his mind, she ran away. A convent took her in, but the nuns were cruel there, believing she was just a simple beggar. They beat her and made her work until her hands cracked and bled. Still, she was good to all she met and gave everything she had to those even less fortunate than her.

Then one day, an army came to the gates to take Kwan-Yin back to her father's kingdom. There, he gave her this choice: accept the man he'd chosen and rule, or die. Kwan-Yin was executed that very day.

Upon her death she was sent to the gates of heaven. The angels and gods and goddesses who dwelled there bowed to her and said, "In your infinite goodness you surpass all who dwell here. You may rule here as a goddess."

But again, Kwan-Yin refused. She said she could not enter heaven when there was so much suffering on earth. Instead, she said, she would sit upon a mountain peak inside a lotus heart and listen to all appeals for mercy, offering what aid she could. She would only enter heaven after all earthly suffering was eased.

"SO," MY MOTHER SAID, "if ever you're afraid or suffering, you need only to pray to Kwan-Yin, who sits on a mountain, listening for the cries of those who need her help. She won't rest until every living being has attained enlightenment."

"What's enlightenment?" I asked.

My mother thought. "An awareness that transcends suffering," she said. "A consciousness that lets you rise above it."

UNTIL I WAS NINE YEARS OLD, I'd been terrified of lightning. When it stormed I'd hide in the bathroom, which was the most interior room in the house. During one particularly intense storm, my father coaxed me out and took me to where my mother sat on the porch. "Your mother isn't afraid," he said. "Look at her. She loves the storm."

My mother was curled in a chair, a blanket wrapped around her against the chill, her eyes bright with rare happiness. She saw me and smiled. Another bolt of lightning split the sky, and she began counting aloud: "One one-thousand, two one-thousand, three one-thousand," and when she got to six one-thousand, she turned to me and exclaimed, "Now, Katherine! The thunder is coming now!" And just then the thunder cracked.

"How did you know?" I gasped. I was so astonished that I forgot in that moment to be afraid.

"Come here and watch with me," she said as she unwrapped the blanket that surrounded her, and opened up her arms, and let me scamper in. I leaned back with a sigh of happiness.

For the rest of that afternoon she let me sit in her lap, her arms loose around me, except when lightning streaked across the sky, and then her arms would tighten, and she'd hold me close. It felt as if we were part of the storm that way, and it was exhilarating. She taught me how to count the seconds between lightning strikes and cracks of thunder and told me the shorter the time between the two, the closer the lightning was to us. We tried to guess the patterns to predict when the lightning would come, and when we guessed right, we shouted with laughter, and I imagined we were the ones controlling the weather, making the light flash against the sky. I was hooked. From that moment on, I stopped flinching at the sound of thunder and anticipated it instead.

THE NEXT WEEK, we checked out a book on lightning from the public library, and I learned a bolt of lightning contains one billion volts of electricity and is five times hotter than the sun. I learned that lightning is electricity that opens a hole in the air, a channel that collapses back in on itself when the current leaves it, causing the boom we call thunder.

"The air shakes," I explained to my mother. "That's what makes the noise."

"What causes the lightning, though?" she asked. "What makes it hot?"

So I showed her the part in the book that said clouds are tiny droplets of water that hang together in the sky, and how when bits of ice move around and collide, they create an electric charge, which fills the cloud. The particles in the cloud separate, and the lighter positive particles rise toward the top while the heavier negative ones fall to the bottom. In the end, lightning is all about attraction: the low-hanging negative charges in the clouds pull on the positive particles in the ground, which climb as high as they can up anything that stands up, like a lightning rod, or a person, or a tree. The attraction between the sky and the ground builds and builds, until the electrical charges finally burst toward one another, tearing a hole through the air in their haste to connect.

"What are particles, though?" I asked my mother. "What's a positive or negative charge?"

We went back to the library to find a book about protons and electrons, and I learned everything in the world is made of particles, of atoms, and charges that hold us and the entire universe together. It would be a while before I learned about the math underlying these relationships, but that's how I began to learn about wind currents and weather, the stars and the sun. Whenever it stormed, my mother and I went to the porch to watch. My mother never instilled in me a sense of family history or tradition, but she did give me a reverence, an awe for nature—and the belief that I could get closer to it by learning how it worked.

MY FATHER HAD NOTED my interest in science and was always showing me little things—how if you put a marble in an empty light socket and then flipped the switch on, the marble would shoot out with a pop. He built me a combination lock out of wood, and a burglar alarm that went off when you opened the lid to its box, as well as a little train set that went round and round. I still have a scar on my cheek from when we blew the cap off a bottle with acetylene and water—my father lost his grip on the bottle and accidentally pointed it toward me as it burst off. I felt no pain when it sliced into my cheek, but I remember my father shouting in alarm. A moment later I put my hand up to my face and felt something slick and warm on my fingers. When I looked at them, they were shiny and red with blood.

"Oh dear," my father said, kneeling in front of me and wiping my face with a dirty rag. "Let's not tell your mother how this happened."

Injuries notwithstanding, I loved these projects my father took on and always wanted to be a part of them. One day, he brought home a pile of the parts needed to build a ham radio and asked if I wanted to help him put it together. It took us a week, and we built it at our kitchen table, which meant that for that week we ate dinner on our laps in our living room, our plates warming our legs, our water glasses on the floor. We ate with the windows open as the breeze blew in, and we watched our neighbors tending to their gardens and sitting on lawn chairs, or children riding their bikes, shouting.

After dinner, my father went straight to the kitchen table where he'd left a mess of wire and cables and vacuum tubes, and got to work. I started by helping my mother clean up, but then I went over to him, leaning over the part of the radio he was working on to study the diagrams and assembly instructions.

Once the receiver was built, we took it into the garage and built a simple transmitter. Then we studied for the radio license, quizzing each other on Morse code and electrical principles and radio wave characteristics every night. My father already knew all of it from the war. He'd been a radio operator as a soldier, and he told me how radio waves could go far, far out into space—and how a few years ago two radio operators from opposite sides of the world had sent messages to each other by bouncing them off the moon.

After we received our radio licenses, we spent many nights sitting side by side in the garage, picking up radio stations and messages from other amateur radio operators. There were so many messages floating around, waiting to be picked up: Are you lonely? How are you? What's the weather like there? There were reports of shipwrecks, and messages from as far away as Canada—and we decoded each message as it arrived. Nowadays, when communication is so instantaneous, I cannot help remembering with nostalgia how my father and I turned the knobs to the contraption we had built as the messages came in through our complicated machine of vacuum tubing and plumbing wire. We recorded the taps as they came in—and I marveled that each tap traveled only a little bit slower than the speed of light. *Tap tap tap* came the pulses of radio waves into our earphones, and I transcribed the taps as fast as I could into letters, watching them gather into words and then sentences. It was the closest thing to performing magic that I could imagine: manipulating the radio waves that were all around us to talk to someone across the world.

That radio was also my first taste of anonymity: no one knew what I looked like, or how old I was, or whether I was male or female, adult or child. When these things did come up, my fellow ham radio operators were always surprised to discover I was a girl, but their manner toward me rarely changed, at least insofar as I could notice. The sense of belonging I felt because of that was freeing in a way I have never experienced since.

My father and I never told each other what we were saying over the radio, and I never decoded his messages. As far as I know, he never decoded mine. We took turns, sitting silently for hours, keeping each other company into the night. Sometimes I leaned into him, and he reached his arm around my shoulders and operated the radio one-handed. It was, I suppose, such a small and regular thing—to sit at a table in a garage next to my father every Sunday evening, taking turns transmitting messages. But in those moments I felt closer to my father than I ever had, or ever would again.

Chapter 4

THE SUMMER BEFORE I ENTERED TENTH GRADE, MY mother left my father. That's always been the official story, as if it was primarily a marital rift, as though when she left my father, she didn't leave me, too. She left while I was at the library—she packed up and went, taking our only car, without warning, without saying good-bye.

"Why didn't you stop her?" I asked my father, when he told me she was gone. "What were you thinking?"

He sighed. "When someone wants to go, you can't stop them." Pausing, he seemed to consider what he was going to say next and continued, "She'll come back for you. When she's settled, she'll come back for you and take you with her." He looked so sad, and I imagined him alone in our house, and the thought was unbearable.

"Daddy," I said, and I went to him. "I don't understand."

"It's just the two of us now," he said. He was trying to sound cheerful, but his voice was listless and defeated.

"We'll be all right," I said. I was shaken, but also sure she would return. In my mind, the three of us were alone in the world. We only had one another. It was inconceivable to me that she was really gone.

THE DAY BEFORE SHE LEFT, she'd spent the afternoon with me, looking at trees in our backyard. "Spend a minute," she had said, "looking at the trees. Don't talk, don't think, just look at them. I'll tell you when the minute is up."

And so I'd sat in the grass, my mother beside me, looking at the trees—the way their branches reached out and swayed their leaves in the breeze, the way they shivered and bounced. I'd looked at how the light filtered down and danced through them, and listened to their soft rustling.

When the minute was up, my mother asked, "How do you feel?"

"Calm," I said. "Happy."

She smiled at me and touched my head. "Okay," she said. "Now turn around and stare at our house. I'll let you know when the time is up."

And so I looked at our house—the grooves in the wood, the gleam of the window, the paint chipping at the corners, the gutters filled with leaves.

When my time was up, my mother asked, "Did it feel different?"

"Yes," I said. "It felt harder, somehow, like everything I was looking at was surface, like my mind couldn't just go in, except through the glimpses in the windows."

"Okay," my mother said. "Now I want you to turn around and look again at the trees, but now I want you to imagine that the house is looking at you as you watch." I did this, and immediately felt the little hairs on the back of my neck rise. I felt the house looming over me, watching me; I felt like someone could come out of the house and do me harm while I had my back to it. I couldn't concentrate on the trees at all.

"I don't like this as much," I said, though my mother hadn't said it was time. "I feel like the house is creeping up on me, like it's closer than it really is."

"Interesting," my mother said. "I want you to try just one more thing. Try imagining the trees are looking at you as well as the house, and that you are looking back at both."

"But I don't have eyes in the back of my head," I said.

My mother smiled. "Just throw your awareness backward," she said. "You know it's there. You know what it looks like."

And so I did. I looked at the trees—their leaves and branches, their strong, fine trunks. I looked at the way their roots reached into the ground, while their branches reached for the sky. And I felt them looking back at me. At the same time, I cast my mind backward toward my house—the surface of it, the shingles on the roof, the way the foundation dug into the ground. And I found I could cast my mind inside the house as well, our little kitchen—my mother's armchair, my room on the second floor. I was overtaken by a revelatory feeling—of understanding, of being part of something huge. I could feel the trees, but also the horizon behind them. And I could feel the house, and the horizon behind it too. It felt like doing math—like sensing all the things I couldn't see, but knowing they were there.

"Time's up," my mother said. "How did this one make you feel?"

"Like the world got larger," I said. "No, like my mind expanded. Like my mind was holding the world, and the world was holding me."

"Your mind beheld the mind of the world," my mother said. "And it recognized yours in return." She smiled. "I hope when you are older, you will think of me sometimes when you consider the trees, or when you feel them regarding you in return." Then she reached over and did something she almost never did. She kissed me on the cheek.

I wondered afterward if that afternoon was my mother's way of saying good-bye. But every time I thought this, I banished the thought from my mind. I refused to believe that in exchange for her absence, she made me a gift of those trees.

THIS WAS IN 1957, and my mother's departure became the great scandal of our town. Everyone knew by the end of three days that she'd left. "Another man," the car salesman said when we went to buy a new car. "You can't trust foreigners. No loyalty."

"It must be the Chinese blood," a classmate said when we returned to school. His friend piped up, "My mom thinks your mom's a commie spy."

He said it confidingly, as if I wouldn't care. But it made me aware of how uncomfortable the town had been with my mother's presence, and how gleefully they talked about her once she was gone.

It reminded me of something she'd said once, when we were walking by a pond, which was covered by a thick net of tiny green leaves growing on the surface of its water. They were smaller than my fingernail and dotted with small, fragile white flowers.

"Where I come from," my mother said, "we called this kind of plant duckweed. Look how thick it is, so that you can't see anything underneath it. It comes from nowhere and takes over the pond, covering and choking everything, and then it disappears." She took a stick from the ground and pushed it into the duckweed, which trembled but did not break apart. "Sometimes I think I am like that duckweed," my mother said. "Floating without roots to hold me anywhere, disconnected from everything that I used to think was permanent."

The feeling she described came over me: chaotic and rootless.

"What about me?" I said. "Aren't you connected to me?" But my mother had already stood and begun walking away.

AFTER MY MOTHER LEFT, I felt like my heart had been infested with duckweed: I felt rootless and disconnected, and my thoughts were tangled and messy. Still, as time went on we fell into a new rhythm, and while the town didn't forget what had happened with my mother, that fall its attention turned to the news that the Soviet Union would be launching a dog into space. Almost everyone in those days in my town was invested in the space race, but the source of my obsession was the dog, Laika. She was a stray with a pointed muzzle and stand-up ears that pricked forward, and a sweet, taut body.

They had a million nicknames for her: Kudryavka, or Little Curly, Zhuchok, or Little Bug, and Limonchik, or Little Lemon. I was careful not to enthuse about Laika at school: given the suspicions my classmates continued to harbor about my mother and my own foreignness, I figured it was safest to pretend I wasn't paying attention, in case they considered me disloyal for loving an enemy dog.

At home, I read everything I could about Laika. If I've ever dreamed of being a spy, it was during this time—when I harbored fantasies of entering the Soviet Union with the mission of rescuing her. I knew that scientists were gradually training her to live in a tiny space built inside the heart of the rocket they were launching her in, with only enough room to lie down. The enclosure was stocked with a special food, a gel that she could lick out of a container. A harness would monitor her vital signs. A bag strapped to her hindquarters would catch her waste. Finally, the day came, and they put her into the small dark box that was her home inside the rocket, a home without even a window, and flung her into orbit. It made me sad to think of all the endless stars around her, and no way for their light to reach her.

After the launch, I looked for her night after night in the sky, listened for the signal of her rocket on our ham radio. But none ever came.

On the sixth day into her flight, the Soviet Union reported she had died. When I read the news, I burst into tears. It came to me suddenly that it was possible my mother would never come back to us, and I cried so hard I started to hiccup. I realized I had been wrong about everything: I had thought Laika would survive, but she'd died. I'd thought my mother loved us, but she'd left. I took out a piece of paper and wrote, "The truth is crippling, it does not set us free." I tucked the paper into the leaves of my German notebook. I stared out the window for a long, long time, thinking of my mother, and of Laika, and how it was possible to fall into the space that someone left behind, and be crushed inside, like air falling back into itself within a clap of thunder.

Chapter 5

A mathematical proof is absolute once it has been written and verified: if the internal logic of a proof holds, it is considered unassailable and true. The underlying structure of my family was something I'd never questioned. It had formed the foundation of my life. When it suddenly dissolved, I was unmoored. It had never occurred to me to question my mother's love for me, or our relationship to each other. I had believed these things were absolute.

Still, when my father introduced me to Linda, I hadn't yet given up hope that my mother would return, and I regarded Linda with hostility. She was the opposite of my mother in every way: she was blond and busty and talked all the time. She had been born and raised in New Umbria, and her husband—her high school sweetheart—had passed away eight years earlier, and she'd been alone ever since. When she was at our house, I could hear her stomping around upstairs when I was downstairs, and when I was upstairs,

I could hear her opening and closing doors downstairs with great force. When she wasn't talking to another person, she was talking to herself, or singing. The food she cooked was always drowning in sauce, and she made my father laugh in a way my mother never had. After my father started dating her, our neighbors began inviting them to dinners and barbecues, as they hadn't with my mother. My father always tried to persuade me to join, but I refused.

When, six months after introducing me to her, he told me that he and Linda were getting married, I retorted, "Don't you have to get divorced first?"

My father looked away uncomfortably, then looked back at me. "Listen," he said. "I didn't want to tell you this, but your mother and I were never officially married."

"What?" I was bewildered. "Why not?"

"It's not that we didn't want to. It's that we weren't allowed."

"Who didn't allow it?" I asked. "Your parents?"

"No, our parents were dead," he said. "But it was illegal for us."

"Oh," I said. I felt the power behind the word *illegal*, the way it delegitimized my parents' relationship. The way it delegitimized me. "Why was it illegal?"

"Because your mother and I met in Virginia, which didn't allow whites to marry Orientals," he said, using the word that, back then, was used to describe anyone of Asian descent. "And by the time we moved here, we had you. We were already a family. And we couldn't just go to court and get married—we didn't want people to talk."

We looked at each other. "Legally," I said, "am I considered Oriental?"

"Of course you're not!" my father said. "At least I don't think you are." He rubbed his face. "I mean, what's important is that you're my daughter." He reached out to put his hand on my shoulder, but I shook it off.

I went upstairs. In their bedroom, the things my mother had left behind were still there: the creams in front of her vanity, her hairbrush, and next to it, her wedding ring, smooth and golden. I slid it onto my finger, but it stuck halfway down. I tugged it off. I opened her dresser: the few shirts she'd left behind were still neatly folded in rows, a handful of dainty flowered handkerchiefs tucked beside them. *What had she actually taken with her?* I wondered.

Inside her closet were a few old dresses and a small suitcase filled with papers that turned out to be old grocery store receipts. There was also a tiny spoon bent in half, a stick of wax, and some stamps. *Junk*, I thought. She'd left behind junk. Some shirts, some dresses, a broken spoon, a wedding ring, my father, me. I felt worse than I had before. In the corner, caught up in the dust, were a few strands of her long black hair. I picked them up and shook them off, but they were limp and dusty and felt dead in my hand, and on my way out of my parents' room, I tossed them into the trash.

Linda and my father married two weeks later, just the two of them in front of a judge. She moved in that day, crowding our house with her boxes, pushing aside our things for hers with gusto. Linda's brightly upholstered chairs were shoved between our old couch and my mother's armchair. Her dishes were stacked upon our dishes. It cheered my father to see her things, to have them in our home. He kept saying, "Isn't this great?" but his happiness wounded me. There was less room for me, and no longer any room for my mother to return. As for Linda, she made overtures of friendliness, but I looked away when she was near. Sometimes, I left the room. I mumbled when I spoke to her. I knew it was not her fault my mother had left, that she had nothing to do with her absence, but I resented her for filling that place in my father's life, and I wanted to make clear that she would never fill it in mine. Without articulating it, I think I believed that if I suffered enough, if I believed in it enough, my mother would eventually return to us. So when I had to be home, I was usually in the garage, tapping out messages to strangers, asking them about telescopes.

Our local librarian, Ms. Lorain (may all the librarians of the world be blessed!) had slipped me a copy of the magazine *Sky & Telescope*, and I'd been obsessed ever since. I'll never know how she knew that would be just what I needed—a magazine filled with diagrams of lenses and mirrors and instructions on how to build your own telescope as well as pictures of the glossy ones available for purchase. The only problem was that telescopes were fabulously expensive. Even the parts needed to build one myself were far beyond my reach. I satisfied myself with descriptions of what I would see through them: planets, stars, entire galaxies, invisible to the naked eye. I was a jumble of grief and longing, and I yearned to find my place in worlds beyond my own, to ground myself in science, with its fixed rules that never changed and never lied. I longed to see things on a larger scale, a cosmic scale. The Katherine scale was too close.

I'D ALWAYS KNOWN I wanted to go to college one day, but after Linda moved in, I began to pursue that goal with single-minded purpose. It was the one thing I knew that I wanted, and I aimed myself at the goal like an arrow. One day, as I sat at the kitchen table filling out applications at last, Linda sat down across from me. She said, "Katherine, I think we have to talk."

"What do you want to talk about?" I asked.

She chewed her lip. "I've tried to give it time, I really have, but I know you'll likely be gone in a year. I just want to say while there's still time that I'm not the enemy. I'm not the evil stepmother. I'm not the reason your mother and father didn't work out. Or the reason she left."

I knew I'd hurt her feelings over the years. I had even started to feel guilty about it, but now I clenched my hands together. "Please don't talk about my mother," I said.

"This is what I mean," she said. "I'm not trying to start a fight. I'm trying to tell you something."

"Listen," I said. "I don't blame you for my mother leaving, okay?" This was true. I blamed her, however unfairly, for my mother not coming back.

"But I don't believe you," she said. "Listen to how angry you sound! You blame me, I know it. And I think you think something that isn't true. You don't even know where she lives, do you?"

All I wanted to do was get up and leave. When I thought about how my mother had left us, how we didn't even know where she lived, I felt weak, like all the strength had gone out of my body. But now I wondered what Linda was getting at. "No. Do *you* know where she lives?"

"No," Linda said. "But I do know some things you don't."

I felt a prickle of apprehension. "Like what?"

"Well, for one, she wasn't your real mother."

"What do you mean?"

"I mean she wasn't your real mother," Linda repeated. "Your father needed someone to take care of you, and the woman you thought was your mother agreed to do it."

"That's a lie," I said. I felt a crack open inside me. In the span of a breath, Linda had upended everything.

"It's the truth." Linda said.

"I don't believe you," I said, but for some reason, I did.

"I'm telling you now so that you can let go," Linda said. "I've always wanted children, you know, and when I married your father, I thought maybe we could be friends." Her voice was trembling now.

Rage blossomed inside my chest and spread through my limbs. "We'll never be friends," I said, and though my arms and legs were shaking, I got up and left.

I still don't know what Linda was thinking, telling me that the way she did—as though she thought I would thank her for it. As though she thought that would solve, not exacerbate, my hostility toward her.

Still, I realized I had underestimated her—I'd thought of her as an irritant to be borne, someone whom my father loved who had nothing to do with me. But in just a few minutes, she had reconfigured everything I knew and set up a powerful new equation: my mother ≠ my mother. It was a staggering revelation. She might as well have told me Katherine ≠ Katherine.

I felt as if my whole past was lost to me—that there was no ground to stand on, and my mother was no longer mine, had never been mine. And if that was the case, then I was Katherine-from-no-one, Katherine-from-nowhere, Katherine-doomed-to-be-lost.

I SPENT THE REST of the afternoon in the bathroom, vomiting. When my father came home from work, he stood inside the doorframe, watching me as I heaved and cried in turns.

"Katherine," he said, and he knelt down next to me. He put his hand on my back and sighed. "My poor sweetheart. Linda told me what happened," he said. "I'm sorry you found out this way, but she doesn't know the whole story. It's complicated."

I wiped my mouth. "So tell me," I said, my voice raw. "Is Mom my real mother, or not?"

My father rubbed his face. "Katherine, I know this must be confusing for you, and I'm sorry. I wish Linda hadn't said anything, but your mother and I were not entirely up front about everything. Your real mother died right after you were born, and your mom offered to take care of you."

So it was true. "Why would she do that?" I asked. "Who was she?"

"Well, she was close to your real mother, but she couldn't have children of her own. She'd known you since you were born, and after your real mother died, your mother and I grew close."

"Who was my real mother, then? How did she die?"

"She died in childbirth," he said.

"So it was my fault."

"No," my father said. "No, no, I shouldn't have said that. Listen, Katherine, that's why I never wanted to tell you these things. I knew they would hurt you. It doesn't change anything. Your mother was your mother in every important way."

My mind was racing. Real mother, false mother. True story, false story. I'd been living in a false story all my life. There was nothing I could count on. "If that's true," I said, "then why did she leave me?"

My father exhaled slowly. "That had nothing to do with you," my father said. "She loved you more than anything else in her life." He reached out and took me in his arms.

I let him hold me for a moment, my head tucked under his chin. I was so confused. I understood, intellectually, that my mother wasn't my real mother, that she hadn't given birth to me. But she was the one I missed, the one I longed for, the one I still struggled to understand.

"She's not coming back, is she?" I asked.

I felt him shake his head. My tears spilled over.

"What can I do?" he asked. "How can I help?"

"What about my real mother?" I demanded. "Where is she buried? What was her name?"

"Katherine, don't ask me to do this right now," he said. "Give me time."

"You've had time!" I cried. "If you don't tell me the truth, I'll never know anything. I'll never know who I am."

"You're my daughter," he said firmly. "That's all that's important for now."

I still felt a sick clench of dread in my stomach, but I was actually relieved not to learn more in that moment. And I let my father pull me up off the floor and wipe off my face with a towel. I let him lead me back to my room and tuck me into bed, like a child.

Mathematicians used to believe that all statements that exist within mathematics could be categorized as true or false, and that we could use those statements to construct an accurate description of the world. And then Gödel proved all second-order language systems were incomplete, overturning David Hilbert's second problem—dismissing the hope that mathematics was without internal contradictions, that everything in the universe could be described in pure, mathematical terminology. He didn't solve Hilbert's problem so much as he obliterated it.

Some historians say Gödel shook the foundations of mathematics, but that isn't exactly right. What he shook was our understanding of the foundations of mathematics, our perception of them, but that was enough to cause a major crisis of faith.

All my life there had been topics we didn't talk about in my family. I saw now what lies that silence had been meant to hide, but I still didn't know how to break through it. And I was devastated by what I had already learned. So I gave up. I closed and locked the door to that part of my life and stopped asking to know.

A FEW WEEKS LATER my father bought me a telescope, an Endo Astrola, and set it up in the backyard. The Endo Astrola had a 6-inch mirror and both 10 and 25 mm eyepieces. It came with a tripod and weighed about thirty pounds. I couldn't stop touching it.

"How did you know to get this for me?" I asked my father.

"I've seen the magazines you bury your nose in," he said. "I've picked up all the sketches you left around the house. I pay attention. I've been planning this for some time." He reached out and ruffled my hair. "I know the last couple years have been tough on you."

I wanted to tell him that this gift fixed nothing, that I still felt bereft and abandoned. That I was still confused. But my father smiled at me, his eyes lit with hope. So, leaning against him and tilting my head to rest on his shoulder, I said, "Thank you."

I spent every clear night I could outdoors in our backyard looking up at the stars. When my father came out to join me, I showed him Saturn's rings and the spiral arms of the Andromeda galaxy. Around that time I received a scholarship letter from Purdue University, and over the course of the following few days, three more acceptances from other colleges followed. Together, those admissions letters and my telescope promised expansion to me, and freedom. On those nights I felt I had cast my mind out so far that I couldn't care about what was happening on our lawn, or in our house. We were so small compared to the immensity of time and space.

Linda never asked to look through my telescope, and I never offered to let her, though I would have let her look without resentment, I believe, if she'd asked. I wouldn't—I don't think—have begrudged her a closer view of the heavens. I tried not to think about what she had told me and also stopped obsessively waiting for my mother to return. Instead, I turned my attention to the sky. Through an instrument made from polished glass, I could look at stars light-

Chapter 6

THE FIRST UNDERGRADUATE MATH CLASS I TOOK, I took on a dare. I arrived at Purdue University a week before classes began and spent it walking around campus. I loved everything about the university—the sprawling green lawns, the red brick buildings with their accents of limestone, and the great pillars of Hovde Hall. The day I arrived, I walked up and down each aisle of the university bookstore, picking up books and putting them down. A handsome, neatly dressed young man—blond hair slicked back—approached and said, pointing to a lovely light blue book in front of me, "That's supposed to be the hardest undergraduate course in the whole school."

I met his eyes for a moment, then picked up the book—*Real Number Analysis*. I opened it to a page full of pictures of functions. They were lovely, I thought, in what they suggested—a visual representation of an idea, an ordering of a thought.

"Trust me." The boy broke into my thoughts. "That's not for you. The professor fails half the course."

"Do you work here?" I asked.

"Good God, no," the boy said. He grinned. "I'm a student."

"How do you know so much about the math curriculum?" I asked.

"I'm a math major," he said, nonchalantly, like he expected me to be impressed.

"Which class are you taking next?" I asked.

He looked sheepish and proud at once. "Real Number Analysis," he said, nodding at the book I still held. He held out his hand. "My name's Blake."

I ignored his outstretched hand. I smiled. "Thanks so much for your advice." Then I turned away from him, and walked to the counter to pay. As I handed over the money for the book, I couldn't help glancing back. Blake was standing in the aisle I'd left him in, still watching me, a rueful smile on his handsome face. I turned on my heel and walked home to my residence hall.

ANALYSIS IS CONSIDERED the study of limits, but before it was called that, it was called the study of the infinite. When I got home and looked inside the blue textbook, I found definitions of infinity and density, and proofs showing that the set of real numbers is both infinitely large and infinitely dense, and—most astonishing for me—that there are even different sizes of infinity. I flipped through the pages with growing excitement. There were descriptions of convergent series: sequences of numbers that go on forever, getting closer to limits they never quite reach, as well as divergent series, those unbounded by limits. I felt for the first time that I was looking at mathematics as it was meant to be done: here was a book that wasn't meant just to instruct, but to open a door.

The class, when I arrived on the first day, was all male except me. I sat by myself in one of the middle rows, and the boys came clustered in pairs and groups, as cliquish as any girls. No one sat near me. Two boys sitting a few rows in front chatted with great animation about how parallel lines could intersect. I leaned forward—I'd only learned Euclidean geometry up until then.

I said, "Excuse me, I don't mean to interrupt, but could you please explain? I thought the very definition of parallel lines is that they don't intersect. Are you talking about a different kind of space?"

And one of them—I'd later find out his name was Gerard—paused in his conversation, turned back, his eyes lingering on my face and then my chest, and when he was finished looking, he smirked a bit, and said, "Girl."

Ironically, years later, I came to be known as something of an expert on the mathematics of the curvature of space-time, but at this moment, I didn't even know that such a thing existed. When I told this story to a female colleague in the prime of my career, we laughed until we cried. Poor Gerard, who in the end failed the course. Poor Gerard, bested in the end by a girl.

There was only one person in that class who would talk with me, and it was Blake, the boy from the bookstore. Those of us taking Analysis could usually be found in the math library, and at first Blake sat with the others, sauntering in later than the rest of us, and leaving much earlier. But after the first few weeks of sitting with the rest of our classmates while casting sidelong laughing glances my way, which I haughtily ignored, he came over to my table and sat—not across from me, but next to me, and leaned over the homework I was doing.

"Excuse me," I said. "Do you mind? I'm trying to work."

"Ah, Katherine, don't be so cold," he said, smiling disarmingly. "Let's be friends. How are you doing on the problem set? What did you think of the lecture today? The prof went on and on about pointwise convergence a little too long, wouldn't you say?"

And despite my pride, I laughed—and thus began the closest friendship I'd had in my life thus far. It turned out Blake came from a family of math royalty—he was the son and grandson of mathematicians who were celebrities in their ways. His father was a professor at Princeton and had been friends with Einstein; his grandfather had written the primary textbooks on algebra still used in colleges today.

"Mathematics is in my blood," he used to say, as if it was a biological imperative rather than a field of study. He said he didn't regret it, exactly—his relationship to numbers was an extension of his being, as natural as hunger or thirst—but sometimes he wished that his family did not loom quite so large, that he'd had the opportunity to test out whether any other subject might exhilarate him as much. His talent felt like a generational obligation, as if his name was not his own, to do with what he wished.

I had always been an outsider, but now, for the first time, I was friends with someone who seemed like the ultimate insider. He told me without restraint what he cared about, what he thought, and how he felt. It was exhilarating. I could finally unleash my mind and not be careful, not explain, but just really *talk*. I was infatuated, but didn't know what to do next. I was afraid to say anything and ruin the only friendship I had. And I didn't want more, not yet. I would have been happy to stay as we were, forever.

In those first months of friendship we went on long walks together; we watched thunderstorms from the sunroom in the giant apartment his family had rented him, and I told him how my mother and I had watched lightning together. When he asked where she was now, I told him she was dead. I regretted the lie immediately, but Blake said, "Oh, Kath, I'm so sorry," and wrapped his arm around me, and I felt such relief against his shoulder that I let myself melt into him. Thus freed from my family, freed from my past, I felt that I bloomed into a new person, one who was defined primarily by being friends with Blake. If not for him, I may have become a physics major instead of studying mathematics, but I took class after class with him and discovered in doing so that what I found most exhilarating was figuring out how to make the mathematical tools that explained the logic underpinning natural phenomena—to do the science beneath the science. I was fascinated by the physical world as well, but what I was really interested in was how to turn it into an abstraction, to reduce it to its most elemental form.

I told Blake about my ham radio and telescope, which I'd reluctantly left behind in the garage at home. One Saturday night that fall, we lay on a blanket watching the Leonid meteor shower until the curfew for the female students on campus. We talked about Hubble's discovery of the expansion of the universe, and how Einstein had included a cosmological constant in his equations for the theory of general relativity because he'd assumed the universe wasn't expanding, and how he later called that the biggest blunder of his career. Much later, it'd turn out a cosmological constant was necessary after all—because of dark energy—so Einstein would have been right anyway, though of course we didn't know that then.

In the winter Blake and I bundled up and raced each other in the snow, we drank steaming cups of coffee until we shook from the caffeine, we smoked cigarette after cigarette, and I watched the elegant way Blake carried himself, so lean and long and impeccably dressed, always draping himself over the furniture as if he could make a room glamorous just by being in it.

I adored him, but I always felt he had the upper hand, and this embarrassed me. He was so comfortable and confident everywhere he went: he knew how to dress, how to talk, and how to make friends. I could never quite believe that he wanted to be friends with me too.

When he asked why I'd entered college relatively less prepared in mathematics than him and our fellow students, I explained to him that our high school simply didn't have as advanced a curriculum as his, and I felt ashamed. He asked why the teachers hadn't sent me to a nearby university, or encouraged me to study on my own or take correspondence courses, and I replied there was no university near me. I told him about my experience with Mrs. Linen, explaining, "My experience wasn't like yours. A lot of the time I felt punished for doing well."

Blake was aghast at my story. He said that when he was in elementary school, his teacher had made a child in his class wear a dunce cap all day. When Blake's mother found out, she'd been so outraged she'd called the principal to complain and insisted he reprimand the teacher. She also requested both Blake and the dunce-cap child be switched to another classroom.

"That's great," I said. "Good for your mother." But I remembered how my parents had looked in Mrs. Linen's classroom, squeezed into the small furniture, and thought to myself that even if they had complained on my behalf, the outcome wouldn't have been any different.

Still, I liked Blake's perspective on things, his confidence that the world would bend to his will, the way that nothing ever seemed like an obstacle to him. It made things that had never seemed possible seem possible. Blake was the first person to mention graduate school to me as a thing I should do. To put things in perspective, notoriously few women who studied mathematics as undergraduates went on to study it at the graduate level. And there were very few of us to begin with: I was almost always the only woman in any math class I took—at most there were one or two others. Elite universities like Princeton and Yale wouldn't even take undergraduate women then, not until 1969. Blake said he'd go with me wherever I got in. It never occurred to either of us that I would be admitted somewhere he was not. In any case, we drew up a dream list: Stanford, MIT, NYU, and the University of Chicago, and I daydreamed about going to one of these programs with him. In my fantasies, we were always a couple.

The more time we spent together, the more I was convinced he must return my feelings. I was baffled by why he never made a move and wondered if it was because I was Asian or because I did not meet the standards of a girl that he could be with, no matter what his feelings. Perhaps to be with someone like me would embarrass him. I was always on the brink of confessing my feelings or demanding he explain his, but I held back, afraid he would say I was not good enough to be his girlfriend: I only fit into his life as a friend.

I told my father about my friendship with Blake, and our plans to go to graduate school. My father said, "That's great, but don't get ahead of yourself. Even if you are admitted, it's possible that afterward no one will want to give you a teaching job over a man."

But Blake disagreed. The world was changing, he said, and just in time for me. Women were infiltrating science—growing up he'd met a handful of women mathematicians, including the physicist Lise Meitner, who'd discovered nuclear fission along with Otto Hahn, and Maria Mayer, who had discovered the subatomic structure of an atom and would win the Nobel Prize in a couple years hence.

Blake's life was so different from mine: it overflowed with money and ease, and I was impressed by his casual and dismissive attitude toward his own privilege, and eager to sympathize with his complaints. I was jealous of what he had, and it seemed noble to me that he could wave away the winters he'd spent skiing in Vermont, the adolescent afternoons in the company of the most famous intellectuals, politicians, and artists of our time. But his feelings about his upbringing were ambivalent. He was jealous of my relationship to my father, he said. His father had not paid much attention to him or shown him any affection. His father had not even applied pressure to follow in his mathematical footsteps. No, Blake said, the pressure had come from his environment, from where he'd come from and who he was.

I never told him this, but the thing he wanted most to escape was what I most wanted for myself: a sense of importance, a sense of belonging, a history I could root myself to and claim—and more urgently, something or someone to claim me. What I'd inherited from growing up with my mother and father was a kind of separateness from other people, a sense of yawning interiority that made me feel always alone. I wanted what Blake had—a sense of history and belonging, the feeling that I was doing what I was meant to do—and I was grateful for the proximity to this he provided. I was astonished and moved to discover that who he was and where he came from came with certain expectations that were unspoken, like mine, and were thus—for him as well—impossible to answer.

BLAKE WAS MY BEST FRIEND and only love interest, but he went on many casual dates. To me he said these girls were just for fun, and "If a fellow really wanted to marry someone, he'd want to marry you," which sounded like a compliment, but I took as an insult—because why couldn't the person you wanted to marry also be the person you spent time with for fun?

My one consolation was that these dates never amounted to anything: Blake came to be known as something of a heartbreaker, but

I was the only girl he spent time with regularly. Those other girls he took out to dinner, and occasionally for other nocturnal activities, but he did not see them otherwise. Because I never had to see him with anyone else, I was able to distance myself from that Blake—the heartbreaker—while remaining devoted to the Blake who was mine.

One day, he was telling me about a date with a girl the previous evening, and he said, "The problem is she isn't smart. No one's as smart as you."

I laughed in his face when he said it, but the laugh was edged with hurt. I wanted people to think I was smart, but I wanted Blake to see me as more.

He touched my arm with his hand and said, "No, really, I mean it." He caught my eyes with his and gazed at me intently.

I didn't know what to do. Lean in or pull back? I felt caught in the moment, and breathless, and deeply self-conscious. My pulse beat so hard I could feel it in my fingers. Awkwardly, jerkily—not at all like the movies, not at all like I had imagined, I leaned forward and kissed Blake on the mouth. I had never kissed anyone before. It was only a moment of contact—his lips were so soft—and then behind them, his teeth, which I banged with mine. He smelled like laundry soap and pine needles.

We both pulled back, and I turned my face away. I stole a look at him, wondering what he would do next. But he just stroked my hand, and when I finally looked back at him, he smiled sweetly, and said, "Not yet, Kath. Not yet."

That moment disoriented me. What did he mean, not yet? Was he letting me down gently, or was he saving me for later? My infatuation intensified after that moment, and I read meaning into everything he said or did: even the most casually tossed aside comment or gesture became something to consider and interpret. Mostly, I wanted to touch him again, to lean against him, to crawl a little bit closer. I wanted to feel the softness of his mouth. I heard stories of how he flirted and danced and laughed with girls who were not me and wondered what he meant when he said I was the marrying kind.

IN THE SPRING SEMESTER of that year, one of our professors asked us to come to his office after his class. I went with no trepidation whatsoever, but I noticed Blake was uncharacteristically quiet, that as we walked he kept buttoning and unbuttoning his shirtsleeves and, once we arrived, kept pacing outside the professor's door. He was prone to fits of neurosis, however, so I didn't ask what was bothering him, but waited quietly.

I smiled brightly at the professor as we entered his office, but he didn't acknowledge me at all. He did, however, put his hand on Blake's shoulder briefly before closing the door.

"I'm here to discuss a very serious offense," he began, as soon as we were seated.

I waited, a little alarmed by his opening, but still mostly curious and expectant.

"Plagiarism is punishable by expulsion," the professor said, looking sternly at each of us in turn.

I nodded, wondering if he was going to tell us someone in the class had plagiarized. Then he placed my problem set in front of us, and next to my problem set, he put Blake's. Realizing what the professor was implying was exactly like when my father told me my mother had left us—disorienting, unreal, an actual shock that ran through the length of my body.

"If it was only the one problem set," the professor continued, "perhaps I could be convinced of your innocence. But all three problem sets you have turned in so far have been identical, including minor errors, and that cannot be a mistake or coincidence."

Blake looked up. "I don't know what to say," he said. He paused and seemed to be thinking. Finally, he said, "I felt bad for her. I wanted to help."

My confusion was so great that for one panicked moment, I actually thought Blake was talking about the kiss. Why was he telling the professor this?

The professor nodded. "I suspected that's what you'd say," he said. "And I can't say I don't admire you for wanting to help your friend, though it puts me in a difficult position."

I heard a rushing in my ears. My fingers felt numb. I opened my mouth to explain, to defend myself, but the professor was still talking.

"The only reason I'm not failing you, Blake, is that you have a marvelous future ahead of you. Your solutions are very unique—you don't think the same way as everyone else, and this—in the end—will be your greatest strength. You shouldn't have shared your work, but I daresay we have all had lapses in judgment when we were young, and it would be criminal to see you fail because of a girl."

Those were my solutions he was praising, and though I knew the professor wasn't speaking to me, I was naive enough to think that once everything was sorted out, that once the professor understood that the problem set was mine, he would transfer that praise—his belief in the author of the homework—to me.

"But I didn't do this," I said. "I didn't cheat. Tell him, Blake." I put my hand on Blake's arm.

He pulled it away. That's when I knew for sure that he'd done what he did. A small sound escaped my chest, like the chirp of some tiny creature, and I clamped my mouth to shut it in.

I didn't understand. Blake was smart enough to do his own work—I knew this to be true. But I remembered times when I would go to the bathroom and come back and see him fiddling casually through my papers, searching for pieces of gum in my desk, or looking for something to write with when he already had a pen in his hand. He had never asked for my help, but if he'd ever needed it, I would have been happy to do whatever I could. In fact, I'd been hungry to do so, to offer him something in return for the gift of his friendship. But he'd always acted like everything was easy, like it took no time—laughing at me while I pored over my books at night.

The sunlight streamed in from behind the professor's back through the tall leaded windows. I knew I'd lost something that would take me a long time to work out.

The professor glanced at me and saw the tears on my cheek. He said, "The tears of females have no place in this university," but I knew he meant *I* had no place in the university, not just my tears.

"I'm sorry," I said, feeling ashamed of my tears, and for the first time, like the female my classmates saw me as. "Can I just explain?"

The professor rolled his eyes. "There is no explanation I am interested in hearing," he said. "I hope you understand, young lady, that if this ever happens again, you will fail the course and be reported to the expulsion board."

The word *expulsion* shot through my heart. Any defense of myself died on my tongue.

Several more excruciating seconds passed before he cleared his throat and said, "Very well now, you may leave."

I STOPPED GOING to classes for the next several days. I avoided the dining hall: I didn't want to run into Blake. I remembered his outrage at my story about Mrs. Linen and wondered if he knew that what he'd done was much worse. I thought of his story about his mother going to the principal and wondered if I should go back to talk to the professor, or even the Dean, but I remembered how cold the professor had been at our meeting, how convinced he'd been that I was the one who had copied, and I felt frozen with dread. What if I was expelled, after all?

Instead of going to the professor in person, I amassed all my class notes, and the notes I'd taken on my way to solving my problem sets before I transferred them cleanly onto the papers I turned in. I compiled these notes and wrote a letter to my professor in which I said, "I thought you might be interested in these notes, which show the work that went into solving my problem sets." I didn't mention Blake at all. I slipped the folder into my professor's mailbox when class was in session and I knew I wouldn't run into him, or Blake, or any of my classmates. I waited a few days for a response, but a response never came.

While I was waiting, I took up the old German notebook my father had given me, which I'd slowly been going through the process of translating, page by page. Most of the text was math speak, defining terms or explaining certain moves, which didn't help me place the math in a context of any kind. But there was one page, near the end, that was just three lines, all in text, and on my fifth day of hiding out, I skipped ahead to translate that instead.

After some toggling between the page and the German-English dictionary, I was able to translate:

Be kind. Everyone you meet is fighting a great battle.

Let everything happen to you, beauty and terror. Just keep going. No feeling is final.

I discovered later that these were quotes. But at that moment they read to me like a direct order handed down through time from the author of the notebook to me, and I took this as a sign.

THE NEXT DAY I took a shower and got dressed. I caught up on my homework. I went to the dining hall at the same time as I always had. I would not change my schedule for him. When I got there, Blake was at the same seat at the same table where we had always sat together, except now he was sitting with another girl. So he had not had the decency to change *his* schedule, I thought. He had not had the decency to hide. I sat at another table alone and recited the lines from my notebook silently to myself like a mantra.

Toward the end of my meal, Blake approached, smiling, as if to speak. I stood up and hissed, with a viciousness that surprised me, "Get away from me, cheater." His blue eyes widened, and he backed up so quickly he knocked into a group of students. After that, he stayed away.

We sat far from each other in class for the rest of the semester, but when our grades were posted on the door, I paid attention to his scores, making sure to note that I outdid him on each assignment. On the exams, again and again, I broke the curve.

I kept waiting for the professor to admit he'd been wrong, to make the smallest gesture when he handed back my homework or my exams, but he never did. He said nothing, and when I tried to catch his eye, he turned his head and ignored me. This was what made me angriest—not that he never apologized or admitted or said even once, "Good job," but that I expected him to, that I waited and waited, and was wounded by the waiting, like a fool.

If there is an upside to what happened with Blake, it's this: I worked harder in the following year than I ever had before. I became more disciplined. When I went home for summer vacation, my father said, "Relax. Do you need to study nonstop?" But I wanted to dominate so completely that my record would speak for itself, and no one would ever be able to assume I'd relied on someone else for my work ever again. When I returned, I was unapologetic and ferocious—hungry for the problem—and not only for the problem, but for victory as well. I devoured my textbooks, I laid waste to my homework, and when I rose to the top of my class, I felt a cold, triumphant thrill. By the end of my sophomore year I was on track to graduate a year early from college. *Let them gossip about my accomplishments*, I thought—let them know they had been right to fear my arrival. I wanted them to see that my ambition and hunger were no different from theirs, but that my will—and my nerve—were stronger.

I began to speak out of turn in classes, not waiting to be called on, but anticipating, jumping in, and asking for clarification. I had learned that if I waited to be called on, my turn would never come. I pushed myself even harder, and if at first I was met with resistance, I would persist and stumble upon something interesting to say—something that would communicate my seriousness and my commitment—show that I had really thought through the topic at hand. Then the professor would pause for a moment, surprised, and look at me—and something between us would shift. It happened again and again. Sometimes I said something stupid or obvious, but I made myself face those moments unflinchingly, nodding calmly when I was corrected, as if I was unembarrassed, as if I was grateful for being told my mistake. It worked.

"Our own Kovalevskaya," the professors said. "Our own Sophie Germain." I was their pet, their novelty, their very own girl-prodigy, and with the exception of the one professor who'd accused me of plagiarism—he simply would stare off into the distance whenever I was near, as if I didn't exist—they were delighted by me. Still, I had stopped looking up to professors, stopped seeking validation from them.

"If only you were a man," one said, "I'd ask you to be my assistant next year." Said another, "If you were a man, you'd have a brilliant future ahead of you." I let such comments roll over and past me like a wave I had nothing to do with. I compiled a list of women mathematicians from the past: Hypatia and Kovalevskaya, Noether and Germain.

In the fall of my junior year, I applied to the graduate programs Blake and I had once planned to apply to together, alone. I took classes on complex functions, algebra and rings, field theory and logic. In the spring I was accepted everywhere I'd applied. I took number theory and became entranced by prime numbers. It was then I first learned about the Riemann hypothesis. It's called a hypothesis instead of a theorem because it's unproven, but it's not a conjecture because so many theorems have woven the Riemann hypothesis into their proofs that the assumption of its truth now forms the foundations of entire fields. If it is ever shown to be false, proofs in every field of mathematics will fall. The drama of this has always appealed to me, as has the glory. By the time I graduated, I had promised myself that I would make my own attack upon it one day.

I was so focused during those last years of college that I never really fell in with a crowd or made another intimate friend—but I told myself not to be sad about that. I decided my people were not in college, but still out there waiting to be found and to find me. They were the ones who knew—or could discover—secret things. I would find them and discover secret things of my own.

Chapter 7

I WAS ASKED TO GIVE A TALK AT MIT IN 2005, AFTER LAWrence Summers, then the president of Harvard University, gave his infamous speech on the natural abilities (or lack thereof) of women in the sciences. I agreed, happy to return to the place where I'd received my graduate degree, and exasperated—not for the first time—by the remarkable arrogance of a smart man. In his speech, Summers had speculated that women might lack "the science gene" and then wondered out loud whether it explained why there were far fewer successful women than men in science.

I had known Larry for at least twenty years by then, and when I heard what he had said, I wanted to go and find him and shake him by his ears. Setting aside all the research negating what he'd said, just simple common sense, I would have hoped, might have made him consider other factors first: for instance, how women hadn't been allowed the same access to education historically, to say nothing of societal pressures even to this day for women to behave in a certain way and pursue marriage and family above everything else.

Summers's speech was a poorly argued, lazy analysis based on historical prejudice in lieu of rigorous study, and while he was duly punished for it, I couldn't help but wonder why so many intelligent men aren't more embarrassed to speak on topics they know nothing about, or why anyone would listen to an economist on such a matter in the first place. How are they so sure of themselves, and why are so many people so eager to listen? I've always wished I had the confidence to speak with half the conviction on subjects I'm actually competent to discuss.

In any case, the talk I was invited to give was organized in response to Summers's remarks, and I was asked to talk about my career and the history of women in math as well as the challenges facing women today. The event was widely publicized in the furor that followed Larry's speech, a furor which struck me as hypocrisy because the notion that women are inferior at science has long been a sentiment widely held and firmly defended in the Academy. If anything, it seemed to me that the furor and outrage over those remarks had been manufactured to camouflage that fact.

As I stood at the podium waiting to begin, I looked out at the auditorium into the faces of so many women, their faces upturned, both young and old—and my legs suddenly went unsteady. Over the years I'd grown accustomed to giving lectures to audiences that were almost exclusively made up of men, and now I was surprised by the impulse to tears. I had to breathe quickly and blink several times before I could speak.

I held the edges of the podium tightly, and as I stood there, the memory of the evenings I spent as a child sitting next to my father operating our ham radio came powerfully back to me. I had always thought that my father's gadgets and experiments were his own hobbies, projects he wanted to take on for his amusement alone, and it wasn't until the middle of that talk—so many decades later—that I realized these were things he'd done for *me*, so that we could share the experience together, so we could have those moments that, in part, helped turn me into a scientist.

I remembered now the feeling of hope that had coursed through me when we sent out our first signal, waiting for some response—any response—and not knowing from where or when or if it might arrive. Afterward, the question we most often came upon and the question we most asked was: Are you there? And after a lifetime of solitude as one of the only women in my field, it took my breath away to look out at the audience and see the answer to a lifelong question: Are you out there? Are you listening? Am I alone?

I KNOW NOW, of course, that I am not the only woman to have felt alone for much of her career. That is one of the sad hard facts for many women pursuing careers in science—or any male-dominated field, for that matter. The first time I visited Harvard was in 1963. I had just started graduate school nearby at MIT, and when I stood in front of the hallowed buildings of Harvard grown over with ivy, I thought—*What beautiful places men have built for each other with the intention of keeping women out.* And my joy at being there was diminished by knowing that this was a place that was meant in fact to exclude me.

"Hypatia," I said under my breath that day, as if her name was an incantation, a magic spell. Hypatia was a woman born between AD 350 and 370 and had been a mathematician, philosopher, and astronomer who became the head of the Platonic school at Alexandria. She had been born to a famous scholar father, and as she grew, she overtook his reputation, becoming both the leading mathematician and leading philosopher of her time. She is the only woman in history of whom such a claim can be made.

She worked to preserve Greek mathematics and philosophy during a time of immense conflict between the Christians, Jews, and pagans; she was a Neoplatonist who championed the belief in an ultimate underlying reality that could only ever be partially grasped through science and human thought. She drew enormous, diverse crowds and taught that the purpose of life was to deepen our understanding of this underlying reality. She famously declared herself married to this endeavor, and vowed to remain a lifelong virgin. At first, Hypatia seemed destined to happiness—beloved by her friends and the public, a woman of noted virtue and beauty and brilliance, who wielded rare influence and power—the only woman allowed to set foot into the Senate. But like many women who rise to unknown heights of celebrity, she was destined for a quick and brutal fall.

In the political struggle that arose between church and state in Alexandria, Hypatia was branded a pagan for her belief in science and learning, and when Cyril, the bishop of Alexandria, banned Jews from Alexandria, and Orestes, the governor, condemned this, it was Hypatia, as a friend and advisor to Orestes, who was thrust into the center of the bitter conflict. A forged letter in which she decried religion was circulated; rumors and testimony began to spread that she was a satanic witch. And so Hypatia, celebrated for years as a shining virgin, a paragon of virtue and learning, fell from grace for the very same reasons and was pulled from her carriage one afternoon by an angry Christian mob.

In my mind I see Hypatia sculpted in marble, as untouchable and white as the Greek statues I've seen in photographs and museums. But she was not marble: she was flesh and blood, mind and spirit. The book she wrote has been lost. None of her papers remain. But reports of what that mob did to her have endured. Her countrymen gathered around her, and pulled her from her carriage by her hair. On the street, they swarmed her body; with tiles from the roofs of nearby buildings, they peeled away her skin, strip by strip. They claimed their trophies eagerly—each clump of hair, each ragged piece of skin—then set her limbs on fire.

Hypatia of Alexandria. All that is left is her name.

Chapter 8

THEY SAY YOU NEVER FORGET THE FIRST TIME YOU SEE the woman you're meant to marry, but I would have remembered you no matter what." That's what Peter Hall said to me once, when we still thought that one day I'd be his wife. In any case, at that time in my life, being remembered wasn't a problem. In fact, I'd be shocked if any of my classmates didn't remember me—every single person who attended our orientation, down to the last man. I was the only woman in our entering class of graduate mathematics students—a skirt in a sea of pants.

I'd won the inaugural Emmy Noether Award for a paper I'd published in my last year of college on invariant theory, and along with full funding and a living stipend for five years, I was also written up in the campus paper and interviewed by a local radio show in the first week after my arrival. This was a great honor, of course, but for a long time both this prize and Noether's name were a painful subject to me.

Perhaps I should have been grateful that such an award existed at all, for "a young woman of extraordinary promise wishing to pursue a career in science." But back then I was the only young woman in my year studying mathematics at my university, and though I was grateful for the award and the stipend that came with it, all the attention that came with the prize seemed designed to highlight the fact of my womanhood rather than my talent, as if I couldn't hold my own with the rest of the students, who of course were all men. I still remember how indifferently the president of the university shook my hand when he was introduced to me at the dinner held for the winners of prizes that year, and how warmly he greeted everyone else. At every turn I felt humiliated by the prize and the comparisons it brought up, and so instead of feeling grateful and humbled as I learned more about Noether, I came to resent her instead.

Her life should have inspired me, but the more I came to learn, the more I understood that Noether was one of a kind, comparable to no one, truly unique. She'd made fundamental, revolutionary contributions to mathematics and written a theorem on symmetry that remains one of the most beautiful and deepest results in theoretical physics. She was a woman who had succeeded in all the ways I feared I might fail: against all odds, she'd gained the respect and support of her peers. I felt there wasn't room for both of us, and that I had already fallen behind. The people she'd known, the things she'd accomplished all rose up in reproach, casting their light on my inadequacies. I was jealous—and ashamed of my jealousy. I didn't know yet what enormous arrogance that was on my part, or what a regrettable waste of time.

I WANTED TO MAKE an impression my first day of graduate school, and I planned what I would wear, how I would walk, where I'd sit, and where I'd direct my eyes. I'd filled out in my final years at college and had been made aware that I had come to be considered attractive. I understood the choice was be seen or be invisible. I decided I wanted to be seen.

I wore a white silk blouse and a pencil skirt and pumps with skinny little heels. A watch, some lipstick, and a string of pearls. I sat at the front of the giant hall, in the first row, so that no one would miss me as they walked in. There's a picture of our class from that first day, and even now when I look at it, I can see the defiance in the way I stood—shoulders back, gaze level at the camera, studiously conspicuous and also unconcerned.

Ah! There I am in all my youth. That way I had of standing so that you had to take me in all at once: a cloud of dark brown hair (almost black) framing an angular, rebellious face—curious, unwavering, not-entirely-friendly eyes—a compact graceful body, and lovely legs that I still vainly remember a classmate once claimed had been made to break his heart.

What a disturbance I caused! We were all serious students then, but the first week you wouldn't have guessed it. The men in my classes—and there were only men—ogled me and talked about me. I was the constant target of speculation and assessment, both kind and unkind in nature. By turns my classmates were aggressive or circumspect, but always guarded and unnatural. Never again have I been so alienated as I was in that first year of graduate school, or made to feel so absolutely foreign. My opinions were never asked about anything, and yet I was always watched, as a symbol of something—an outsider who'd somehow made it in.

EARLY ON, a classmate of mine named Richard told me a joke I've since heard again at various moments in my career. Back then there were only two or three women mathematicians from history whom anyone had heard of. The first was Emmy Noether, and the other was Sofia Kovalevskaya, a Russian mathematician who'd written several important papers on partial differential equations, the dynamics of Saturn's rings, and elliptic integrals and who was best known for discovering the Kovalevskaya top—one of only three cases of integrable body motion.

We were at a department gathering, all the graduate students awkwardly standing around a buffet table while the professors chatted in corners, when Richard blurted from across the table, "Hey, Katherine! Have you heard this one? There have only been two women in mathematics, and one was not really a mathematician, and the other was not really a woman."

It took me a moment to get the joke, that Sofia Kovalevskaya was "not really a mathematician," and that Emmy Noether was "not really a woman." I felt a flash of irritation.

"Come on," I said. "Why would you say that to me?"

"Oh, come on yourself, it's a joke, Kat," he said, shortening my name. "Lighten up."

"Whatever you say, Dick," I said, shortening his.

That silenced him for exactly half a second, and then he burst out laughing and punched me lightly on the arm, shaking his head. "Not bad, Miss Kat," he said. "Not bad at all."

For a moment I was tempted to cling to my outrage. But then I looked into his laughing face and relaxed. He had meant no harm. Not that the joke itself was without harm, not that in his hands it wasn't a weapon, whether he knew it or not.

But by then I was resigned to these jokes, to the constant reminder that I was an anomaly, an outsider, a kind of freak. I was aware that even if I contributed to our field, my name would also become a punch line. I didn't know how to resist, except to make clear that I wasn't trying to fit in, that I knew I was different, and to highlight that difference to make it clear. For instance, I always wore skirts, never pants—even on winter days when the wind blew through my long, thick coat and wrapped itself around my legs, I persisted. I'd bought the longest, most luxurious coat I could find in a deep chocolate brown that I knew set off the darkness of my hair. That was the one decadent thing that I owned. The rest of my clothes were sometimes elegant, almost to the point of being severe, but cut, always, to fit exactly—if not to accentuate, to acknowledge the fact that I was a woman in a woman's body. No prim or prissy outfits for me. No nun's shapeless shift. And over it all a coat to go to the opera in.

Emmy Noether had done no such thing—she displayed no interest in her own femininity and flaunted neither her looks nor her clothes. Here was a woman who had succeeded in all the ways I aspired to, and all Richard saw fit to make of her life was a dumb and ignorant joke. This was nothing new of course: after she died, a full page was devoted in her tribute to the fact that she'd died alone and had never—to anyone's knowledge—had sexual relations. And during his eulogy for her, the famous mathematician Hermann Weyl, who'd been one of her closest collaborators, stood at her grave and talked at length of her triumphs and genius, but closed with a treatise on how she lacked all the charms of the "gentler" sex, outlining her mannish appearance, her simple nature, and how she was unfit to feel love for a man, and incapable of sparking his passion. What injustice these men did her, her colleagues and friends, with their affectionate, condescending, deliberate, and delicately worded gibes about how no one wanted to seduce her! As if that was the last word, as if they weren't bespectacled savants in baggy clothes themselves. I wonder if that was what ultimately allowed them to accept her into their ranks—a deficiency in one sense that let them accept her as a genius in another. Does there always have to exist, in the end, such a choice?

Chapter 9

SAY THERE'S A GIRL AND A BOY, AND THEY'RE MADLY IN love with each other, but they live on opposite sides of a lake that neither of them can cross. The boy wants to marry the girl and buys a ring to propose. There's a ferryman who goes back and forth on the lake. In his boat he carries a box on which you can put any lock. If you put something in the box, he'll take it across to the other side, but unless the box is locked he'll steal whatever you give him before he reaches the shore. Either way, he can go back and forth across the lake as often as you ask him to. The boy has one lock and the key to his lock, and the girl has another lock and the key to her lock. How does the boy get her the ring?

I SOLVED THIS PROBLEM for extra credit on my final exam in Peter Hall's class my first semester of graduate school. Peter liked to give freebie brainteasers at the ends of his exams for anyone who had extra time, which few people attempted since they were generally entangled in the actual problems, and because the extra credit questions were worth very little, points-wise. This one had been worth the constant e (a little less than 3 points in a 100-point exam); another had been worth π. In any case, Peter Hall called me into his office after the exam, and when I walked in, he said I had received the highest score in the class on the exam by $e + 5$ points. He congratulated me.

"I've never received an irrational test score before," I quipped (the number e had been named after Euler, who'd proven its irrationality in the eighteenth century).

"Ha," Peter said, in a way that made me immediately wonder how many students had made the same joke before me.

I looked at the equations on the chalkboards behind him, and then down at his gleaming wood desk. I felt tongue-tied and inexplicably shy.

"You should know that the extra credit problem you solved is one of the foundational problems of modern cryptography," he said. "And you were the only one to solve it." He reached across his desk, and shook my hand. "Congratulations. I've got my eye on you."

I blushed.

You have to understand: he was Peter Hall. The most famous mathematician on the faculty, maybe in America, appealing in that rumpled scientist way, and he had his eye on me. He'd written a problem that in our class only I had solved, and he'd couched it in the language of love then revealed it to belong to the domain of cryptography—I was in over my head before we began. The problem I'd solved—that I felt sure he'd written for me—had drawn me in as only a mathematical problem could: bounded, defined, it was a puzzle to break your head over until a solution appeared—everything leading up to it a struggle, but the answer itself effortless as a drawn breath.

Let's take another look at the problem: the boy and the girl across the lake. He can get her the ring if you find the solution. No need to rush: this isn't a timed exam, and in the story the girl and boy never age. Nothing will happen to them until you've figured it out—no one will fall in love with anyone else, no war will break out to take anyone away, no one will fall sick or die. So take your time. Later, when we come back to them, they'll still be there, the shining lake and the old ferryman between them, waiting for us to bring them together.

Chapter 10

PETER HALL AND I DIDN'T SPEAK AGAIN UNTIL THE FALL semester of my second year, when I took his class on celestial mechanics. The course dealt with dynamical systems, which I'd become interested in by eavesdropping on the physicists whose offices were across the hall: my office was located right at the border between the departments, and unlike my own officemates, my neighbors were always in their office or in the physics lounge, which was next door. Even when I shut my door, I could often hear them talking and joking. The mathematics lounge was pristine, but the physics lounge was filled with gadgets and wiring and models, and a rotating ceiling that a former student had built, pierced with holes in the exact arrangement of constellations in the night sky.

The students in the office directly across from mine had built an elaborate train set that took up their entire room—"because the engineers have one," they said—and they were constantly tinkering with it. The circuitry for the train set was underneath the table the train ran on, and so they spent most of their time down there, like mechanics in an auto shop, a row of feet poking out as they talked.

All their gadgets reminded me of the things my father had built for me growing up, and I came to appreciate their friendly banter coming through my walls like disembodied radio voices. Sometimes I would linger in front of their office door, listening and trying to track their conversations, until one day, they caught me.

"We've got a guest," a dark-haired young man announced, scooting into a sitting position out from under the table. He sat up and smiled, a warm, open, dazzling smile. "I'm Rob," he said and wiggled the shoe next to him. "That's Leo."

"Hello," I said, holding out my hand.

"Well," Rob said, getting up to take it. "For the sake of all that's holy and good, tell us your name—we've enough mysteries on our hands as it is."

I laughed. "I'm Katherine."

"Pleased to meet you," Rob said.

"Welcome," said Leo, crawling out from underneath the table with a grunt. He was disheveled and covered in dust, and clutching tools in his hands, but when he looked up at me, he blinked into the light and smiled.

I spent many afternoons in their office, crowded around the big table with physicists and books and the menagerie of exotic houseplants Leo was cultivating to serve as forests for the train set. I liked the social atmosphere, and it was the first time I'd been invited to join a group so easily—as if I already belonged. I started wearing pants so I could go under the table with them and stare at the dazzlingly complex circuitry they'd set up to keep the train running, the gates going up and down, the lights in the houses blinking, and so on.

They occasionally asked me to explain some math they needed

for whatever they were working on, and I was only too happy to be useful. Leo and Rob were generous with their ideas and shared them openly. Their train set was a model for how they worked: anyone at all was welcome to come and tinker with it—to add something, to change something, to make the circuitry more efficient. I learned a lot watching them work, and I observed how this ethos translated to their research as well—it was as if no one had authorship or ownership of a single idea—they threw it into the pot for everyone to attack together.

Sometimes when I was with them I thought with a pang about my father, and how much he would enjoy meeting them. But whenever I called him, he wanted instead to talk about the future, and then he said things I didn't want to hear. "You have to think of how difficult it will be to get a job as a woman," he said. "Most departments aren't going to want to hire a woman professor."

"So I'll do something else," I said.

"I think we should talk about this," he said.

"I'm done with this conversation," I said. And I called him less than I had, and when it came time for vacations, I found myself saying I was too busy to go home.

CELESTIAL MECHANICS fell outside Peter's field of expertise, but he preferred to teach classes on subjects he was unfamiliar with—to use his classes as an excuse to learn something new. He was an exciting, charismatic teacher, and on the first day, as I entered his classroom, I felt a jolt when I saw him standing there in front of the room, frowning down at his desk, and scribbling furiously. Back then, he was always in motion, pacing across the room, covered in the chalk dust he picked up by brushing against the board or rubbing his arm absentmindedly while he held a piece of chalk in his hand. And when he broke it writing on the board, which he often did, he would kick it across the room, so that it'd ricochet against the walls or the chair legs of the students in the first row, and when class was over there'd be pieces of chalk strewn all along the floor, little hazards that people sometimes slipped on or crushed into powder beneath their feet.

On that first day, though, Peter waited until five minutes after the official start time, until the room was packed to bursting and there were students standing up on the stairs along the edges of the rows. The first day was always like this for Peter, with both undergraduate and graduate students eager to see him in action, whether they were registered in the course or not. The room was loud with the buzzing of voices, but when Peter stopped scribbling on his paper and stood back on his heels to look at us, we were immediately silent. He paced up and down the length of the room, looking at us, his gaze running along the rows of students who had come to hear him. For a moment his eyes rested on me. For a moment, they paused. But then his eyes slid away and moved on, searching other faces.

"The way I like to choose a problem," he began, "is to take two ideas that seem very far apart, and try to find the connection that brings them together." He held his hands wide and brought them close. "I was told earlier today," he continued, "that there are several nonmathematicians in this class. I was just trying to see if I could tell them apart from the mathematicians." He paused, and I felt an uncomfortable prickling under my skin, afraid of being singled out like Richard's joke had singled out Kovalevskaya and Noether. But then Peter smiled and shook his head. "I couldn't. You all look alike."

Everyone laughed, and I joined in relief. He grinned back at us. He seemed eager for us to like him, and simultaneously confident that we would. Humble and arrogant at once. He began again, energized now, and pleased that he had gotten his first laugh. "As we all know, the closest distance between two points is a straight line, but sometimes the closest distance between two ideas is a long and winding path. Perhaps you will feel that way in this class."

And he laid out the basic framework of what we would be studying in the class, beginning with the founding of celestial mechanics and Poincaré's assertion that the solar system is unstable, to Kolmogorov's argument that the solar system actually tends toward stability. We'd cover the Boltzmann equation, partial differential equations, and the laws of thermodynamics. We'd be looking at microscopic physics and macroscopic physics, reversible and irreversible phenomena, and predictions and observations in theoretical physics that were still waiting for mathematical explanations.

All semester long, that class was magic, and not just for me, but for everyone who stayed in the course. We grew closer than a class usually does—talking long after the class time was up, sharing ideas, even meeting out for the occasional group meal. Peter became especially close to Leo and Rob, quizzing them in class to fill in his own gaps of knowledge in physics. As a result, they came to class incredibly well prepared, studying ahead of time, to anticipate what he might ask of them. They took to bringing ten books between them, as references, and Peter took to throwing chalk at them when they were too slow or came up short. There was a lot of laughing and high-spirited argument in that class, and it bred a camaraderie among everyone that Peter became famous for, and as his students, it spurred us forward. As for me, there was an extra little buzz that surrounded everything he did. For years, I could remember entire lectures he'd given, word for word, everything he'd said and exactly how he'd looked when he said it.

DURING THE WEEK, Peter would often invite Leo and Rob to the faculty lounge to sit and talk with him, and to make use of the giant sliding chalkboards that lined every wall of the room. In that room, you could go round and round, sliding those chalkboards up in a spiral that rose above you. After those meetings, Rob and Leo would stop by my office, exhilarated.

They'd begun to pick up his mannerisms—the way he had of suddenly leaning forward before he asked a question and fixing you with his eyes, or the way he broke whatever he was holding in his hands—chalk, pencils, bits of paper—into smaller and smaller pieces as he thought. I found myself flirting with them on the days they came back from spending time with Peter.

Rob, who was married, flirted gently and amusedly back, but made it clear, quite firmly, that he was not interested. Leo, who—it is possible—had never had an extended conversation with a woman before I joined their duo, and who may not have noticed I was a woman until that moment—was baffled, enjoyed it, and tried hard not to care. But mostly, we were all obsessed with Peter.

"He's brilliant," they said. "He grasps everything immediately, intuitively. He could be a great physicist if he wanted. You too, Kat. You could be good at anything you put your mind to, if you were a man."

They had taken to adding that last bit—"if you were a man"—as a joke to everything after I told them about the professor in college who'd said he'd make me his assistant, if only I were a man.

"Very funny," I said.

ONE DAY, I was in Leo and Rob's office when Peter came by looking for them. I was perched on the edge of a plush leather armchair, and when he came in, I straightened up. "I was just heading out," I began, starting to rise.

"Nonsense," said Rob. "You weren't doing any such thing. Don't be a spoilsport, and come with us, won't you?"

I looked at Peter.

"We're talking about parabolic curves," he said in the tone someone might say *we're having cookies* or *we're having champagne.*

"Okay, I'll come," I said. And then we just stood there, looking at each other. The blood in my body rose and grew warm with his nearness.

Leo cleared his throat. "Shall we get going then?"

Peter and I blinked and broke eye contact. But in that long look had been a promise, and I'd recognized it for what it was—the kind of intimacy that precedes intimacy.

LEO BROUGHT A FOOTBALL with him. I knew he liked to toss it around in the math faculty lounge. "All that wasted space!" he'd crowed after his first day with Peter. Now he groaned, "We won't be able to, with her," nodding at me and twirling the ball between his hands.

I plucked the ball from his hands and tossed it to Rob. "What, is this how it works?"

Rob laughed and tossed the ball to Peter. "Gotta keep your eye on the ball, Leo, or you're going to have it stolen right out of your hands," he said.

"Yeah, Leo, you throw like a girl," Peter said, tossing the ball back to me. He winked. "No offense."

"So do you." I hurled it back as Rob and Leo hooted with laughter. "And none taken."

Leo leapt for the ball, Peter dodged and tossed it back to Rob, who kept it away from him, running along the perimeter of the room with Leo chasing and yelling at his heels. The door opened, and Rob jumped aside quickly, but Leo ran right into Paul Mapleton, the chair of the department, and a very serious man.

"What's going on here?" Mapleton cried. "This is the faculty lounge! For the faculty!" Then his eyes focused on Peter, and he did a double take. "Sorry, Hall, didn't know you were in here."

Peter laughed. "Apologies are mine to make," he said. "We were working out a problem on arcs and trajectories, that sort of thing."

"I see, of course," Paul Mapleton said. "Well, carry on."

So we settled down and got to work, talking and laughing and brainstorming ideas to solve—as it turned out—some problems having to do with arcs and trajectories. The time passed so quickly I didn't notice the afternoon turn into evening, and then it was dark outside and dim in the lounge, and Rob started and looked at his watch and said he had to go home to his wife. Leo also took his leave. "I should be going too," I said, after a brief pause and followed them out.

I couldn't concentrate when I returned to my office, so after half an hour or so had passed, I gathered my books and my coat to leave. I'd taken less than five steps in the hallway, when suddenly a brisk footstep joined mine. Peter was next to me, smiling.

"I was just heading out as well," he said, and we walked through the long hallway and down the stairs without speaking. When we reached the door, he leaned over and took my coat from my arm, shook it out, and held it open for me. I stepped into the arms of my own coat as easily as if it we'd rehearsed it. He smoothed it over my shoulders, and when I looked up to thank him, I was suddenly aware of everything around us—the wood paneling of the interior of the building, the smell of floor polish, the dying light filtering in through the old lead-glass windows—and I felt dazzled by the moment of acute perception, as if I'd finally stepped firmly into the real world, into my life.

Outside it was winter, and the lamplight shimmered on the bits of snow that clung to the frozen blades of grass, which crunched under our feet. We started walking without any destination in mind, and after a while I realized we were walking in circles around campus. All the while, we talked. We talked about what the other students and faculty members were working on, and sparred over a controversy that had arisen within the ranks in response to a recent article condemning the "new" way math was taught to elementary school students. When I interrupted to note we'd circled the campus three times as we argued, Peter laughed, and said he would walk me home. But when we reached my apartment building, we were still deep in conversation, so we turned around and walked all the way back to campus. We went back and forth like this until the sun had sunk all the way down, and the evening had turned into night.

I couldn't stop looking at him: people passed us on the sidewalk, cars drove by on the road, all of it an impressionistic blur—only Peter stood out, exuding a glow under the streetlights that seemed to strike others as well, because people kept stopping to turn and look at us as they passed by. But for once I didn't care about being stared at. I was with him so it didn't matter. I was happy.

THAT NIGHT PETER TOLD ME how his family had lost both of his older brothers in the war when he was ten years old, and how he'd grown up in the shadow of that loss. Rick, the eldest, had been a popular high school and college football player, and he'd been lost for six months after a battle in Italy before they finally identified his body. Johnny had been nineteen years old, and just proving himself as a talented mathematician, when he was killed in France. A week after the news of his death, a series of letters had arrived containing a mathematical proof of rare insight and reach. His parents had sent the proof along to a professor at Princeton, who'd verified the importance of the results, and who'd had the paper published in a major journal. Twenty years later, and Peter was brilliant, famous—more than fulfilling the promise of his lost older brother, but haunted by the sense that no matter what he did, he could never make up for the loss or match the sacrifice. He was always competing with a ghost.

When we got close to my apartment building on our last circuit, Peter turned to face me. "You're shivering," he said. "I've kept you too late. I'll let you go in this time." He smiled. The streetlight fell over his face and hair, slantwise, so that the part of him that was lit up seemed brighter than anything around us. He took a deep breath. "Come to my office and work with me," he said. "Whenever you like. Starting tomorrow. I have an extra desk and could use the company."

"All right," I said. I felt a surge of happiness—to be seeing him tomorrow, to have had this walk with him. I turned and ran to my building, calling out "Good night!"

Chapter II

When I was a child, maybe four or five years old, my father used to let me sit under his desk to read or draw while he worked. For the most part we ignored each other, though sometimes I'd lean my drawing pad against his legs and line my colored pencils up between his socked feet. Sometimes while I read, he'd reach out one searching foot and poke me in the side with his toes. I'd bat him away, declaring in my most irritable grown-up voice, "I'm working!" There was a Do Not Disturb sign I'd post to the side of his desk, and I'd crawl under there even when my father was elsewhere, for the feeling of calm delight it gave me, puffed up with self-importance at being allowed to work in the proximity of his work on my own all-absorbing tasks.

When I first started working with Peter in his office, I went four times a week. On the days he taught Celestial Mechanics, I went to class separately and spent the rest of the day in my office. The rest of the week, the routine went like this: we spent the morning in silent contemplation, then we had lunch together, and then for an hour in the afternoon we told each other what we'd been working on, throwing ideas around. If I had another class or he had a meeting, we took our leave wordlessly, and just as wordlessly came back. Sometimes we called one of the graduate students or faculty members in to get their take on whatever we were doing. Then we took a walk, exactly the same walk of about forty-five minutes, either the two of us or a little parade of mathematicians and scientists, and when we returned we either kept working until evening or went our separate ways—I to my office, he to his, or I to my apartment and he to his house. Then we both worked separately, deep into the night. We would meet again in the morning and start over. That was it.

My favorite part of the day was the mornings, when we worked silently, without looking at each other, putting our heads down until it was time for lunch. Then he'd get up without saying anything, take his coat, and leave. He'd return with two bowls of soup from the cafeteria, one of which he'd place on the ground in front of my desk. Sometimes I would be the one to leave and return with two sandwiches, one of which I'd place on the ground by his desk. When we were both ready, we'd take our soups or our sandwiches and move to the little table he had in the corner of his office and eat them there. We never deviated from this routine.

Peter's favorite part of the day was always when he got to stand at the blackboard and Figure Things Out (though I teased him that it was when he got to stand at the blackboard and Show Off). The difference between our preferences was due to the fact, I think, that Peter was fundamentally social in nature, while I was an introvert, preferring to work things out in privacy—and sometimes near secrecy. But it was good for me to learn how to work the way Peter did: I saw how progress could be made more quickly in collaboration with others, and it also taught me how to think on my feet (pun intended). Whereas before I had been cautious, preparing for hours before I put forth a thought, I learned now to be flexible, to throw out ideas to be questioned relentlessly so they would become more robust as they developed.

Another thing I learned from Peter was his capacity to be interested in anything and everything. His understanding of math was both wide and deep, and he seemed to comprehend new concepts with the most minimal explanation. At the time it seemed to me that math was his native language, whereas for me it was something I had to painstakingly learn. Now that I'm older, I wish I hadn't wasted so much time making such comparisons. I tell my students that it isn't always the dazzling talent who ends up doing the great work. Sometimes people grow into their work, sometimes people burn out, and you never know who will stumble on the right problem at the right time. It's a matter of engaging fully, of persevering.

On the romantic front, despite the proximity, nothing had changed. It was particularly maddening because everyone assumed Peter and I were lovers, though since the night of the long walk we hadn't so much as brushed against each other accidentally. We were always together, but with at least a foot of distance between us. This distance was torture for me: I always wanted to be closer to him. I felt like the air between us was ionized, magnetized, pulling me inexorably toward him.

I experimented with that distance, stepping an inch closer to him as we stood side by side, facing the chalkboard. I leaned forward, he leaned back. And the opposite—I stepped away, he stepped closer, as if an invisible elastic band kept us linked and separate at the same time. In the bathroom, at home, I examined my face in the mirror, I examined my body. I found myself reading beauty magazines. I started wondering what kind of girls Peter liked, if he would find me more appealing if I was shorter, or taller, or more slender, or voluptuous. It was an agonizing time.

I deferred to Peter on nearly everything. He was my professor, my mentor, my crush, and my hero. The only place where we ran into conflict was also perhaps the most critical one. I had asked Peter to be my thesis advisor, and he had enthusiastically agreed, but when I told him I wanted to work on proving something called the Mohanty problem, which involved proving that at least half of the zeros of the zeta function lay on Riemann's line, he blanched.

"Katherine," he said, "the proof you're talking about requires very complicated analysis and would be a major step to proving the Riemann hypothesis. It's a rather large topic for a thesis. Don't you think you should start a little less ambitiously?"

I found myself flushing. He thought I was too ambitious, not knowing that I was after more than the Mohanty problem—that I wanted to one day tackle the Riemann hypothesis itself. Even now, I can't help but smile at my youthful audacity.

Still, I said, "Why not? What's the point if not to go after the big fish?"

Peter smiled, gently. "Listen," he said. "This is a problem that's broken mathematicians greater than either of us. Is this really how you want to begin?"

I swallowed. "It's just that I think I figured out a way to tackle it by improving Selberg's formula," I said. "I think it's all we need to get us to the next step." I started putting the formula up on the board, but Peter held up his hand.

He said, "Hold on a moment," and started a long explanation of why I had to tread carefully, how difficult the kind of work I was proposing was, how quickly things turned, and how easily mistakes could be made.

"I'll be careful," I assured him, still wanting to explore it further, but for the first time, he was impatient with me, unwilling to go through each step.

"I'm your thesis advisor," he said. "Trust me. Great mathematicians have wasted decades of their best years on this problem and gotten nowhere. This is the kind of calculation where you won't even know if you're making progress until you're there. Take my advice. Let this go."

Unconvinced, I decided to work on it on my own. But around the same time, he invited me to work with him on another problem, and so, jumping at the chance to collaborate closely with him, I let go of my idea for the moment, and told myself I'd come back to it later.

The problem Peter identified for us to tackle was fun and dynamic, and we maintained a surprisingly good balance between us in terms of equally contributing to the work. I only gloated to myself once or twice about what my classmates from college would say, how jealous they would be to know I was working with Peter Hall on a paper. We finished the paper over the course of a year, and afterward it was immediately accepted for publication. We were invited to present our findings at a conference in Chicago in the spring after its publication. The thought of traveling with Peter exhilarated me, but I wasn't sure how I'd be able to bear the proximity, the possibility—I thought all the time about saying something to him, about crossing our invisible boundary and placing my hand on his arm. I developed a strange extra sense—I could tell where he was at all times; even when we weren't in the same room I could tell when he was close by, an extrasensory perception that extended only to him.

Then one day a college student named Jeannie came by his office. She was dark haired and tiny—as pretty and light as a bird, her bones so delicate that her whole body seemed translucent, as if the light incandesced through her. Her eyes were enormous. If I had been a man, I thought, I would have fallen in love with her. I stayed seated at my desk, transfixed. Her eyes flicked over me and she blinked once, then she directed her eyes to Peter. She smiled.

"Hi, Peter," she said.

He looked up, and then back down, raising his left hand to signal her to be quiet as he finished what he was writing. I felt vaguely triumphant. But when he was done with his sentence, he leapt up and said with real delight in his voice, "Jeannie! How are you? I've been wondering about you!" He practically bounded across the room to her. Then, without saying good-bye or so much as glancing at me, he placed his hand on her tiny shoulder, cupping it under his palm, and propelled her out the door.

For the rest of the day I couldn't read or work. I sat at my desk trying to focus so if he came back and asked what I'd done, I would have a list of interesting ideas to impress him with. It didn't work. Finally, I packed up my books and, defeated, went home for the day.

The next day I kept waiting for Jeannie to reappear. She didn't, but late that night I couldn't stop worrying about whether or not he'd gone to meet her somewhere, if he was spending time with her. I thought of how large his hand had looked on her shoulder and longed for him to cup my own shoulder, so I could lean my cheek against his fingers, so I could feel his skin on my skin. I couldn't concentrate. I couldn't do my work.

After a week or so of this, I broke our implicit rule of never interrupting each other's work, and after a long minute of watching him work from across the office at his desk while I sat at mine, I said, "So I haven't seen that pretty girl around in a while."

Peter barely looked up. "Hm?"

"The girl who was here last week," I said.

"Hm."

"Jeannie, was it?" I pressed.

"Mm-hmm."

"Who is she, a student of yours?"

"Former student."

"Hm," I said. And then, "I was thinking perhaps I should start working from my own office again."

That got his attention. He looked up immediately. "Why?"

"I thought maybe you'd want your own space."

"No, I work better with you here." A pause. "Do you want your own space?"

Now it was my turn to look down. I pretended to study the papers on my desk. "No," I said. "I mean, maybe. I don't know."

"That would make me very sad, but if this isn't working for you, you should say so."

"Thanks," I said, thinking I'd gone too far. I hadn't meant for him to turn it around on me. "I was just thinking that if you're going to have girls over here often, it would be more comfortable for everyone if I wasn't around," I said in a rush, digging myself deeper.

"Girls?" Peter asked. He started to laugh. "Since when do I have girls over here?"

I shrugged.

"Do you mean my student Jeannie?"

"Maybe."

"Katherine, what's this about? Do you have a problem with Jeannie?"

"Never mind. Let's talk about it later," I said.

"I think we should talk about it now."

In all the many conversations I'd imagined us having with each other about this, I had not imagined it would go so awkwardly or that I would feel so foolish. It was both terrible and strangely pleasurable to have him focus all his attention on me at last.

He pressed on. "Why don't you want me bringing girls around here?"

"I can't answer that question," I said.

"Why not?"

I looked down. I was embarrassed. "I'm going to go back to doing work now."

"That's really not fair," Peter said. He was looking at me intently from across the room.

I didn't answer, but continued to shuffle the papers on my desk, feigning absorption. But I could feel my ears burning.

After a few minutes, I heard Peter push his chair back and cross the room. I ignored him. Then he was behind me, looking over my shoulder. I felt him lean closer, so close I could feel his breath on my neck. I went absolutely still.

He pushed my hair to the side, and my whole body filled with heat. Neither of us moved. In the room, it was still enough to hear the ticking of his watch, and the even sound of his breath. He swiveled my chair around to face him, and I was so used to watching him sideways from the corner of my vision, that it was almost too much to be looking at him straight on, and so close. I tried to focus on a freckle at the top of his cheekbone, I looked down at his mouth, I looked back at his eyes. I couldn't look away—everything in my body clamored to touch him, and as he held my gaze, I felt as if he was pouring himself out of his eyes into my eyes, and I was filling up with it, with him, and there was no room for anything else, nothing to do but pour myself back.

It was like this with everything else: he kissed me, and having started, we couldn't stop—once his lips had touched my lips, I felt like they had to keep touching, keep passing this current between us. And once we held hands, we couldn't stop holding hands, and—later—once we made love, we couldn't stop making love, marveling at the energy that sprang up between us and flowed at every point of contact, as if together our bodies were a closed circuit of spirit.

Math had always seemed miraculous to me because of the beauty it revealed underlying nature, because of the deep sense of rightness that came over me when I understood something all the way through, as if for a moment I'd merged with the grace I only ever caught glimpses of. Being with Peter was like that to me: I looked at my fingers splayed against his fingers, felt his legs tangled in mine, tucked my chin into the space between his neck and his shoulder, and thought—there was a matching part of him for every part of me. Sex was the proof of that, a revelation: his body pressed against me, inside me—each inch of my body clamoring to touch each inch of his, his breath so close it felt like my own.

That time was a blur of joy during which I thought we could talk about anything. We talked math, we talked love, we were astounded by the things we had in common: we had, for instance, matching scars on the insides of our elbows—like crescent moons, about half an inch long and curving up in a smile. His was from a fishing accident, the origin of mine was unknown. When he was a child, he'd been tied up with a belt by a doctor who came to his house to give him a polio vaccination—I'd been strapped to a chair by a dentist who pulled four of my baby teeth to keep the teeth coming out beneath them from emerging crooked.

I couldn't have left Peter in those months if I'd tried. He could have rushed at me with an ax and I would have stayed immobile, gazing at him with eyes overflowing with love. Yes, I said, to everything he asked, to anything he wanted. All the space between us was alive with that word. Yes. Its reverberations echo still.

CHAPTER 12

THE FOLLOWING MARCH, PETER AND I WENT TO CHIcago for the conference to present our paper's findings. We went a week early to meet an old friend of his and to see the sights, and we booked a room together, as Mr. and Mrs. Hall, and it surprised me how easy it was to lie. Nobody at the hotel questioned whether or not we were married, nobody asked for evidence. I thought of my parents and wondered if this was all that marriage was anyway, if it was this easy, if everyone accepted it as true just because you said it was so.

When we arrived at the hotel, I was treated so courteously, and with such solicitude—Mrs. Hall, will you be needing anything else tonight? Mrs. Hall, please let me carry that for you—that I began to wonder if this was the reason women, in fact, got married at all. It wasn't just that doors were opened and bags were carried, but how—there was something in the eye contact, the tone of voice, the tip of the hat, as if now I was a person of consequence. I told Peter this, and he smiled broadly. "Maybe one day it will always be so," he said, missing the point. For my part, I was torn between explaining it to him and wanting to swoon.

The afternoon before the start of our conference, we walked from our hotel to the lake. It was laced with ice, and endless as an ocean. I couldn't see Indiana or Michigan: the water went on and on to the sky. A frigid wind blew from it, and though I wrapped my coat around myself, it chilled me to the bone. Peter rubbed my hands vigorously. He grasped me by the arms and jumped up and down, pulling me with him until I was breathless and laughing and warm.

"Let's walk," he said, and we wandered a whole hour on the lake path from downtown Chicago to Hyde Park, where we strolled around the campus of the university until it was time to meet Peter's friend Sal for coffee.

Sal was an engineer Peter had worked with on thermonuclear weapons at Los Alamos, and the first thing he did when we entered his office was lean forward and ask, "Peaceniks still giving you trouble?"

Peter laughed, and said, "I've got one with me right now." He put his hand behind my back and thrust me forward.

Sal rose from his desk, grinning. He was a big man with red cheeks, and I expected his hand to be clammy when he took mine in it, but it was smooth and delicate and soft. He held on a beat longer than I expected, smiling warmly.

"Sit," Sal commanded, pointing at one chair and pulling another out for me. He sat in front of us, his legs spread wide and his elbows on his knees. "So," he said, looking from Peter to me and smiling that slow grin, "tell me everything."

Everything, of course, was work, and Peter launched into a summary of every paper he'd read for the last month, and the things he was working on, and what he wanted to work on next. During the recitation of this long and exhaustive list, Sal asked a few pointed questions, and he and Peter went back and forth in an easy rhythm. Occasionally they'd loop me in with a question, but I was content to watch them go. Peter was loyal to Sal, loved him—it was Sal who'd taken him under his wing in Peter's first year of graduate school, and Sal who had taken him to Los Alamos.

Sal had immigrated to the United States in the 1930s from Germany and was—as Peter told me—a true intellectual. His father had been a famous chemistry professor and his mother had been a piano virtuoso. Sal had sung the theme of a Bach cantata at the age of ten months old and had been something of a violin prodigy. (Like Einstein, like Sherlock Holmes, he played every day to clear his mind.) He had taught himself eight languages and crossed Europe as a teenager on a tour of scientists' homes across the continent. He was eighteen when he came to America, but he spoke with no discernible accent.

Sal had no wife or family. His father had remained in Germany, certain that his name would protect him from the Nazis until it was too late. Sal's entire extended family had been killed. Peter thought Sal never married or had a family of his own as a kind of penance for surviving when everyone else he knew had died, and while there may have been some truth in that, we discovered many years later that Sal was gay.

Just looking at him, though, you couldn't have guessed at all the things he had lived through. He was free and generous of manner—and so trusting in his nature that I couldn't help but respond in kind. Peter had opened up to Sal because of this kindness. He'd had other teachers who'd recognized his formidable talents, but it was friendship that Sal offered before anything else, and it was this friendship that Peter had grasped with both hands.

Peter's parents had always been unimpressed by his accomplishments. He had been born late in their lives, long past the time when they were expecting children, and so he was always treated like a disruptive and not entirely welcome surprise. As the youngest child of a household long accustomed to functioning without him, he'd always felt somewhat overlooked by his family, but when both his beloved older brothers died, that had been the end. While they'd been away fighting, Peter and his parents listened to the radio together, read the news, scoured the names of the missing and the dead. Peter had been the one to find his brothers' names in the newspaper one after another. By some cruel fluke, his family had not been informed before their names had been printed. Peter had sat stunned and disbelieving: his brothers hadn't even been in the same countries—what kind of coincidence could this be? It seemed impossible. He kept closing and reopening the newspaper, and when his father—annoyed at the rustling noise—asked him to hand it over, Peter had folded it up and refused.

"Give it here," his father had said, impatient and unknowing, and Peter had sat on the paper and pushed his father away from him with shaking hands. All he knew with any certainty was if he let his father read it, it'd be true. He didn't remember what happened after that, didn't remember his father finally taking possession of the newspaper and reading what he had tried to hide from him, or his mother receiving the news. He had blocked it out.

What he knew was that in the days and months that followed, his mother became increasingly anxious about his physical safety—opening and closing his door half a dozen times at night and standing over his bed to make sure he was breathing. He would wake with a start to her hand a few inches over his mouth, feeling for his breath. Every time he opened his eyes, she would leave the room without a word.

For Peter, everything was tied up with that initial tragedy. When, as an undergraduate, he met Sal, whose age was the midpoint of his two siblings, Peter felt like he'd acquired an older brother. Sal teased and played pranks on him. He talked to him about math, but also gave him lessons for an hour a day on his piano, and told him to feel free to borrow any of his books. Sal introduced him to all the faculty as "our newest most brilliant colleague," and when Peter was despondent, Sal told him to buck up, that he'd win the Fields Medal one day, which turned out to be true. So Peter's loyalty to Sal was fierce. And when Sal asked him to come with him to Los Alamos to work on the hydrogen bomb, Peter didn't think twice. He believed in Sal, and also that the only way to achieve a lasting peace was to develop as many weapons as possible and to use them to enforce the peace.

When his brothers had died, he'd been too young to stand beside them, to contribute to the war. He'd been too small to protect his family. His willingness to help build bombs, to strengthen the military, came (I have always thought) from the desire to make it up to them somehow. He was in opposition to many of the scientists who'd worked on the first generation of nuclear bombs, who had reversed their positions and were against developing any more.

Long after the project was over, Peter would be made to defend his choice over and over. A few times he'd been the target of anti-Vietnam activists who'd accused him of being paid by defense funding, and of turning MIT into a branch of the military. Neither of these things was true, and in fact Peter was against the war in Vietnam, but against his critics he always responded the same way: World War II had been a different beast, and he'd helped build the hydrogen bomb to secure the nation's future and keep America safe. He was a patriot who wanted to serve the country that he loved.

I was convinced of the sincerity of his feelings, though I didn't agree with the conclusions he drew from them. They seemed too simple, too innocent, even. When he had been at Los Alamos developing the hydrogen bomb, I had been in grade school, getting

I wanted desperately to meet Grothendieck, who was already on his way to becoming a legend, mostly for his mathematics but also for his radical political views. Starstruck, I hung back and felt shy. I had told Peter to socialize without me, feeling nervous about being seen as his girlfriend instead of his collaborator—as a woman instead of a mathematician. But now I felt stranded, unsure of how to approach. I worked my way toward the group Grothendieck was standing in, but lost my nerve. I stood at the edge of the crowd and listened awkwardly.

He was talking about the étale cohomology theory of schemes that he'd recently developed and would later use to prove the Weil conjecture. The following year he would lecture on category theory in the forests surrounding Hanoi while it was being bombed to protest the Vietnam War. I was fascinated by him. I suppose all of us were. He had a nervous, passionate way of shifting from one leg to the other as he talked. He'd been born in the 1930s to anarchist parents and grown up in internment camps in France, which he'd escaped as a teenager with the intention of assassinating Hitler, and then he'd been hidden in a village in France where he'd been allowed to attend secondary school and first became fascinated with math. His mother contracted the tuberculosis that would later kill her in an internment camp; his father was sent to Auschwitz, where he perished. After the war, Grothendieck went to Paris, where unpolished, lacking formal training, and coming as he did from such a deprived and tragic background, he shocked onlookers by ascending to mathematical stardom. I did not know any of this background then, only what he had accomplished, and that upon being invited to Harvard he'd famously refused to sign a pledge promising not to overthrow the United States government. When he was told he could be sent to prison, he'd cheerfully replied he didn't mind as long as he'd have access to his books.

I wish I'd had the nerve to talk to Grothendieck when I had the chance. Soon after the conference, upon learning his position was partially funded by the military, he would quit his job as a professor. From there he'd grow increasingly estranged from the mathematical community, eventually cutting off contact, rejecting prizes, yet continuing to produce monumental works in isolation. All the while he'd denounce a scientific culture that he claimed was governed by competition and hierarchy, and the outright theft of ideas.

By the time I saw him at the conference, he already felt—he would later say—that he was living and working in a golden cage. But all I noticed then was how the people crowded around him, wooing him, and felt too constrained myself to join. *This must have been what Cinderella felt at the ball before she danced with the prince,* I thought: I had dreamed of being in the presence of so many of the people attending, and now here I was, eavesdropping on their conversations. I lurked on the outside fringe, watching the clock, fidgeting and feeling out of place.

Someone asked me once if the loneliness I always felt came from being alone in a field in which there were no other women, but that wasn't it, exactly. I wasn't alone. There were in fact two other women at the conference, but by unspoken agreement, we avoided each other. This was pure instinct, an understanding that by being seen with each other we would draw attention to ourselves as women, and that would do us more harm than good. I caught glimpses of the other women from time to time—one of them always at the center of attention, talking loudly, putting herself forward—the other hanging back at the edges of things, like a girl waiting to be asked to dance—like me. I always turned away when I saw one of them, and I suspect they did the same when they saw me.

Which is why, I think, from the moment I met him, I wanted

to be friends with Charles Lee. He was not a star like Grothendieck, but he exuded an outsider aura that I responded to with a feeling of fellowship. I met Lee in the elevator on the morning of the second day. We were wearing our name tags for the conference, so though we had never met, we recognized each other as fellow participants. I was so startled to see another Asian face that I said, "Oh!" out loud. He gave me a slight nod and then stood facing forward, observing a polite but alert and friendly silence—until the elevator gave a sudden small lurch. I yelped and put a hand out to the elevator wall, but nothing else happened. Lee assumed a crouched and ready stance, hands up, knees bent—as if preparing for a fight. I hadn't looked at him directly until this moment, but now I watched him rise back to his full height with fluid grace.

He was a small man, five five or five six maybe—an inch or two shorter than me—and as slim around the waist as a girl. I would have guessed him to be in his forties, though it turned out he was already in his midfifties.

"Hello," he said, turning toward me. "I think the elevator broke." He turned back to the front of the elevator. He bounced up and down on his toes, gently, as if to test it or to prove his point. He spoke with an accent that reminded me of my mother's, and the way he smiled felt comfortably and unexpectedly familiar. I felt not only at ease, but trusting—as if he would get us out of this.

I looked up at the ceiling, pressed my hands against the door. "What shall we do?"

"Well," he said, looking all around us—at the door, the ceiling, the walls—"I guess we press this button." And he pushed the red Alarm button on the elevator panel. Immediately, an alarm inside the elevator started ringing, shockingly loud and insistent.

We both covered our ears. "Turn it off!" I cried, laughing.

He pushed the alarm button again and again to no avail. It kept ringing. He returned to covering his ears with an exaggerated shrug. After a couple minutes of uninterrupted ringing, the alarm finally stopped.

"My God, what was that?" I laughed again. "Why would they sound the alarm inside the elevator when we're the ones who pushed the button?"

Lee leaned against the elevator wall in mock exhaustion and relief. He gave me a wry look and shrugged. "Perhaps someone will come now to fix the elevator and let us out."

"I hope so," I said. And then, "I'm Katherine."

He gave a slight bow. "I'm Lee. Are you here for the same conference as me?" Here he pointed at my name tag. "I ask, but I know the answer. What are you presenting here?"

"I'll be presenting on elliptic cohomology with Peter Hall," I said. I realized he was the first person to ask me what I was presenting on—the first to assume that I was. "But I'm also working on the Mohanty problem."

Something in Lee's face grew more alert. "A very interesting problem." He smiled. He seemed about to say something, but then there was banging from the elevator shaft and voices shouting down at us.

"How many of you are there?" the voice called.

"Two," Lee shouted back.

"We'll be lowering you manually," the voice called down.

"Did he say manually?" I said. "As in they're lowering us down in this elevator by hand?"

"Not the most efficient or reliable method, but perhaps the speediest one available to us now?" he said. And then we were going down, jerky and slow, with a sudden dip that made me gasp out loud before we lurched and steadied. The door was forced open by two sets of hands. Lee and I looked at each other. He smiled at me and gestured with his hand to exit first.

We had only been lowered to the eighth floor, and I groaned, "We're going to have to go down six flights of stairs."

"It could be worse," said Lee. "We could still be in the elevator." He laughed cheerfully. "Or it could be worst, we could be splattered inside the elevator, crushed at the bottom of the chute." And with that, he bounded down the stairs.

MY PRESENTATION WITH PETER went well: the room was full to capacity, standing room only, and afterward we were inundated with congratulations, well wishes, and every kind of attention. But as it turned out, we were overshadowed by another presentation that became the talk of the conference. In the hallway, we ran into a guy named Mac, a former student of Peter's who had been at Lee's lecture. "It was incredible," he said. "There was this old Chinese number theorist whom no one had ever heard of before, and he proved part of the Mohanty problem, the one everyone said would take at least two more decades for someone to solve."

"Could you repeat that?" Peter asked as I gasped out loud.

"How did he do it?" I asked.

Mac went on to describe precisely the approach I had originally proposed to Peter.

This kind of thing happens fairly regularly in mathematics: Bolyai, Lobachevsky, and Gauss came up with non-Euclidean geometries at the same time, independently, for instance. And Gauss was constantly one-upping Legendre, who—practically every time he proved something—would be met with Gauss's maddening, "Oh yes, I came up with that result myself years ago and never got around to publishing it!"

To write a proof or discover a new object or tool or start an entire field is not the same as creating or inventing a truth: it is more like being the first to arrive at a truth. And yet it is still a creative act, one that requires your imagination to arrive at a previously unknown understanding of a deep problem. It is something like designing and building a spacecraft, figuring out the necessary path you need to chart through space, and flying to some location you don't yet know exists, a location it feels like you discovered but also invented because it is an idea or an understanding more than an actual place.

"Lee's solution was ingenious," Mac said. "He set up a specific case of the general question, and then using the specific case, he was able to solve it for all even numbers." As he described the process, it became clear that he'd proceeded along the lines of the proof in exactly the way I had originally proposed.

I looked at Peter and he looked at me. He reached out and took my hand. I squeezed it.

I could tell Peter felt much worse about the whole thing than I did. If anything, I felt vindicated, and pleased that it was Lee who'd done it. There was a momentary pang of regret that I had not been the one to solve the problem, but it was mostly outweighed by the pleasure I could take in having my thinking confirmed.

"What about for odd numbers?" I asked.

"Not yet," Mac said. "Because obviously it's a trickier case. But it seems inevitable that that will come next."

"Yes," I said, feeling some relief that it wasn't all over, that there remained further work to be done on the problem I'd wanted to tackle.

I didn't get the chance to talk to Lee again at the conference: every time I caught a glimpse, he was surrounded by other conference-goers and he looked tense and uncomfortable.

The story circulating about Lee was that he'd never really been accepted by mathematicians before. He'd been something of a star in graduate school, but then he'd had a falling-out with his graduate advisor and had been unable to get an academic job. He'd worked as a janitor and a florist and chopped vegetables at a Chinese restaurant in his town. It had been hard for him to hold down a job. He was unkempt and distracted, and when he ran out of paper, he wrote notes on the backs of his hands. Even now that he'd proven this important result, what most of the other mathematicians felt for him was a reluctant admiration coupled with a sort of alarmed and curious contempt.

What I felt for Charles Lee was neither curiosity nor contempt, but kinship. Even now, after his triumph, he was alone. I wanted to approach him, to break through the crowd to ask him when and how he'd solved his problem. But I was aware that I was nobody, and that I'd already told him I was working on the Mohanty problem in the elevator. I didn't want it now to seem like I was trying to claim something that wasn't mine, so I stayed away.

EVERY CULTURE HAS ITS FAIRY TALES: the same is true for mathematics. The most famous math fairy tale goes like this: Once upon a time, in a tiny town in South India, there lived a husband and a wife who were so poor they slept on the dirt floor of their hut. They wanted very much to have children, but year after year, no child came to fill the wife's womb, and so she went on a trek to pray at the temple of her family's goddess. While she was there she was blessed with a dream that she would bear a son who would speak in the language of the gods.

Soon after, a boy was born to them, and they named him Srinivasa Ramanujan. He did not speak a word until he was three, but then he spoke in sentences and could write words in the sand with a stick. His parents by then rented an extra room in their hut to two students studying at the college nearby. Ramanujan, while still a young boy, read the books that these students left behind, and in this way he discovered the divine language: he discovered mathematics.

He was a star in high school, the best student anyone had ever seen. Much was expected of him when he went to the university, but Ramanujan became fixated on mathematics and only mathematics, and studying that to the exclusion of all other things, he failed out of college. Shocked and despairing, he ran away to live alone in a hut where he filled notebook after notebook with notes.

Alone, destitute, half dead with despair, he finally mailed pages torn from his notebooks to strangers he hoped would help him: a clerk, a deputy accountant, a professor. To those with any understanding, his pages were magic spells containing a rare power: they were keys to another realm. And so the clerk, the accountant, and the professor became his champions.

With their help, he sent his notebooks across the sea. In Cambridge, England, lived several famous mathematicians, and he wrote to all of them. The first two did not respond. A third, by the name of Hill, wrote back: "You have some talent, but clearly lack formal training. You will never have the foundation to be a real mathematician."

But a fourth mathematician opened the notebook that had been sent to him, and saw what lay behind a seemingly nonsensical formula: $1 + 2 + 3 + \ldots + \infty = -\frac{1}{12}$. Rewritten as $1 + 2 + 3 + \ldots + n + \ldots = 1 + \frac{1}{2^{-1}} + \frac{1}{3^{-1}} + \ldots + \frac{1}{n^{-1}} + \ldots = -\frac{1}{12}$, it was in fact the calculation for Riemann's zeta function $\zeta(s) = 1 + \frac{1}{2^s} + \frac{1}{3^s} + \frac{1}{4^s} + \ldots$ when fed with the number -1. The fourth mathematician, whose name was G. H. Hardy, was astounded. "Prove to me that you are who I think you may be," he wrote back to Ramanujan. "Send me more."

The notes Ramanujan sent next were stunning and strange and written in a wild notation. He claimed he could calculate the number of primes up to 100 million with an error of just 1 or 2. Hardy couldn't believe it. This nobody from India had conjured up part of the Riemann hypothesis all on his own: Had he also solved it? It turned out he had not, though he had solved a dazzling number of other problems. But he didn't know the language of proofs: he didn't know how to show his work. Later, Hardy said his association with Ramanujan was "the one romantic incident in my life." He said he had known Ramanujan's theorems must be true, "because if they were not true, no one would have had the imagination to invent them."

So a ticket was bought, and Ramanujan boarded a ship to England. There he became Hardy's student—a student whose intuition surpassed that of his teacher. He had never been taught how to write a proper proof, but in some ways he seemed liberated by not knowing the rules—he seemed to simply know things so complicated, to recognize patterns so deep, and to find them so obvious, while the mathematicians around him labored for weeks on each declaration, just to check if he was correct.

If this sounds like a happy ending, beware. After all, every fairy tale has its dark side. At Cambridge, Ramanujan was cold and hungry and homesick. A strict vegetarian, he had difficulty finding food to eat. His British patrons thought him fastidious and ungrateful, a savage rescued from the wilds. His fellow students scoffed at him, made fun of his clothes, his food, how he always hunched over, how he always ate alone and without a knife or a fork. He didn't even use a blanket, they said, shivering like a fool on top of his bed, a simpleton who had slept on the dirt and in the heat his whole life. Because he'd taught himself everything he knew—essentially deriving all of modern mathematics himself, sitting on the ground in a hut—there were huge gaps in his education. So what of his dazzling mental leaps, if he didn't know the least of what any schoolboy in England did?

Ramanujan was aware of his enemies. He knew that he was a laughingstock. Like Kafka's ape who learned to talk and drink and smoke cigars, he was a novelty act, expected to explain over and over again how he came to be so clever, while his audience patted themselves on the back for having discovered him. Oh, Ramanujan was celebrated, but he was always the object, he was always the prize.

And he was a sickly prize at that, always in and out of the hospital, always shivering, undernourished, always sad. After throwing himself facedown in front of a train that braked, however, and did not hit him—he was taken to a mental hospital. In the hospital, he was told they would only give him firewood to heat his room on the days he was mathematically productive. He was not productive. Still, he could perform parlor tricks. When Hardy came to visit him, Ramanujan blinked awake from his stupor. "Your cab number was 1729?" he said. "How interesting. Have you ever noticed it is the smallest number expressible as the sum of two cubes in two different ways? $1^3 + 12^3$ and $9^3 + 10^3$."

Luminaries had brought Ramanujan to England, but he only wanted to return to his heathen land, to India, back to the sun, the dust, and his mother's voice. Hardy and his colleagues could not believe it. Did he not understand he was sabotaging himself? Did he not understand the marvelous opportunities before him? But Ramanujan had had enough: he would go home. And yet the fairy tale would not release him, and the man who said "An equation for me has no meaning unless it represents a thought of God" was dead a year later from the tuberculosis he contracted in England. He was thirty-two years old.

Graduate students and researchers still pore over his notebooks, and at some point someone discovered in one a list of all the primes up to 100 million that Ramanujan had compiled. But there was no formula, no notes to give them a clue as to how he had constructed it. In death, he was given the respect—even reverence—he was often denied in life. I've heard it said that you can judge a society by how it treats the lowest of its members. Let me say now, I've often been dismayed at how we treat our best.

Chapter 14

THE SUMMER CAME SOON AFTER THE CONFERENCE: A blur of weeks and studying and exams, and then my third year of graduate school was over. Leo and Rob left for summer jobs at Bell Labs, and I stayed on at MIT as a research assistant to Professor Pearce, a geometer working on multidimensional cones. Those early months of summer were glorious: I had many hours free to work on the Mohanty problem, which had been the first thing I read upon returning from the conference and which I had been thinking about ever since. Meanwhile, the weather mellowed out from the fragile warmth of spring into a string of progressively hotter days, and Peter and I spent nights at each other's places, running the fans all day and all night long. Without classes or the structure of school or the attention of students and faculty around us, we went on picnics, we went on walks, pleasure and work flowing through our talks and long hours together.

One day, Peter and I went to the park to have a picnic and to work. We sat side by side, our papers secured by rocks we'd collected from the edge of a riverbank. I had on a red hat that kept blowing off. Peter was wearing my sunglasses. We were surrounded by huge trees, their branches creaking in the wind.

I taught him the exercise my mother had done with me with the trees, and at the end of it, Peter said, "Wow. I feel so calm."

I smiled and leaned into him. He put his arm around me.

"Tell me more about your family," he said. "I feel like you know everything about me, but you never talk about your childhood."

"There's not that much to know," I said.

"That can't be true," Peter said. He squeezed me tight. Back then his physical proximity was still enough to make me swoon, and I caught my breath and laughed.

"What do you want to know?" I asked.

"Well, how'd you get so good at math?" he asked. "When did you get interested in science?"

I told him about the ham radio my father had built for me. I told him about my mother and the lightning. "You know," I said, "I always thought it was my father who encouraged my interest in science, and it's true that he did. But I don't think I ever understood how much I got from my mother. She's the one who taught me to start paying attention to things. She's the one who encouraged me to think."

"That's wonderful," he said, and then he frowned. "Have you ever tried to track her down?"

"I've thought about it once or twice. But I don't know where to start." I paused. It was difficult to say the rest. "The thing is, I don't think she wants to be found. It's not like we moved. It's not like we don't have the exact same home address and phone number. She could have written or called at any time. If she wanted to see me, she could. So I can only assume that she doesn't."

Peter rubbed my shoulder.

Eager to change the subject, I said, "Actually, could I show you something?" All our talk of childhood had reminded me of my German notebook, which was in my satchel. I took it out and opened it. "It's a relic from the war that my father saved for me," I said. "Do you see anything familiar in there?"

Peter flipped through the pages. "I'm not sure what this is," he said. "Whether it's original work or notes picked up from a book or a talk or random doodles. It's not really clear."

"Yes, it's hard to tell," I said. "I don't know, either, and I'm not sure where it's trying to go, but I see some familiar theorems, like here." I flipped through several pages. "Here are the Friedmann equations, and look here, that's the Boltzmann equation."

"Yes, but I can't tell what he's trying to do with them," Peter said. "How old is this notebook?"

"It says Göttingen 1935," I said. "See? S. M."

"It'd be interesting to track this fellow down. But I can't tell just from a quick glance how promising this is. What else did you find?"

I showed him another equation. "This also seems familiar, but I don't know from where," I said.

Peter tapped his pencil. "Yes, I've seen it too," he said. "It's from invariant theory. When we get back to the office, remind me to pull out one of Klein's monographs. I believe I saw something like this in there." He rubbed his chin. "I don't know what the equation has to do with the rest of it, though."

We sat next to each other, our arms touching, flipping through the pages of the notebook and trying to make sense of it together. A lone beetle with bright yellow geometrical markings circled the edge of the table, the filaments of its antennae waving wildly. "Look at that guy go," Peter said.

Watching him watch the beetle with a delighted smile on his

face, I felt as happy as I'd ever been, like someone was finally helping me put something from my childhood back in order. It was more than that, of course—I was in love, I was making progress in my work, and I had the companionship and support of an important mathematician. I felt as if I'd imagined my life into being, as if my luck would keep growing, and never run out.

THAT SAME SUMMER I started work on the second part of the Mohanty problem—the extension to odd numbers. This time, Peter was on board and excited, but I didn't invite him to collaborate. I felt a little selfish not offering, but I wanted to do it myself, and Peter was only too happy to let me do this, as penance, I think, for his earlier discouragement. He insisted, however, on talking through my ideas with me, on helping as much as he could while leaving the main work to me.

We saw only a handful of people—Pearce, the professor I was working for, made almost no demands of me, and so I was more likely to see him socially than at school. We entertained only once, when Maria Mayer happened to be passing through Boston. She was an old friend of Peter's—she'd worked with him and Sal at Los Alamos, and she was one of three scientists to propose the nuclear shell model for the atomic nucleus. I was excited beyond reason to have her and her husband over for dinner: she had won the Nobel Prize in Physics during my first year of graduate school, and I'd sent away for her speech with a feeling of gratitude and pride for what she'd accomplished.

Maria Mayer had been born and raised in Germany and started out studying mathematics at the University of Göttingen, where she met her husband. But she was seduced by the nascent field of quantum mechanics and switched her focus to physics. When she and her husband moved to the United States, first to Johns Hopkins, where she was introduced to chemical physics, and then to Columbia, neither of these universities would consider hiring her as a faculty member, so she took what she could—a modest assistantship at one and an office space at the other. When her husband moved to Chicago, she was again denied a paid position so she worked as a volunteer professor for the Institute for Nuclear Studies at the University of Chicago, and eventually as a half-time Senior Physicist at the Argonne National Laboratory. Here, she learned nuclear physics, and like a fairy story, where all the elements come together in the unlikeliest way at the end, this is how Maria Mayer would end up winning the Nobel Prize: the combination of mathematics and physics and chemistry that she acquired led to the discovery of the subatomic structure of an atom. "San Diego Housewife Wins Nobel Prize," her local newspaper read. Peter always told the last bit of the story with a disbelieving laugh.

In any case, it was with great expectations and excitement that I prepared to meet Maria Mayer. I chose my clothes and rubbed rouge on my cheeks and lips, like a girl preparing for a date.

Meanwhile, Peter went grocery shopping and came home with charcoal and hamburgers for the grill, and a case of beer. We sliced vegetables and slid them on skewers. He laughed at me for being so nervous to meet her. "She's the most down-to-earth woman in the world," he said. "You'll love her, you'll see." Still, I was nervous. Back then, I didn't know how rare it is for a person to actually meet your expectations, but Maria Mayer did. She exceeded them.

She was in her sixties and wearing a simple linen suit. She had frizzy curls she hadn't even attempted to tame. She had two children around Peter's age, and she treated us with a sort of maternal fondness that put me immediately at ease. It's that ease I remember now, along with her astonishing graciousness. Her husband, Joseph, was just as easygoing and warm.

"I want to sit next to Katherine," Maria said as we escorted them through the backyard and settled them on matching lawn chairs. "Tell me all about yourself," she said, leaning forward.

For the rest of dinner, she ignored everyone but me, focusing on the food in front of her and my descriptions of the paper Peter and I had published together, and the problem I was working on now.

"How interesting!" she exclaimed. "Bravo for you! This is why I love talking to young people. Are you going to go on the market in the next couple years?"

"That's the idea," I said. "Though my father's convinced a math department isn't going to hire a woman faculty member. Not that he's an academic."

Maria nodded thoughtfully. "Well, in my experience, he's not wrong," she said. She shared that she hadn't gotten her first tenure-track job until six years ago. She'd done the bulk of her work for free. "It isn't that I didn't try to get paid," she said. "At first the universities said they couldn't hire me because of anti-nepotism rules. They all wanted to hire Joseph, you see," and here she shot her husband a wink.

Her levity astonished me. "But doesn't that make you angry?"

"Angry?" she said.

"That you were turned away. That you had to work for free when you were so much better than everyone else who was getting paid. That it had to be so much harder for you."

"Oh, it could have been much, much worse," she said. "I mean, at least I got credit and the Nobel Prize! How many women were denied their medals and not even acknowledged? There was poor Rosalind Franklin and the double helix, God rest her soul. And

Peter!" Here she reached over and slapped him on the shoulder. "There's your friend Chien-Shiung Wu, who disproved the law of parity. Even you said it was a shame Wu wasn't included on the Nobel Prize. And don't get me started on how women get written out of textbooks. Oh, Katherine, don't kid yourself. Among the rare subset of women who could have won a Nobel Prize, I am one of the even rarer ones who was actually recognized with one."

"This is all turning out to be a much more depressing conversation than I'd expected," I said. "And here I was thinking you were going to say something encouraging."

She laughed. "How's this? I got to do science," she said. "I didn't have a paying job for most of the time, and I do think I had to work a little harder than everyone to get my foot in the door. But I got to do science, and that was the most important thing."

"It isn't fair you had to work harder," I insisted, but I felt very aware of Peter and Joseph. I wondered if this was the same conversation we'd be having if we were alone.

"Oh, Katherine," she said. "Life's not fair." She said it very simply. "I could have spent my time fighting the unfairness of it all, or I could dedicate my time to science. There wasn't time for both."

AFTER MARIA AND HER HUSBAND LEFT, Peter and I had our first argument. We'd cleaned up and settled down together on a blanket outside in his backyard to watch the fireflies blink in and out above the lawn.

"I can't believe she didn't get paid all those years," I said. "Her and Emmy Noether!"

Peter nodded. "Luckily, it turned out just fine for both of them," he said. He nuzzled my neck.

I pulled away. "That's not the point," I said. I thought of my father telling me he couldn't imagine any department hiring me over a man. This was a source of immense anxiety, because I had no idea if I would be able to make a living. If I didn't get an academic job, I'd have to get work doing something else. "Don't you think that women should be paid for the work they do?"

"Of course I believe women should be paid, and equally," he said. "But just to play devil's advocate, Emmy Noether claimed she actually liked not getting paid, because she didn't have to do any of the additional duties official faculty were required to do."

"Oh, Peter, you're a smart man, please don't be stupid," I said.

"Don't blame me, I'm just repeating what Noether said!" He laughed.

"Come on," I said. "That's a nice story, but what was she supposed to say? She didn't want to make everyone she worked with uncomfortable, and she had to fight so hard just to be in the room. What time or energy do you think she or anyone had left to fight a battle she'd never win about money? I'd take that comment of hers a lot more seriously if she'd been offered a salary and then turned it down."

"Whether or not that's true," Peter said, "you make it sound like these women had terrible lives. Noether was so happy and generous! And Maria is wonderful, you saw for yourself. They both had incredibly productive, enviable careers."

"It depends on how you look at it," I said. "They both accomplished enough to make anyone jealous, it's true—but do you think that the men who were at their level would have been content to never have held a permanent position while they were doing their most important work, or consented to work without pay, or suffered all the indignities of having to beg to be able to be in the room when they were clearly better than everyone else? Would you, Peter

Hall, agree to do what you do for no money, while everyone else gets paid?"

"Well, Maria was supported by her husband, and Noether had some money from her father," Peter said.

"Exactly," I said. "Their circumstances allowed them to work for no pay. What if they hadn't? What would we have lost as a scientific community, without their contributions? I'm not saying they had terrible lives, but they were certainly exploited. Why can't we admit that, soberly and matter-of-factly?"

"Settle down," Peter said. "I'm on your side! No need to get worked up."

But I was getting worked up. "I don't know why you want to pretend that these women weren't taken advantage of, and that women now as a class aren't currently being taken advantage of." I wanted to say more, that I felt doomed by this pattern—not just of getting taken advantage of as a woman, but Peter's failure to recognize it as such.

"Come on now, Katherine," Peter said. "We both know you're here on a very generous fellowship that was made just for women. I think you're doing just fine. How are you being taken advantage of?"

"I'm not talking about me. I've been very lucky so far," I conceded. "But remember, the Kennedy Commission reports that women make fifty-nine cents on the dollar that men make for the same job. Just so you know, that is the current state of affairs."

He shrugged. "Well, that's all changing now," he said. "For instance, you are here now, so clearly we're making progress as a society to right some of our historical wrongs. Let's not fight about this. I promise I'll support you. I'll make sure you get everything you deserve."

"That's not the point," I muttered, but he wrapped his arm

around me and pulled me close. Soon, he fell asleep, the rhythm of his breath tickling my neck. Darkness had fallen, and the fireflies had gone away. I lay in the dark with my eyes open, watching the stars, feeling the thud of my own heart beating against my back.

LUCK, OR HAPPINESS, or nearly everything in this life, I've found, is largely a matter of perspective. I learned this when my mother left—how one action can shift everything on its axis. From the moment she was gone, I always saw the past and our family through the lens of her departure. The depth of her unhappiness, her capacity to leave us, how little I knew her—the question of who we even were to each other, and what we owed each other—colored everything backward. And when I remember that argument with Peter, which wasn't really an argument, I still find it difficult to locate the disagreement. What did I want from him then? To see things he couldn't see, to see things even I couldn't see? There is the story you think you are living in, and then there is the invisible, secret, unguessed-at core of that story, around which everything else revolves.

Chapter 15

All too soon the summer was over, and Rob and Leo and all the other students returned. Classes resumed, and my fourth year of graduate school began. One day early that fall I was in the library searching for a monograph when I accidentally heard two men talking about me. I was standing in the darkness of the stacks, a pile of books in my arms, when I heard my name. I froze.

"You know she's sleeping with Peter Hall," one of them said.

"Yeah, he puts her name on all his papers now," the other responded. And then they snickered.

I wish I'd walked out into the light and confronted them right then and there. But I didn't, I was flooded with shame. So I stood in the shadows, ears burning with humiliation, until the voices were quiet, and I guessed it was safe to sneak out. The problem with that, of course, was I never knew who had said those things about me—whether they had been faculty or students, or even friends or acquaintances of mine. And because I didn't know, I suspected everyone.

IF THERE WAS ANY SOURCE of awkwardness that arose between Peter and me, it came from that overheard conversation and the very successful paper we had published together. As the year progressed, it became clear that Peter was receiving all the credit for the paper, and I was getting none. My name was right there next to his, and yet when the paper was cited, my name went unmentioned more often than not. Men described my own paper to me, calling the results "the Hall results." It was as if I'd been erased. Everyone just assumed he'd done all the work. And worse, Peter didn't seem to notice, even when it happened in front of him.

I tried to take it in stride, focusing instead on the Mohanty problem, but I found myself beset by the mounting anxiety that everything I did would be seen as a bone that Peter had thrown my way, that my accomplishments would always be compared, unfavorably, to his. So it was, when on the recommendation of an old college professor I was offered a visiting fellowship at the University of Bonn for the following year, I was immediately tempted to go.

Peter, however, was strongly against it. "Why would you break up this momentum we've got going?" he said. "Not to mention, I'm the most productive I've been in years, and you've been doing extremely well for yourself. Do you really think you'll find a better mentor in Germany, who's more invested in your future than me?"

I prickled. "You said yourself that studying abroad as a student was one of the most formative experiences of your career," I said. "You said it shaped your intellectual life."

"Things were different then," he said. "Nowadays mathematicians from all over the world come to us. Back then it was the other way around. And I was alone—I wasn't leaving anyone behind."

This also rankled. It wasn't Peter's fault, of course—who wouldn't resist their partner going across the world for one to two years, whether there was a clear benefit or not? But I felt constrained in ways I couldn't explain and didn't fully understand, and though none of these things were his fault, I'm afraid he took the brunt of my frustrations, as partners usually do. "Are you saying you won't be here when I return if I go?" I asked.

Peter, bless him, laughed out loud. "Where else would I be?" he said. "I'm just saying if you wait another two years, until I'm up for sabbatical, then maybe we can go together."

"And what will I do while I wait? Not to mention I don't think they'll hold the fellowship open for me."

"You can go as a postdoctoral fellow. Or if they don't invite you again, I'm sure I can get myself invited, and then you can come with me. If that's what you want, I promise, I'll take you."

I sighed. "But that's not what I want. I want to go on my own invitation, not as someone who happens to be appended to you."

"Well, maybe it isn't ideal," Peter conceded. "But if you're part of a team, sometimes you have to make compromises."

I wish I hadn't said what I said next the way I said it, but I did. I said, "I'm not sure I want to be part of a team."

Peter looked immediately and deeply hurt. "You don't?"

"Not if it means you think I should sit around waiting for two years," I said. "I want to be with you, but I don't want to be the one who always has to compromise. Sometimes I want to stand on my own. To make it by myself first, the way that you did."

"I see," Peter said slowly. "I didn't realize you felt like you were always compromising." He was silent. I felt terrible.

"I love working with you," I said. "But look at the paper we wrote together—people talk to me about it sometimes as if I wasn't one of its authors."

"I tell everyone how much work you did on that paper," Peter exclaimed. "I tell everyone you're the smart one between us."

I rolled my eyes. "No one takes you seriously when you say that, Peter. And I feel like if I stay here, I'll only ever be your sidekick."

"So do something of your own, but stay here," Peter said. "Do you want me to withdraw as your advisor? I'm happy to withdraw. You don't need me for your work, Katherine. I know that."

But he sounded so wounded that I didn't believe him. "No," I said, "I don't want anyone else as my advisor. I like working with you. I just—wanted to try something else." I felt as if I had damaged something between us, and just kept cracking it further.

"Can I tell you a story?" I asked, and I told Peter about Blake and his copying my problem set when I was in college, and how the professor had accused me of being the cheater. Afterward, I felt shaken, as if by telling him the story I had invited him to stand judgment, to weigh in whether or not he also thought I had cheated.

"That's terrible," Peter said. "Why didn't you take it to the head of the Math Department?"

"That professor was the head of the Math Department."

"Why didn't you take it to the dean?"

"I don't know," I said. "It never occurred to me."

Peter was quiet for a moment. "Do you want me to get in touch with them now?" he asked. "I could say something."

I laughed. "What does it matter? What difference does it make?"

"Maybe I can get them to revoke Blake's degree," he said. "Or blackball him. He should pay for what he did."

"That would be ridiculous," I said.

"What's his last name?"

"I'm not telling you."

"Why not?"

"I don't want to stir things up," I said. "It doesn't matter. I did fine. I graduated. I'm here."

"I could probably call over and figure out who this guy is," Peter said.

"Please promise me you won't."

"Why not? I could probably call his parents—you said his dad was a mathematician?"

"Peter, please."

"If I promise, will you tell me his name?"

"No," I said. "I don't want you to know anything about him. I'm not telling you this so that you can do something about it. This isn't yours to handle." I felt bad all over again, the same shame about how everything had unfolded. "What I really wanted to tell you," I said, "was that for months after, I'd go over the problem sets Blake copied, over and over, quizzing myself, to make sure each answer was mine. I mean, I knew they were mine, I'd done them, but something about Blake and the professor uniting against me made me doubt myself, made me wonder if somehow I'd remembered everything wrong."

There was a long pause. "I'm sorry that happened to you," Peter said. "Why didn't you stand up for yourself?"

I found myself at a loss for words. "I didn't feel like I could," I said. "The professor didn't believe me, it was my word against Blake's, and frankly I was made to feel lucky that I was allowed to stay on at all." But I felt now a second prickle of shame at Peter's question. Why *hadn't* I stood up for myself? "I guess I thought," I said slowly, "that working hard and succeeding, beating him and doing well was the best way I had of standing up for myself."

"I see," Peter said.

"It's not that I want to go to Bonn," I said. "Or that I don't want to be on your team. I just feel like I won't ever feel safe until I can stand on my own."

There was a long pause, and then Peter said, "I can't believe you don't trust me."

I reached out and took his hand. "That's not what I meant," I said. "It's not about you at all."

After a week or two of consideration, I told Peter I wouldn't go to Bonn after all. And he said, "Are you sure? I don't want to hold you back."

I said I was sure, and he said he was glad, but I felt that something had come between us. That I had planted distrust or dissatisfaction in him, and I regretted it sorely. Still, we moved on, and the conversation was forgotten—or at least dropped—and we went on as before, though it seemed to me that Peter henceforth held back just a little, that he tried to give me more space—which wasn't at all what I'd wanted. But I wasn't sure if he really was doing these things, or if it was all my imagination. I see now, of course, that he was trying to give me what I'd asked for: that he was hurt and afraid I would leave. All I could see then was my own fears—that I would lose him, or I would lose my career.

ONE EVENING LATER THAT SPRING, as Peter and I sat in my kitchen working, Linda called me, weeping. At first I couldn't figure out whose voice it was, but the grief in it frightened me. "Who is this?" I said. "Hello?"

"It's Linda," she gasped. "I'm calling about your father."

"What is it?" I asked. "What's happened?"

Linda cried into the phone. "Your father's had a heart attack."

Everything in me went still. "Is he all right?" I asked. "Linda. Is he alive?"

"Yes," she burst out. "He's in the hospital."

"Thank God," I said. "How serious is it?"

"They're running tests," Linda said, gasping. "But I've never seen him like this. He started clutching his shoulder after dinner yesterday, and staggering around crying out your name. He was bumping into the furniture and the doors and I was right there beside him but I couldn't make him see me. He just kept gasping and moaning your name, and now he's better, but I can't be here on my own, alone with him. I can't."

"Okay," I said. "I'll come out on the very next flight. I just need you to give me the doctor's name and for you to write down everything he says when he comes in so I can look it over." I didn't know anything about medicine, or heart attacks, but taking charge like this helped me feel calmer.

"Okay," Linda said, "I will do that," and I could tell she felt calmer too.

When we hung up, I turned to Peter and said, "I need to go back to Michigan tomorrow. My father's had a heart attack."

"Sweetheart," Peter said, when I told him what had happened. "My love." He wrapped his arms around me.

I wriggled out of his arms. "I have to pack," I said, pushing him away. "I'll have to go to the airport and get a flight out tomorrow, but I should still get packed and ready to go."

"Of course, Katherine, we'll do all these things. But why don't you just stay still and take a few deep breaths. Relax for a moment."

But I didn't want to relax. I wanted to keep going, keep active, because there was a ball of grief, hard and aching in my chest, that I could ignore as long as I had something to do.

"Do you want me to go back to Michigan with you?"

"No," I said. "They don't even know about you. Let's wait."

The last conversation I'd had with my father had been a fight.

I'd asked him to tell me more about the woman who'd given birth to me, and he'd refused. Then I'd asked him to tell me more about my mother, the one who'd raised me. "Stop pushing it," he said. "Let it go. You never know when to stop."

"And you never know when to give in," I said. "I have a right to these stories. I deserve to know what you know." And then I'd told him I wouldn't come home again until he agreed.

And now I felt sick to my stomach, almost as if my father had actually died—as if the thought of his death had made it come closer. I regretted not telling him about Peter. I regretted never introducing him to my friends Leo and Rob. He had never been to my apartment. I hadn't even told him when I was in Chicago, just a few hours away from him by train. When I went to see him this time, I decided, I would do whatever he asked. I would not push so hard.

Chapter 16

I RUSHED TO MY FATHER THE NEXT AFTERNOON. WHEN I entered his room, Linda stood by his bedside. My father sat up in his bed, the beat of his heart beeping steadily beside him on a monitor. He smiled. "Katherine," he said. "My love." It was probably the influence of medication that had made him speak to me that way, in a voice that was like a caress, but tears sprang to my eyes anyway. "My darling," my father said. "I've missed you so much, and there's so much to tell you." He held out his arms. "But first, come here, and let this old man put his arms around you."

I went to him immediately, leaving my suitcase at the door. There were two empty chairs, one by the bed and one a little farther away, and the room was divided by a curtain, beneath which I could see the legs of another bed, on which lay another patient with his own visitors. I sat in the chair right by the bed and leaned into my father. He wrapped his arms around me, pressing me into his chest. The pajamas the hospital had given him were coarse and scratchy.

He smelled different than I remembered him, less sweet and more metallic.

After a moment, I tried to pull away, but my father said, "No, Katherine, stay here for a moment."

"I'm sorry I didn't visit enough," I said.

"You're here now," my father said. "And the last few days, I've been thinking about the past, about what I did wrong and what I did right."

"You weren't so bad," I murmured.

My father waved his hand. "It's not about good or bad," he said. "But I have two great regrets in my life. One is not taking better care of you. The other is not being able to make your mother happy."

"You did all right taking care of me," I said in a small voice. I glanced at Linda.

She cleared her throat and stood up. "Do you think it'd be all right if I stepped outside for a moment?" she asked my father. "Just to give you and Katherine some privacy?"

"Yes, please," my father said, and as she passed by, he took her hand in his and kissed it.

I waited a moment after she'd closed the door behind her. "Why couldn't you make Mom happy?" I asked. "Didn't you know how?"

"Oh, Katherine," my father said. "I wanted to, but it was sheer arrogance to think I could. And ignorance to think that she wanted me to."

He sounded sad, calling forth none of that false cheerfulness he'd always put on when talking about my mother. I reached out and squeezed his hand.

"I tried to make her happy too," I said.

"You did make her happy, as much as it was possible to do so," he said. "I know it's long past time to tell you what I know of her life, but I lived with her for over ten years and she was always a mystery to me. I thought I could change what I knew—the trajectory of her life, I mean—but that was stupid of me. That's where I went wrong.

"I'd been honorably discharged after being wounded in Germany and had returned home to care for you. You were not even a year old, and motherless, and I was afraid all the time of hurting or killing you by accident. It didn't help that my own body was still healing—and sometimes I would lose my balance or a wave of vertigo would overtake me. For a long time, I found it hard to hold you except when we were both safely seated in a chair. I have sometimes worried that perhaps my uncertainty harmed you in some way, made it hard for you to feel steady and safe. But you were always a good child, quiet, and alert, and when I sat by your crib and read to you, you would listen as if you understood, watching me, as if I was telling you the secrets of the world.

"Sometime that year, I was invited to Washington to receive a Medal of Honor for my courage in battle. So I took you to DC along with your babysitter. After the ceremony I attended a dinner where I was seated next to a general who had recently returned from a tour in the South Pacific.

"He and I talked all through the dinner: not about the war, but about movies and books and places he had visited, and also, of course, about you. Later, after the dinner was over, he invited me to have a drink with him in the bar of the hotel we were both staying at, and I said yes, why not.

"As soon as we'd sat down in a little table in the corner, far from the other patrons, the general's demeanor became serious, and he said, 'Son, I have a favor to ask you.'

"I said, 'Anything in my power, sir.'

"'I'd like you to meet a woman,' he said. 'I've been thinking that since your child is motherless, perhaps this girl could serve as her caretaker.'

"'Excuse me, sir?' I said. And then I told him you didn't need another caretaker, that I was managing with the help of a neighborhood woman.

"'Please,' the general said. 'As a favor to me, just meet her. She has a room in this hotel, and I could have her come this instant.'

"I must have looked alarmed, because 'Relax,' the general said, reaching across the table and putting his hand on my shoulder. 'Just meet her. You need not agree to anything. Let me tell you her story, and then you can judge whether or not she deserves a chance.'"

The General's Story

"I discovered her in Coro Bay, that paradise of crystal seas and sand. We had won our first major battle there—and the Japs had abandoned their base. They'd left behind their *ianfu*, their comfort women—girls they'd kidnapped or bought from all over Asia, and whom they kept in the barracks for the pleasure of their soldiers. Our men were hungry to be with these women, ragged and thin as they were. But they were just girls, starving and covered in scars. There were seventy of them in all, sick and grieving and unable to go home. One had been branded with a hot iron in her privates. Several others had gone out of their minds. Those rocked back and forth, tore out their own hair, buried themselves into the dirt, writhing and weeping, and the soldiers had to hold them down just to feed them their meals.

"For the most part they withdrew from us when we approached, drawing back, blending in as much as they could to their surroundings, disappearing into each other. They retreated, became as invisible as possible, except for one, who met our gazes, indifferent, angry, and as cold as ice.

"Her name was Meiying, and the first time I saw her all her

clothes hung off her body in dirty, shredded rags. Her bones were sharp and raised, as if they were sawing upward through her skin. Her eyes were two black and shining holes. It was hard to see the beauty she would become, and yet when I saw her, I felt a shudder of recognition shake my bones, and perhaps she felt it too, because when she saw me looking at her, she stood up in her bare feet, shaking the lice from hair. Cuts ran all along her body: someone had carved her up, but they had left her face alone. One cut on the inside of her thigh was infected, and that one was deep and gaping, stinking and leaking pus. When I touched it, she flinched away, and her skin was swollen and hot, so I took her to the medic, who gave her medicine and covered her body in poultices layered over in gauze and tape. She acted as if she was not aware of his touch, looking away into the distance as he tended to her wounds, her eyes set and hard. I watched her and was moved by her and brought her to my house to be cared for.

"I fed her from my hand the first few times, like a sick fawn, but she insisted on learning to eat with a knife and a fork as I did. I let her. Over time, she grew sleek and shining. The scar on her thigh remained dark and purple against her pale white skin. But oh, her eyes, her cheekbones—from her ravaged body emerged the beauty I'd sensed the first time I saw her, a beauty that surpassed anything I'd ever seen before. I became half mad with desire for her.

"I taught her English. Every night, I taught her words. And she learned so quickly that I realized she'd been learning on her own, for many months. Then I told her what my feelings were. I pressed my hand over hers. I could not resist pulling her close and kissing her fine, shining hair. I touched her as a father would, chastely, and with great care. I cannot tell you what joy it gave me when she yielded in my arms and gave herself to me of her own free will, the resistance in her body melting to softness.

"For a year we lived in that tropical paradise, but when I saw how the other men began to eye her, I knew something would have to be done. I sent Meiying to America with my own personal secretary, but in the last month, my wife has found me out. So this is why I am asking for your help. She is my greatest treasure, and there is nowhere I can send her, nowhere she can go. But if you're willing to help me, perhaps she can help a poor motherless girl like your own."

MY FATHER FINISHED THIS STORY and sat back in his bed, and took a deep breath, as if it had cost him something to recount it. "After the general told his story, I sat in silence for a long time," he said. "I would be lying if I said I wasn't curious about Meiying.

"'Very well,' I finally said. 'I will meet her. Please bring her down.'

"But now that the general saw that he had me, he said, 'I think it is better if she doesn't come down. It will be better if I don't have to watch. No, it's better if you go to her yourself.'

"I thought this was strange: Would he not want to protect her, to chaperone the interaction, to make sure I would be kind? But he was the general, and I was used to obeying, and so I agreed to this plan.

"'Wait here, and I will tell her you are coming,' said the general. 'She is in room 409. It is better if we do not talk again, but leave a message for me at the front desk. Yes if you will take her, no if you will not.'

"And again I was stunned at how easily he would hand over his charge, this woman he had described as his treasure. But I sat in the bar for another half an hour, thinking. This new development had eclipsed my medal entirely, as if this and only this was the reason I had come to Washington. So after half an hour had passed, I rose from the bar to find that the general had paid our whole bill, and somewhat unsteadily I took the elevator that led to the fourth floor, where Meiying awaited."

Here my father paused. The day had passed from afternoon to evening, and behind him, the window that had been bright with sunshine when I first came in was dark. My father's face was lined in shadow and he looked drawn and tired.

"Could I have some water, please?" he asked, and I leapt up, just as Linda entered bearing a tray with water on it, and his dinner.

"It's time to eat now," she announced.

My father looked at Linda and then at me. "Can we continue the story tomorrow?" he asked.

I wanted so much to hear what happened next, but I nodded and said I would wait. We had dinner together in the hospital with our meals balanced on our laps, and I looked at my father and Linda and was reminded of the dinners my mother and father and I had eaten off our laps when we were building the radio so many years ago.

THAT NIGHT, Linda stayed with my father in his room, and I went back to our old house for the first time in many years. I was surprised to find that my room had not been touched—my child's bed, my child's desk, my science posters, all my books, just as I'd left them. The old house seemed smaller and yet more cavernous with no one in it, and it smelled different than I remembered as I went from room to room.

I went into my father's garage, which—though he had acquired more in the way of tools and old boxes—smelled exactly the same as I remembered, of sawdust and electrical wiring, and some deeper scent that was my father's own. My beloved telescope was sitting in the corner where I'd left it the last time I'd visited. The old radio sat on the same small cart as always, its cables wound around itself, dusty from disuse. There were still two chairs in front of it: a large one for my father, a petite one for myself. The sight of those two chairs, sitting so faithfully side by side as they had through my long absence, broke my heart.

The next morning, I hurried to the hospital. My father was awake and looked better than he had the day before. I took up my chair beside him, but he said, “I was thinking that today, Katherine, if you’re up for it, perhaps we could go for a walk around the hospital garden.” He was in his hospital gown, hooked up to various IVs.

“Are you allowed?” I asked. “Can you walk?”

He pointed to a wheelchair. “I thought perhaps you wouldn’t mind wheeling me around while Linda sleeps. She can stretch out in this bed.”

And so I agreed, and we went out into the cool morning air and onto the hospital lawn where drops of dew clung to the grass and wet my feet. I took my father to the gardens, and we found a bench for me to sit on, and I wheeled him around to face me. My father said, “Where did I leave off last night? Shall I continue?”

“Yes please,” I said. “You’d just gotten to Meiying’s room in the hotel when you stopped.”

“Ah,” my father said. “Yes. Our first meeting.

“When I knocked on her door, she opened the door and said, angrily, ‘Very well, come in.’

“I entered her hotel room, surprised at the crispness of her English, the coldness of the tone.

“She gestured toward the seat. ‘Sit,’ she said. ‘And tell me why you’re here.’

“Katherine, I don’t know how well you remember what she looked like, but in those days she was a flower. You could see that to touch her would be to spoil and crush her. But I understood the general's madness, for the moment I saw her, to my shame, it was all that I wanted to do.

"'The general said you were looking for a job,' I managed to say.

"'The general,' Meiying said, with unchecked bitterness. 'The general,' she said again, as if the word itself was a joke. 'Let me tell you about the man you call the general.'"

Meiying's Account

"The first word he taught me was *freedom*: he wanted me to know I was free. The second word he taught me was *liberation*. He wanted me to know who had granted me that thing he called freedom. As if liberation or freedom can have meaning when you are taken from a world of men into a world of men, and all your possible futures diverge into unending other worlds of men, where your body will be used and traded, and words of love will be all that are given to you in exchange, as if this currency has so much value and your life so little that you should be grateful for these words.

"I already spoke English. I only pretended to learn what I already knew all along. My father had been a diplomat: there were five of us children in all, and I was the youngest and the only girl. 'My jewel,' my father called me. 'My rose.' When he returned from his trips, he brought gifts of ivory and gold, spices and tea. I was tutored in Japanese and English. That they would one day be the languages that would seal my fate, no one could have known, at that time.

"The general was so proud of his generosity—and he thought I would be grateful when he offered to one day take me with him to America, or to send me home. But what would be the point of going home? I told him my family was dead. I don't know why I lied, but once I did, I found myself telling the false story as if it was the truth, and who knows—maybe by then, they were dead. I told him I'd seen my family killed before my eyes, and I wept, feeling as if my words themselves had killed them. Misunderstanding, he wept too, dropping tears into my hair. That man was so easy with his tears. I whispered 'fool' under my breath. I still don't know what was worse: the false story I told, or the truth.

"When the war came, I was fourteen years old, and whenever conversation turned to what was happening in our country, my father made me leave the room. Though I wept hot tears at my exclusion, he would not yield. He and my brothers felt it was their job to protect me from knowing what the dwarf-bandits—that's what they called the Japanese soldiers—were doing to the country. But as they talked and worried behind closed doors, I did not feel protected at all. Instead, a strange and terrible feeling began to rise up in my heart, that something bad was going to happen.

"And then one day we packed up our entire household, filling our wagons and sewing gold into our blankets. The war had reached the borders of our province. Taking all our horses, we began our journey to our house in the country. The journey itself was easy: we were never short on food, and when we passed other travelers, my father often gave bags of rice and gourds of wine to help them on their way. At night my brothers guarded our wagons, taking turns awake with their guns. I never felt endangered but was happy to be going to our country house, with its ponds and pavilions, the chrysanthemum hedges and all the green mountains around us, pointing their tips to the sky.

"We had two weeks of peace there before the dwarf-bandits found us. We learned of their approach too late, when we were already surrounded, and there was no way out.

"'Don't fight,' I cried out when the soldiers burst into our house, 'Don't fight,' and I don't know if that was why my brothers stood up slowly, hands free of weapons—if it was my presence or my plea not to fight that was the hinge that everything turned upon next.

"The bandits marched in and took my brothers out of the house one by one, with their hands tied behind their backs. There, in front of the magnificent beauty of our countryside, one of the dwarf-bandits ordered my eldest brother to kneel. My mother screamed when he obeyed, and grasped at the sleeve of the soldier behind him, but he hit her across the face with his hand, and she fell to the ground.

"I was standing in the doorway, watching everything. I knew where my brothers hid their weapons, but I was afraid to turn my back on what was happening. I still thought my being there, my watching them, could keep them safe. The rest of my brothers were made to kneel. The soldiers raised their pistols to the backs of their heads and took aim. It was all so fast. That's when I understood how close the line is between living and not living—a moment and then it's done.

"But before anything happened, my father came out of the house, unarmed and shouting in Japanese, 'Wait!' He took me by the arm and together we ran forward.

"The soldiers turned around, guns still aimed at my brothers' heads.

"'I'll trade her,' my father said then, pushing me forward. 'For my boys. She speaks English and Japanese. You can see how lovely she is, how graceful. I beg of you, spare my sons.'

"'A girl is not worth four boys,' said the officer on horseback, but even as he laughed he looked at me with assessing eyes. I shrank away. He said, 'I will trade her for just one of your sons. I suggest you take the deal, it's the best bargain you'll get.'

"'Leave me the oldest one,' my father said, and his voice broke.

"'All right,' the officer said. And then leaning down to me, he said: 'Come here. Don't be afraid. I will not hurt you.' I stepped forward. As my family watched, I let him take my hand. When he touched my face, I did not close my eyes or flinch. I let him do it.

"'Please spare them,' I said quietly, in perfect Japanese. 'My parents. My brothers. Let them live.'

"The dwarf-bandit's eyes widened. 'You sound just like a Japanese girl,' he said. 'You have no accent.' He glanced back at my family. He turned back to me and nodded once, as if making a decision. He said, 'I will do this as a special favor to you.' To his soldiers, he said loudly, 'Let all of them go.' And then he turned swiftly on his horse, and I let him hoist me up in front of him. I looked back at my parents. My mother's face was smeared with blood, and she and my father were crying, but they said nothing as they watched us ride away. Through the dust and distance, I watched them let me go. That day and the next, I waited for someone to come and rescue me. I waited and I waited, but no one ever did.

"After that, what is there to tell? Whatever you can imagine, happened. Like your general, the dwarf-bandit also claimed to love me. Still, when it was time for him to leave, he did not want to set me free. Instead, he donated me to the comfort station in New Guinea, where he was being sent, so that he would still have the pleasure of me. He said he was doing it to be together, even though he'd have to share me. He said this as if I would be touched at his sentiment, as if I would be flattered by his devotion.

"The men in New Guinea smelled of fire and blood, and when they took us they pounded us with the smell of tears, blood, and rancid sweat, and of never-going-home. Sometimes they wept in our arms, covering us in salt. Sometimes they beat us. There was one soldier who liked to pretend to set all the women free. 'Go,' he'd say. 'Be free.' But none of us ever dared. Until one day a woman who had newly arrived into our company took off running, barefoot in the sand. The soldier shot her in the back of the head, cleanly, one shot, and she flew forward with the force of it, straight onto her face. Afterward, we were made to clean up the mess she left, dragging away her body, dumping water on the sand until the deep red of her blood thinned to the palest pink.

"It was from this so-called comfort station that your general 'rescued' me. After the Japanese left and the Americans and Australians arrived, I saw him watching me for weeks, his face open with hunger. When he finally approached, he thought I spoke no English. He thought I wouldn't understand when he said, 'You beauty, I will make sure you are not wasted here.' Then he put his sweating hand on the gash inside my thigh.

"In Chinese, I said to him, 'At least the dwarf-bandit knew I was his prisoner. Let me tell you now I am not free. I feel no gratitude.'

"The general's eyes lit up. The only words he recognized that I had spoken were *free* and *gratitude*, and his eyes shone at the thought that I was grateful. He was a fool. I thought his weakness would protect me, and no other man would be allowed to touch me. And yet, here we are. He has given me to you."

AT THIS POINT in the story, my father paused and rubbed his arms. I noticed that the sky had darkened and that the wind was picking up. The hairs on my arm prickled, and I realized that my father must be cold.

"Shall we go in?" I asked, rising. My father nodded, and as I put my hands on the handles of his chair to wheel him back, he reached up and grasped my hand with his.

"How are you doing, Katherine?" he said. "Are you all right?"

"Yes," I said, despite the knot in my throat. "I'm fine."

When we got back to my father's hospital room, Linda hovered above him as the nurses eased him into bed and hooked him back up to his monitors right away. As we stood watching the green line rise and fall in time to the steady beep of his heart, I thought about how all we were at the end of the day could be reduced to a collection of electrical signals racing across our brains, precise chemical compounds flowing through our veins and organs. The processes of our bodies were so exact and measurable, while our bodies themselves were so messy.

"You're so cold," Linda said, touching my father's hand and forehead. "Why did you stay out so long?"

"I'm fine," my father said, smiling up at her. "Don't worry." He took a breath and turned to me. "Where did I leave off?"

"Shouldn't you rest?" Linda interrupted. "You've worn yourself out. I wish you would take a nap." She sounded both accusatory and possessive, and my first thought was that she was jealous. But then I looked more closely at her, at the way she stood protectively over my father, and I saw her hands tremble and her eyes water with tears, and I realized she was frightened.

"Dad, I think Linda's right," I said, nodding. "Maybe you can tell me the rest later."

"No," my father said. "I might as well tell it now. There isn't too much left."

"Okay," I said. I scooted a chair next to his bed.

"Come," he said, waving me closer. He took my hand and smiled.

"SO I WAS in Meiying's hotel room," my father began, "and I said, 'I don't want to lay a hand on you.'

"'You're lying,' she said quietly. 'Like everybody else.'

"'It's the truth,' I insisted. I was so ashamed of the attraction I felt for her in that moment—I wanted to protect her, to shield her, it's true, but I also wanted her for myself.

"'I have no desire to touch you,' I said. 'I only came because I need someone to look after my baby, and the general said you might be interested.' I found myself layering lie upon lie, trying to absolve the general, trying to absolve myself.

"'You have a baby?' Meiying said, and something shifted in her face when she said it. Her eyelids fluttered like a captured bird. I wanted desperately to win her over.

"'Wait here,' I said. Then I went up to my room, and Katherine, forgive me, but I woke you up and took you to her. And I swear, when she held you in her arms, something in her face softened. Something in the way she held her body shifted, as if the fight had gone completely out of it, as if it was suddenly at peace."

My father's voice had gone soft. Behind him, through the window, I saw that it was raining. "But she didn't care about me," I said.

"Of course she did."

"Why did she never touch me when I got older, then, if she cared?" I asked. "Why did she leave?"

My father sighed deeply. "In the first few years, she wasn't as sad as she became later. There were days and days where she would walk around, showing you things—the leaves on trees, the ants hiding beneath rocks, the sticks floating down the creek. She would laugh when you would laugh. She was smart and strong, and sometimes I watched her and could see the person she might have been if her life hadn't happened the way it had. I was stupid enough to think that perhaps I would be able to help her recover.

"Her one request when she agreed to be your caretaker was that you would always be told that she was your mother. And I agreed. But I see now how it complicated things. It's hard when you pretend something for the world not to come to believe it yourself. And you looked like our daughter, like you were made of part me and part her—it was so easy to pretend that it was true.

"But I wanted her, and she knew it. At first I slept on the couch in the living room, but after a few months she invited me back in to my bedroom. 'Katherine is old enough to wonder now why her parents do not sleep together,' your mother said. 'I do not want her wondering why that is.'

"So that night I got into bed with her, wondering if the invitation signaled another kind of opening. But as soon as I was in, she turned her back on me, and slid as close to the edge of the bed, away from me, as she could go. From that night on I slept next to her, not touching her, wishing I was anywhere else. I felt so ashamed for what I wanted to do with her, and I was sure she sensed it from me. That was when her nightmares began full force. And they were terrifying—she would wake up screaming, but I couldn't touch her, couldn't comfort her. She wouldn't let me, and I knew better than to try. This is when I began to realize that there was nothing left for us to give each other except pain.

"'Waiting is worse than the thing itself,' your mother said, but it felt like we were always waiting. Waiting for me to transgress and touch her: waiting for you to discover the truth. I felt as if I hurt her every day by wanting her, by loving her, as if everything about me was disgusting. Still, sometimes I wondered if she didn't love me a little, too, if she didn't want me to take her into my arms. And so one day I did."

He paused.

"I didn't force her, Katherine. I just took her into my arms and found that she was willing. She didn't protest, she didn't cry, she didn't pull away. I admit I was uneasy, but I thought that we grew closer during those years. 'You're a good man,' she said. 'I am lucky to have found you.' She never made contact on her own, she never leaned against me, but I thought her past constrained her. If she'd ever said the word, if she'd ever said it hurt her, I swear I would have stopped. That's why I didn't see it coming. But when you neared the age that she had been when she was taken from her home, she said, 'It is too much, I cannot bear it.' And within a week, she was gone."

At this point, my father took a deep breath, but before he could continue, Linda burst out weeping in her chair. They were loud, uncontrolled sobs, and my father reached out his hand to her and said, "My dear, my dear." But she rose from her chair, her hand over her eyes, and left the room, still wailing. We could still hear her, walking away from us down the hall.

I was breathless with discomfort and grief for both my parents and found myself furious at Linda's tears. Who was she to cry over this story? I felt she had usurped something that was mine, taking over something that wasn't hers to have.

My voice was harsh when I said, "You haven't told me yet who my real mother was. What happened to her? How did she die?"

I think I knew the answer before he said it. My father looked away. His eyes darted in the way they did when he was trying to avoid a confrontation or an answer. At last he said, "By the time you came to me, your real mother was already out of the picture."

"What does that mean?" I asked. "Do you mean you aren't my real father either? Where did I come from?"

The beeping on the monitor grew faster and faster, and the moment I noticed it, I knew I could not lose myself in this surge of emotion. "Your heartbeat's getting faster," I said. At the same moment a nurse came in, checked the monitor, looked at my father, and looked at me, and—saying nothing—stood and watched him for a while as his heart rate steadied.

"No excitement," she said sternly, before she left.

I took a deep breath and looked out the window. So this man in front of me was not my father. So I was an orphan. "Never mind," I said. "I understand."

"I am sorry, Katherine," my father said, and his voice was hoarse. "I should have told you long ago."

"Where did I come from?" I asked.

"You came from an orphanage. And I'll tell you the story. I'm not hiding things from you anymore. But I need you to know that no matter what, I am your father now."

I wanted to say yes, I felt in my heart that he was, but I couldn't give him the comfort. It wasn't that I wished to punish him. It was just that to extend that comfort would have meant accepting it for myself, and that wasn't something I'd learned yet to do.

"AS YOU KNOW, I was a soldier," my father began. "And I shattered my arm in combat in the late summer of 1944. I fractured my neck and vertebrae, and shrapnel was embedded all over my body, most dangerously in my left kidney. At first when they brought me in, the medics thought I'd die, and then that they'd have to amputate my arm—but the officer whose life I'd saved during that battle was influential, and he insisted that they wait. There were many surgeries I don't remember, and I was unconscious for weeks. But my injuries were bad enough that when I did awaken, I was told I'd never have to return to war, and I was sent instead to a hospital in the French countryside to recover.

"That was when I learned that my best friend, Tim, from boyhood had been killed in battle. And there was more bad news: my mother had died of a heart attack after learning of my injuries.

My father was already dead. So I found myself alone. I do know what that's like, Katherine—to be adrift in the world.

"As the days progressed, I made a habit of walking the grounds each morning. The hospital was not really a hospital, but the country estate of some French aristocrat. All around, the garden was in disarray, the flowers trampled by trucks full of incoming wounded, the shrubs knocked over on their sides. But sometimes when I'd walked far enough away, I would stand among the olive trees and catch a whiff of the sea that the breeze brought with it, and I'd imagine I was adventuring—trekking through Europe in the olden days.

"I went a little farther every day, and my doctors encouraged me to take these walks and bring back news of what I'd seen. They said it cheered them to see me doing so much better. There was an orphanage at the edge of the estate, though it wasn't an orphanage, really, in the same way the hospital wasn't really a hospital. It was a series of three large farmhouses that had been commandeered by a group of nuns who were looking over three or four dozen abandoned and orphaned children from the war. The children were of all ages—from an infant they had found naked in a field, when they guessed she was maybe eight weeks old, to a sixteen-year-old girl thin and shivering in a threadbare dress. She refused to wear anything else and was always plaiting and unplaiting her hair. All the same, it was a happier place than you might have thought: the children ran through the halls and the fields waving sticks and throwing stones, digging up snakes and chasing frogs. After my first visit, I went often, whittling toys and making kites from bits of wood and paper and rags."

Here my father paused.

"You, Katherine," he said, "were the youngest orphan. You were the infant the nuns had found in a field. A novice named Liliane, barely seventeen years old—hardly older than the oldest orphan, had gone for a walk when she tripped over something in the long grass. She caught herself with outstretched arms, bruising her shin against a rock and tearing her stockings.

"She sat up, touching herself all along her body, checking her limbs for injury. And then, she saw you. A baby. And strangeness upon strangeness, you were utterly quiet looking back at her, still as a hidden fawn.

"It was God who had led her to you, she said later. She gathered you up, wrapped you in her habit, and carried you home. From then on, you never cried, but you never smiled, either, and the other children called you the Baby Who Never Smiled. You were a mystery—a child with Chinese features dropped into France as if from the sky—and these children carried you around in their arms as if you were their plaything, a treasured toy, their only doll. They dressed you in their clothes, fed you their own rations.

"They watched you with great intensity and a simultaneous sort of bored impatience. They spent hours trying to teach you to sit up, to reach for them, to laugh—to grow into a child who could play with them, a child who could smile.

"As for me," my father continued, "it was Liliane I noticed first, the novice who had found you. She was slender and wide-eyed, always hanging back and watching me with a soulful gaze. I had the sense she wanted something from me, and I wanted very much to discover what it was.

"But then the doctors announced that it was time for me to leave. I was well enough to travel, so a date was set, and a flight secured. When I went to the orphanage to say good-bye, we all cried. Oh, it was a terrible scene. The young children clung to my legs when I told them I'd be leaving and wouldn't be coming back. They clutched my shirtsleeves in their hands, only letting go to wipe their eyes with the backs of their fists, begging me to stay."

My father paused to touch his hand to his eyes, raising his old, injured arm, his hand shaking. I thought how young he must have been in the story he was telling.

"I told them I'd come back for them," my father said, wiping his eyes and clearing his throat. "Nicole and Madeleine and Angelique, Matthieu and Pierre and Agnes. I remember all their names, every one. I promised I would look for them and find them when I returned. One of my great regrets, Katherine, is that I never did.

"In any case, Liliane came to me later and asked if she might have a word with me in private. So we walked together toward the outskirts of the property where no one could overhear us. I had no idea what she would say or what would happen next. When at the end of our walk we came to a large oak tree, Liliane took my arm and led me behind it.

"I was young and inexperienced and what I'd heard of French girls—even novice nuns—made me hopeful of what would happen next. I prepared myself to kiss her. But when I saw her only looking down at her hands, twisting them, I knew she had not brought me there to kiss.

"'What did you want to say to me,' I finally prompted her, gently, and she took a deep breath and asked, 'Can you take a child with you when you go home? Just one?'

"It took a moment for me to understand she meant an orphan, not herself. 'Take a child?' I asked.

"'Just one,' she said. 'Will you take the Baby Who Never Smiles? She needs you more than any of the rest.'

"'I don't think I can,' I said, mind racing. 'I have no job, no house, no wife.'

"'None of that matters,' she said. 'When you could save her life.' And then, 'I will tell you a secret that I've told nobody else: not even the other nuns know.'"

Liliane's Story

"I didn't find the baby naked in a field. She was given to me. The day I brought her in it is true, I'd been in trouble with the other nuns, because the night before I'd disappeared for several hours. They assumed I'd been visiting a man, and they'd told me if it happened again they'd expel me from the order. But I hadn't been meeting a man at all, but my sister. She'd traveled to me in greatest secrecy and told me to tell no one she was coming. Imagine my surprise when I met her in the garden shed, and she had in her arms a tiny, newborn baby.

"'Natalie!' I cried.

"'Hush,' my sister said. 'She isn't mine. She's the baby of a German Jew and a Chinese man, both scholars. Our uncle Romain rented them the apartment next door to mine and told me never to speak to them, but when I heard the baby crying, I took them diapers and food. They were so grateful. They spoke passable French and told me they were trying to get to China where the Jewish girl would be safe. They were from Germany and had been trying to get there by way of Bulgaria, but somehow they'd ended up in Paris and found some friends who told them our uncle Romain might be able to help hide them.

"'So they lived next door for two weeks, but someone tipped off the Germans. When they came, the new family did not have enough time to hide. We all heard the heavy boots of the soldiers coming up the stairs, and I ran across the hall to warn the girl and her lover, but they had already heard, and there was no way out, no place to hide. The girl put her finger to her lips and showed me a metal toolbox in their kitchen. Inside it she'd hidden her baby, wrapped in blankets.

"'When the Nazis took her away, a hand on either arm, she went quietly, no fussing. She went with almost no noise, so as not to end up waking the baby. Her lover—also quietly—but with a significant look at me followed by a glance at the toolbox, followed the girl and the soldiers.

"'I bought goat's milk and a bottle, and for two days, I cared for her as best I could. I wish I could raise her as my own, but who would believe me? Uncle Romain says the girl and her man are not coming back. He says if I do not get rid of this baby, he will take it to the authorities himself.

"'Liliane,' my sister said. 'Please take this baby. Keep her safe. You must never tell anyone her mother was a Jew or it won't be safe for her.'"

"'SO YOU SEE why I could not tell the other nuns,' Liliane finished, pressing one of her small hands against my bad arm, so hard that I winced. 'If the Nazis ever come back, I know there will be some who would be all too eager to turn over a Jewish child. As it is, even now we do not take them in.'

"Well, Katherine, what could I do? My parents were dead. I had no family, no one to go home to. The war had battered my body and spirit—days upon days of mankind doing its worst to each other, and now here was this baby who needed my protection.

"'I'll take her,' I said. 'I'll find a home for her.' And then I asked, 'Do you want to come too?'

"Liliane looked startled and shook her head. 'No,' she said. 'But thank you. I have pledged my life to God.' She leaned forward and kissed me quite gently on the mouth. Then she pulled away and took something out of her pocket. It was a notebook bound with battered leather, tied with a string.

"'It belongs to her,' she said. 'It was wrapped inside her blankets:

it's the only thing in the world she owns,' and she pressed it into my hands.

"When I left France, I promised Liliane that I would stay in touch, and tell her where you ended up. I promised to make sure that whoever took you in would love you.

"And I returned, prepared to turn you over to an orphanage, or to some needy family who couldn't have children of their own. But by then I'd watched you grow, witnessed your first steps, seen your first smile. You were the Baby Who Never Smiled, but after you were mine, you smiled for me, and you cried for me, and you clung to me and scratched me like I belonged to you, and for a long time, you would only sleep against my chest.

"I always meant to let you go. But every time I let anyone else look after you, you cried like someone had stabbed you through the heart. I knew you needed a mother, but in the end, I couldn't believe you'd be better off without me. How was I any different from a widower? I asked myself. In the end, I loved you too much to give you up.

"I wrote to Liliane and the children all through the following year, but I never received an answer. After the war was over, I searched for them, writing letters of inquiry and placing many long-distance calls, but I reached no satisfactory answers. The orphanage had been disassembled, the nuns reassigned. The children had been separated and sent elsewhere—some to relatives, some to other orphanages. In any case, there was no way to trace them, no record of where they or the nuns had gone."

Chapter 17

Topology, the field of mathematics that I worked on with Peter, distinguishes itself from other branches through its concern with the positions of objects in relation to one another rather than their shapes or the distances between them. The famous Königsberg bridge problem, for example, takes the city of Königsberg, which is set on opposite sides of the Pregel River and contains two large islands connected to each other and the mainland by seven bridges. The problem is: How can a traveler walk through the city in a way that he crosses each bridge once and only once? The islands can only be reached by the bridges, and each bridge once stepped upon must be crossed all the way. The start and end of the journey need not be at the same point.

Euler solved the generalized form of this problem in 1735—showing that the paths within the island and the city do not matter—it is only the list of land masses and the bridges connecting them that figure in to the question at hand. Land and bridges are reduced to nodes and edges, and from this abstraction, this simplification, graph theory was born, and the foundations of topology were laid.

In topology, you are still working within the realm of mathematics, but here you get to choose a universe in which the connections between things are primary, where the properties of space are preserved despite continuous deformations. Its study is an exercise in ignoring the trees to see the forest—and what it offers is a glimpse from a great distance—a view of the deep structure of mathematics itself. Using notions of preservation and connectedness, it is possible for a coffee mug to transform through a series of continuous deformations into a donut, and because of this, in this system, the object is considered to have remained fundamentally the same.

Setting aside topology, consider that the number 2 can be expressed as 2, or as 1 + 1, or as 4/2. It all depends on which expression you decide to use, and each expression shows us something different about the same number. In the same way, there are theorems that are stated differently but are in fact identical to one another. Approached from different directions, they come to an equivalent conclusion—but the way they are stated reveals completely different things about different parts of mathematics by shedding light on different aspects of a problem. This is, in part, what makes mathematics so powerful—the ability to see the same thing from a different perspective, the ability to see it transformed. That said, there are always limits. Even in topology, if you break the handle off the coffee mug, it will no longer transform into a donut, just as once you cut a string, it can never go back to what it was.

I STAYED WITH MY FATHER for another week, mending many bridges with him. When he was discharged from the hospital, I accompanied him and Linda home. I told him about Peter, I told him about the math I was doing, and as the days passed, he became stronger. I watched how carefully Linda tended to him, and though my old reluctance persisted, I was grateful to her. By the time I returned to Cambridge, I knew it was time to transform. I didn't know how, or what it'd entail, just that it needed to happen. I called Otto Behr, who'd extended my invitation to the University of Bonn, and asked if the fellowship he'd offered was still open.

He said it was, but that if I wanted it, I'd have to take it then and there. I told him I would go.

I realize now how unkind and cowardly it was of me to reverse my decision without discussing it with Peter. But when I told him, I was stunned by his anger.

"Are we together or aren't we?" he asked. "Do we respect each other or not?"

"Of course we are and we do. What are you talking about?" I said.

"How could you make a decision like this without clearing it first?"

"I wasn't aware I needed to clear things with you," I said. "When have you ever cleared travel or work decisions with me?"

"This is different and you know it. It's a whole year, Katherine."

I knew he was right but felt defensive anyway.

"Listen," I said. "I wasn't sure the university would still have space for me, so I called them to check. At that point there was nothing to discuss. But then they said yes, right away, and wanted a decision on the spot. I didn't have time to tell you before I made a decision." This was true—but I knew I had also handled things this way so he wouldn't have the chance to change my mind. Foolishly, short-sightedly, it hadn't occurred to me that I could hurt him. In my mind, Peter was so famous, so established, and held such sway over me, that it was hard for me to acknowledge what power I held over him.

"I'm asking you not to do this," he said. "I think you need to reconsider."

"It's too late to withdraw."

"It isn't too late—just tell them you're not going. Katherine, you need to remember, I'm not just your lover, I'm also your advisor."

"Hold on," I said. "Is that a threat? I'll do what I want, it isn't your choice."

"What do you mean, is that a threat? I'm just warning you now, if you go, you'll come to regret it."

"How is that not a threat?" I cried. "You don't own me, Peter. You can't tell me what to do."

"I know I don't own you!" he exclaimed. "You're twisting my words around. I'm just trying to advise you—I honestly think it's better for your career if you stay. If you leave now, you'll break your momentum, and it will be hard to get back on track. You have so many things going for you. I'm trying to look out for your interests."

"I've already made up my mind. I'm choosing myself for once, Peter. I'm following my instincts, and putting myself first."

He bowed his head. "Well, if I can't make you listen," he said, "then there's nothing more I can do."

I DON'T REGRET going to Bonn, but looking back, I wish I hadn't handled the whole thing so badly. I wish I had taken a deep breath instead and reassured Peter that I still loved him and wanted to be with him. That I couldn't explain, but that something compelled me to go. That I couldn't wait, and that like any creature who seeks transformation, I had to complete it alone. Whether or not he would have understood, at least I owed him the chance.

When I left, it wasn't on terrible terms: we both said at the end of all this, we wanted to be with each other. We tipped our foreheads together and cried. He promised to wait, and I promised to call. But I worried something between us had gone sour, and I was making a giant mistake. Still, I made myself get on that plane. On board, I wondered, was this how my mother had felt, leaving us? That it was a choice—her or us? So much had been taken from her. Maybe it felt good to be the one to decide to leave something, or someone, waiting behind.

I arrived in Bonn with most of my papers and the old German notebook, which I'd tried again to decipher after my father's stories. But it remained incomprehensible. In that way, it was just like the stories my father had told me, something I was doomed to always be circling—held in orbit, unable to get any closer, unable to get away.

I was happy to discover upon my arrival that the program at Bonn offered me quite a lot of freedom. Otto Behr was very kind. He was in his seventies, and quite well known, but solicitous and interested in my work without being overly involved. The graduate students and professors in the program were likewise very open and generous: there was none of the competitiveness and wariness that I had become accustomed to at home—possibly because I was a temporary visitor, and therefore not competing with any of the students for mentorship or funds. The campus itself was unlike anything I'd seen back home—centuries old and sprawling, gorgeous, the buildings and gardens even older than the United States. All around Bonn were enormous, golden trees, punctuated by rubble from the war—enormous piles of stones and dust that used to be buildings. And then there was the Rhine River, wide and curving, grand and timeless, running alongside it all.

The other visiting scholars and foreign students were a joy to meet. We were all there with the sense that we had left our real lives behind, and while I know there must have been those who were homesick or lonely, I threw myself into life in this new place with enthusiastic abandon. For the first time in my life, I found it easy—almost effortless—to make friends. There was Maz, the Iranian classicist and poet; Otto, a brilliant Danish astrochemist; and Leena, an Italian artist with a brutal and beautiful face—not pretty, but mesmerizing and powerful, who attracted both men and women to her with an irresistible force. Then there was Renate, the one German friend in our group: a tall, quiet Sachsen woman with a scar across her face, twisting the edge of her mouth. No one knew how she'd gotten it, and I never dared to ask. There was a strength to her gaze, to everything she did. She was a War Studies scholar working on a book about the children of the war—the Jewish and Gypsy children who'd been reclassified as Christians and Muslims and raised not knowing their heritage; the children in Belgium whose parents had been taken away but survived by hiding in the sewers underneath the cities, living off scraps and trash. The rumor about Renate was that her father had been a high-ranking Nazi officer who kept Jewish servants in his household throughout the war, but as with the scar, no one ever had the temerity to ask her.

The person I grew closest to was a Californian folklorist named Henrietta. She was unlike anyone else I'd ever met. She was lanky and slightly awkward—her body seemed to be arranged entirely of sharp angles—but she used it to her advantage somehow and made it look glamorous. She always wore men's clothes, but they were impeccably tailored and paired with one extravagant accessory: an inky black suit with a purple tie, or men's slacks and a silk shirt paired with a string of giant milky pearls.

She went by the name of Henry, and though she had her own dazzling charm, it was vastly different from the dark glitter of our

European friends. She was all sunshine and mischief wrapped in sumptuous fabrics and, remarkably, was the first Asian friend I'd ever had. She was also the most straightforward person I'd ever met, always going right for the heart of the matter, asking—only a few moments after we met—"You have the look of heartbreak about you. Are you here to get over someone?" And then when I stammered, flustered and aghast, she continued, "Never mind, that was a terribly rude question to ask, though we'll certainly get to it soon, I'm sure—I've already decided we'll be fast friends."

She hammered me with rapid-fire questions and rapid-fire revelations about her own life, but with an openness that entirely disarmed me and spilled over into our every interaction, like when we went grocery shopping together and she grabbed my hand and darted through the crowds on the street, or when she begged me to go to a lecture with her and passed notes to me the entire time.

She had deep dimples on either side of her mouth, and she laughed all the time, and I couldn't stop looking at her. I tried: I knew what it felt like to have people stare, and even now in Germany, people would halt in their tracks for a double take. Children would follow us around, calling, "Chinesische Frau! Chinesische Frau!"

Henry was unfazed by all the attention, and she was also unfazed by me. She knew tons of Chinese people—just her family could form a small country, she laughed, describing her five siblings and many cousins. And as for the attention from strangers, well, she'd gotten used to it, she said with a shrug. In fact, she dressed for it, she added with a wicked grin.

She charmed everyone, and though I was in so many ways the opposite of her—awkward, guarded—she chose me as her friend "at first sight," as she said, and wooed me relentlessly, admiring my looks, telling me she had a crush on me, peering over my shoulder at math textbooks and asking what various symbols and statements meant.

"My father drove an ice cream truck for years," she told me. "He was a scholar and a poet from an aristocratic family in China, but in America, he was no one. So"—and here she gave a wry, knowing laugh—"he was reaaaaally frustrated while I was growing up. But he wasn't a very hard worker, he just wasn't used to it—and so my mother was also reaaaaally frustrated, because she had to do everything."

I was captivated by the way she talked about her family and its difficulties casually, with a knowing, matter-of-fact sense of humor. I always spoke of my family with the utmost gravity, if I had to talk about them at all. Henry would not tolerate evasions, however—she barreled ahead with questions meant to pry open just what you were trying to hide. In the end, I told her everything—about my mother and the stories she used to tell me, how beautiful she was, how I felt when she left. And about my father, and of course about Peter.

I was flattered by Henry's attention and fascinated by the way her friendship transformed the reaction other people seemed to have to me. I was so used to my perpetual status of outsider that I'd stopped questioning in each situation whether this time it was my femaleness or my Asianness or the combination of both that branded me different. Even now, I feel impatient when asked about what being these things mean to me—the expectation that because my race and my gender are often the first things people notice about me, they must also be the most significant to me. When I die, I know the first sentence in my obituary will read: "Asian American woman mathematician dies at the age of X."

For the first time in my life, I had a friend with whom I could talk of such things, and also a friend who understood implicitly, a friend to whom I need not explain. I was surprised to discover that being friends with Henry opened doors rather than closed them: people paid attention to us, wanted to know us, and under Henry's expansive, bubbly protection, I felt myself blossoming. I gave myself over to an endless series of parties and dinners, of walking back and forth between my home and those of my companions, pausing to talk on benches, stopping into cafés for hours, reading newspapers together, and pushing books upon each other.

Our conversations tended to lean toward politics. My new friends were passionately opposed to the Vietnam War and intensely curious about the civil rights movement in America, which I had watched unfold on my television with the sense that this drama was not my drama. But my new friends cared about everything and insisted that the marches and protests and speeches and assassinations of the past decade mattered to them as well. They expected me to talk, soliciting my opinion on every matter, as if everything I said was of interest to them. "And now let's ask our other representative from America," they'd say when everyone had offered their opinions but me. "I can't speak for America," I always began, and they laughed and teased back—wasn't everyone back home just like me? But they were curious what I thought, and I was humbled to be able to talk with such bright and charismatic thinkers about so many things I had until then thought so little about.

Henry, on the other hand, held opinions on everything, and she never stayed quiet. At home she had organized protests and flown east just so she could ride a freedom bus to the South. She had watched a man get beaten by a mob on the street and stood on the sidelines watching in horror, unable to intervene. Afterward she had walked up and down the area where the crowd had dragged him, picking her way around the blood and broken glass, looking for the teeth she had seen get knocked out of his mouth. She had found three of them and cradled them in her palm. She put them in a glass of milk and took them to the hospital, and left them there, though she knew it was probably futile. She had just wanted, she said, for the man to know that someone had been looking out for him. That someone had tried their best.

"You know, until I came to Germany, I didn't really realize somehow that the history going on outside our doors included me," I said. "I just always felt excluded. Our building on campus was protested last year, and even though most of the people I work with are anti–the Vietnam War and pro–civil rights, it didn't matter to the protesters, who were radically antiscience and antitechnology. I felt like they'd already put me on one side, the other side—which to be honest has been what's happened to me my whole life. The truth is I feel freer here in Germany than I ever did back home."

"Well," Henry said. "We're used to everyone thinking we're foreign in America, but here it's actually true. We're not constantly explaining ourselves, and that leaves us a degree of anonymity and freedom we've never been allowed before." She smirked. "Which I really think you should avail yourself of."

Henry had tumbled into bed with at least two men that I knew of in our first month of acquaintance—this was also how she surprised me—how decisively she acted on her own desires, without pause or second-guessing, and how she reveled a bit in shocking me, looking at me sideways with a wicked gleam, teasing me about what she saw as my outrageous innocence. All my friends, as it turned out, found me charmingly old-fashioned. They were free with their affections, physical and emotional, and looked down on anything they found prudish.

They teased me relentlessly about my love life and demanded details about Peter, which I resisted, because as happy as I was to find myself in Bonn, and to throw myself into this new life, the one thing that wasn't going well at all was my relationship with Peter. He didn't answer the letters I wrote him, and on the phone he was distant and withdrawn. He didn't want to talk about everyday things, and he didn't want to talk about math. It was all compounded by the fact that we could only ever find time to talk in the middle of the night for me, or the wee hours of the morning for him. "I'm just not a telephone person," he said. Every time we talked I felt further and further away from him. Had I imagined our connection, I sometimes found myself wondering, or had I just broken it? It was an excruciating time for us, but strangely, I was able to compartmentalize it completely, so that I'd find myself sobbing inconsolably over the telephone, asking him what he wanted from me, and then be able to go out drinking and dancing with my friends two hours later, exultant, as if I were two different people.

And I did feel I was turning into a new person. I found this unfamiliar openness that my friends were so adept in—this talking about anything—exhilarating. In this new environment, it was easy to talk with strangers. I discovered I actually liked parties, especially afterward, when my friends and I would scoop up anyone we'd liked and go to a bar, and after that walk for hours, still talking. So this, I thought, was what Peter had with his friends—this easy camaraderie that I had not acquired in college or graduate school. I sank into it with gratitude.

Among my new friends, my awkward attempts at German and occasional forays into French, all my missteps and ignorance, were met with indulgence and laughter. It was easy to be curious and to bear the curiosity of others. When I rode my bicycle, I did not feel like a woman impersonating a woman riding a bicycle, but like myself, getting from one place to another.

The irony of this, as well as of the sense of freedom and happiness I felt, was not lost on me. Here I was, feeling comfortable and free in the country responsible for my orphaning. And yet I had a feeling—not only for my classmates and fellow foreigners and the jolly band we formed there, but for the buildings, for the streets themselves. Everything was new to me, but everything about the place itself was old. The streets were old, the stones of the buildings were old, even the rubble from the war that still lined street after street was old. And something about the oldness of it all—older than the entire country of America—made it feel timeless, made it feel welcoming. I tried to remind myself that this was a country that was responsible for the extermination of millions (millions!) of people. I was still wrapping my mind around what Liliane had told my father—that I had Jewish blood in me. Here was a secret identity, whereas all my life so many of my identities had been visible and immediate. And yet, despite this (or because of it?), I didn't feel endangered in this country. Instead, I felt strangely at home.

"Göttingen!" Henry exclaimed when I told her I planned to visit there during my stay. "The Brothers Grimm were the head librarians there for years! They're part of the research I came to Germany to do. I want to go there too!" And so we decided we'd go together during the midsemester break.

In the meantime, we went on a pilgrimage to the house Beethoven had been born in; we went on picnics on the great lawn of the university and watched the other students go by; we went to hear musicians playing in the park; we went shopping in men's clothing stores where Henry draped us both in luxurious fabrics.

Amid all this social activity, there was also school. I chose classes to fill gaps in my education, and I ate up anything that might shed light on the Mohanty problem or the Riemann hypothesis. I was delighted by the seminars, which were beautifully prepared and executed and aimed often just above my comprehension, so that I spent hours poring over my notes, reaching for a concept I could barely see the edges of. I made good progress on my own work and even worked up the nerve to write to Charles Lee to tell him I was working on an extension of his proof. It was a risk, just in case he was working on it himself—Peter had told me to keep my work quiet, lest Lee take my interest as some kind of challenge—but once I had something of value to offer, something real to share, I found myself wanting to reach out, to wave to him from across the distance.

The rest of my time I spent frolicking with Henry and meeting and talking with other students, who spoke practically flawless English and were also particularly kind about my less-than-flawless German. I found that talking with them was easier in some ways than it had been with my colleagues back home: I was accorded respect without having to fight for it, without having to prove myself. Even my professors allowed me to drive the conversation in a way I'd never gotten the chance to do before.

I made great strides on the Mohanty problem, and as much as I'd loved working with Peter, I felt for the first time how good it felt to be firmly in charge of my own work—deferring to no one, trying to impress no one, just following my own instincts and interests. A problem can be interesting or beautiful in the way that it is formulated, and it can also be meaningful—the most important ones are both. It was in Bonn that I realized with a thrill that my problem would be both.

There were other welcome professional developments: I had never taught a class before, but in Bonn I was asked to guest teach a course, and after every class, my students applauded by knocking their fists against their desks. They came to office hours and asked me questions with eager, open faces. They wanted to show me around the city. They were excited by what I had to offer them, and when I looked at their smiling, welcoming faces, I thought: *I could live here.* I fell a little bit in love: I told myself this was the country that had produced Bach and Beethoven, Gauss and Einstein, Rilke

CHAPTER 18

PROFESSOR BEHR WAS DELIGHTED WHEN I TOLD HIM I'D be making a trip to Göttingen. "Beautiful town," he exclaimed. "I have happy memories of visiting colleagues there before the war, and taking long walks in the woods." He asked me what I wanted to accomplish on my trip, and I told him that I was going more for the people who used to be there than those who remained, and he said, "Ah, you're making a pilgrimage. Very proper." And he gave me the name of a beloved former student who "alas, lacked the talent for serious study" but had risen in the ranks of the administration there and was now the provost. He promised to write to him to tell him I was coming, and "to see what he could do."

"Frank was never a particularly good mathematician," he explained, "never had the imagination for it, but he was exceptional at every other thing he put his mind to." He continued, "You, however, are a very good mathematician, so though I wish you the best on your travels, I implore you to return after a reasonable amount of time, and do not lose track of your research."

I agreed enthusiastically. "I only have one small lingering hole I'm trying to plug in the paper I'm writing, and then I'll be ready to show it to you and submit it," I told Professor Behr.

"Just don't wait too long," he said. "You don't want to get scooped."

"Of course not," I agreed, but I wasn't really worried. I had a feeling about this paper, a calm confidence that it was *my* paper to write, that it was my time. And when I was done, I hoped it would be enough to establish me—if not among the ranks of Peter Hall, at least within his circle. I wanted to be able to return to America with some kind of crowning achievement. I wanted to see what would happen between us if I returned not as his starstruck student, but as an equal.

In the meantime, Henry had received an invitation in response to her request to access the archives for research pertaining to the Brothers Grimm. She'd gotten permission from her program to go for an extended period of time, as well as to travel to the nearby Harz Mountains where the Brothers Grimm had collected many of their fairy tales.

Aside from my trip with Peter to Chicago, I'd never traveled with a companion before, and Henry and I prepared for two full weeks before we left. We went back and forth about what clothes we might need, how many papers and notebooks, how many pencils and pens. In the end I took a midsize satchel heavy with books: Henry packed two enormous suitcases filled with more things than I had brought for my entire trip to Germany. She had books and clothes and shoes and skin creams and cosmetics, and an additional handbag overflowing with two loaves of bread, a jar of jam, some butter, two rolls of salami, and a bag of pastries.

"Don't you think they will have food in Göttingen?" I laughed, but Henry warned, "Make fun of me, and I won't share."

It turned out she was right: our train broke down on the tracks, and we ate all the food in her bag, and ordered more, as well as coffee, tea, water, and juice from the attendant who came pushing a cart through the aisle every few hours. All day long we sat in our train compartment, and Henry told me fairy tales. I'd seen *Snow White* the movie, of course, and *Sleeping Beauty*—but these were not the stories I'd grown up with.

"Neither did I," Henry scoffed. "It's not like I got these stories from my parents."

"Where did you get them?" I asked.

"The library!" Henry exclaimed. "I read all the fairy tales I could get my hands on, all the different versions from all over the world, in translation. I already knew Chinese, so I taught myself German, and then in college I took Russian and Italian and French so I could read everything in their original language."

"Henry," I said, "has anyone ever told you that you're a little bit terrifying?"

Henry dimpled. "All the time," she said.

Henry was working on a book to collect fairy tales and folktales from all over the world and organize them into archetypes. Every culture, she said, seemed to have a Cinderella story, a Little Red Riding Hood story, a Snow White story. "They're not just stories about rags to riches, powerless to powerful," she said. "They're also really sobering critiques of what we value in women. Do you know in the original Brothers Grimm version, the sisters don't just try Cinderella's shoe on, they hack off their toes and their heels to get them to fit? When they pass the test, they're taken to the prince to marry, except that they're caught when their blood leaks through the bandages and out of the shoes. The prince doesn't care about Cinderella, the girl he supposedly fell in love with at the ball. He would marry anyone who had her tiny feet!" She laughed. "All these stories have these underlying, terrible messages that Disney just erased in his movies and replaced with happy endings, which is arguably worse.

"In the Brothers Grimm version of Snow White, the prince doesn't actually fall in love with her sleeping body—he comes upon her in a glass coffin because she's supposed to be dead, but the dwarves found her too beautiful to bury. The prince doesn't wake her with a kiss—he's loading her onto a horse to take home to look at, like a pinned butterfly or a stuffed animal, and while they're jostling her body, the apple piece she choked on gets knocked loose and she wakes up, and that's when they get married.

"And that's not the only catatonic-girl-in-a-coma story we've got. There's Sleeping Beauty, too, of course—there are all these princes falling in love with the empty, unconscious shells of girls who basically go limp right as they hit adolescence. Sends an interesting message, don't you think? Girls—be as lifeless as possible, and the more likely it is you'll be desired."

By the time our train finally got moving again, it was night. We stretched out in the sleeping car under one of two blankets Henry had packed, our heads propped up by two rolled towels. "At first I was astonished at the amount of luggage you were bringing," I told her. "And now I'm amazed at how much you managed to fit into the luggage!"

We were both exhausted but couldn't sleep because we kept talking and talking. We kept saying, "We need to sleep," but then Henry would say something, or I would say something, and we would keep going on and on, like we were making up for all the years we hadn't yet known each other, all the years we hadn't been able to talk.

"Did you know that the stepmother as a villain is an invention on the part of the Brothers Grimm?" Henry asked. "The original folktales had the mothers as villains, but the Brothers Grimm changed them to stepmothers in the retelling. Just think about that! The original versions were about how dangerous mothers can be, how jealous even of their own children—and then the Brothers Grimm went and sanctified the mother. Also, in the folk version of Little Red Riding Hood, she isn't rescued by a woodsman, she frees herself by tricking the wolf with her wits."

"What? I didn't know that."

"Yes. She pretends she has to go to the bathroom and the wolf says she can, but to tie a string around her finger so she won't get away. She ties the string to the door of the outhouse, to trick him when he pulls it, and then she runs away." Henry stopped here and grinned in delight. "And here's the kicker: it all makes sense when you consider how folktales were mostly told and passed along orally by women, but that the written versions have universally been set down and altered by men, that in the women's version the girl gets away by her wits, and in the man's version she's saved by a hero. Two very different lessons, wouldn't you say?"

"Ha!" I said. "That sort of reminds me of the tenth muse."

"Who's that?" Henry asked.

"You've never heard of her?" I asked. "She's not a fairy tale?"

"Not exactly," Henry said. "The muses are technically Greek myths, but tell me more, I want to hear!"

So I told her my mother's story.

"Ah, I love that story," she said, when I had finished. "I've never heard that one before."

"There's another story I always think of along with that one," I said. "Because it's also about a woman who leaves her family to choose her own fate. The Wise Princess Kwan-Yin. My mother told me that one as well."

"Oh, I know that story!" Henry exclaimed. "It's Chinese. Tell me your version!" And so I did.

Afterward, Henry lay looking at me for a long time. "You know," she said thoughtfully, "the two are almost opposites: the tenth muse is all about fulfilling her own dreams as an individual, and the Princess Kwan-Yin is all about self-sacrifice, or self-transcendence. You know she's a religious figure in China, right? She's a bodhisattva in Buddhism, dedicated to alleviating the suffering of mankind. People have statues of her in their homes. They chant her name in prayer."

"I didn't know that," I said, struck with the thought that I didn't know if my mother had had any kind of religion. We hadn't gone to church—another strike against us in New Umbria—but for some reason I'd just assumed she had no religion. Now I wondered if she'd been Buddhist.

Henry abruptly leaned forward. "Listen, Kat," she said urgently, taking my hand in hers. "Forget princes. Forget men. Let's never get married. Let's stay single and free forever, and do what we want. Let's be heroes or villains, but never the princess. Or if we have to marry, let's be like the girl in Bluebeard, who marries the villain with all the dead wives in the basement, and then kills him in self-defense and inherits all his wealth." She laughed. She was leaning forward and smiling at me intensely, and I felt a little dizzy and breathless, like I was standing at the edge of a precipice and wanted to take her hand and jump.

I pulled my hand away and said, "It's not like anyone's lining up to marry me."

For a moment the air had been alive and electric between us. Now it flattened as I spoke. Henry's smile dimmed and gentled. "Oh, Kat," she said.

I knew then that I had lost some chance, that a door I hadn't been aware existed had closed: Let's never get married. Let's be a pair unto ourselves.

WE ARRIVED IN GÖTTINGEN just as the sun rose, rumpled but bright-eyed, to discover it was a beautiful town with red-roofed buildings and cobbled streets and large sprawling gardens. I was surprised: somehow I'd expected it to be in ruins. America had absorbed so many of the scientists who used to work in Göttingen—so much so that Courant, one such transplant and the founder of the Courant Institute at NYU, had said famously, upon reaching New York and reuniting with nearly all his old colleagues: "It is Göttingen. Göttingen is here."

In fact, the town was in much better shape than Bonn. The cobbled streets were busy with pedestrians and students spilling out of cafés. Henry and I spent the morning of the first day checking into our pension and then walking around, circling the city wall, poking our heads in and out of small stores filled with useful and prettily made things. In the afternoon, we went to the university library where the Grimm brothers had worked before being driven out by the townspeople for inciting political unrest. (A piece of trivia that Henry had recounted with glee.)

That afternoon, Henry stayed to pore over her books, and I left to meet with Professor Behr's former student turned administrator, Frank. Frank was jolly and ruddy cheeked and also clearly swamped with work: in the fifteen minutes I sat across from him at his desk, at least a dozen people needed his attention, coming in and out of the office, whispering in his ear, handing him papers to look at, asking for his signature on various things. In the midst of this hubbub, he gave me a list of people he'd arranged meetings with: the math librarian, the archivist at city hall, and an emeritus professor who'd retired five years ago.

"Professor Behr says you're here on a pilgrimage," he said. "I'm assuming you'll be wanting to visit Gauss's residence, and Hilbert's. I've taken the liberty of marking their addresses for you here on this map." He showed me on a map the marked locations along with a separate list of addresses. "And of course I assume you'll want to visit the house Emmy Noether lived in as well," he said.

"Yes," I said. "Absolutely."

"Now," he said, "is there anything else I can help you with?"

"I'm actually here searching for some people who might have been connected to the math community here in 1935," I said. "I'm looking for information about someone with the initials S. M. and also for a Jewish woman and a Chinese man who might have been here—though it's possible one of them might have been S. M."

Frank tilted his head and looked at me. "It sounds like there's an interesting story behind your search."

"Sort of. It's more like a personal connection I'm trying to track down."

"Understood." Frank nodded. "Hold on," he said. He called his secretary in and scribbled a note on a piece of paper. "Please make a copy of this and send it to the registrar's office, the bursar's office, the chair of the Mathematics Department, and the Office for Foreign Studies," he said. He turned back to me. "I've sent for records, enrollment lists and such. Hopefully they'll help you get to the bottom of your mystery. I'll have everything sent to the pension you're staying in. In the meantime, I recommend you see Professor Mueller, the chair of the Mathematics Department, yourself, and let him know that I sent you."

"Thank you so much. I don't know what to say."

He waved off my thanks. "Any student of Professor Behr's is a friend of mine," he said. "In fact, you must forgive me. I'd like very much to take you to dinner, but my schedule for the next several days does not permit it. Perhaps you could drop by in two days or so to let me know how things are going, and we can arrange it then?"

"Absolutely," I said. And thanking him again for the amount of work he'd already done on my behalf, I took my leave.

THE FIRST PLACE I VISITED was the math library to request access to Emmy Noether's archived papers, as well as Einstein's, Gauss's, and Hilbert's. I was so excited to be in Göttingen, the former mecca of mathematics. There were a few professors, I knew, who remained from the golden years, but the program had been gutted, even more so than Bonn's. It had been one of the first universities to begin firing Jewish faculty when the Nazis rose to power, starting with Noether. The students had protested her "Jewess mathematics" and though Hilbert and her other colleagues had launched a spirited defense via a letter-writing campaign that the absolute best mathematicians had all signed off on, citing her excellence, they had not been able to prevail. It had been the first great shock: the first moment that the faculty realized that their world had changed—that they had lost an influence and power they had not realized could be taken away.

The firings continued. The Jewish students were chased out. Some of the non-Jews began boycotting the classes of Jewish faculty—not just boycotting, but protesting in front of their classes, blocking students' professors from entering their classrooms. Courant left next, then Landau and Weyl. This was when Hilbert famously declared, "There is no mathematics in Göttingen anymore."

And this turned out to be true. When Hilbert finally died, there was nothing to draw the kind of talent that had flocked there before. The program never recovered.

I WENT TO PROFESSOR MUELLER'S OFFICE after the library. He was occupied, but I was told he would be available in an hour. To fill the time during my wait, I climbed the stairs to the math museum, which was on the top floor of the building and was simply an informal collection of objects that various faculty members had collected over the years: telescopes, models of polyhedra and Möbius strips, various optical and electrical devices. I studied the photographs lining the walls. There were pictures of Hilbert, Minkowski, Landau, and Gauss. And among them three photographs of Emmy Noether: in each of them she wore her trademark round glasses, long skirt, and button-down white shirt. Her face was serious but warm, her hands relaxed, her hair askew in its bun.

I stood for a long time, looking at the faces of the students in all the photographs. After a while, I became aware that someone was watching me.

When I turned to face him, he approached with a smile. He was a handsome older gentleman, who looked to be in his early fifties, about my father's age. "I see you're looking at the pictures of Herr Noether," he said, in German.

"Herr Noether?" I said. "I was looking at the pictures of Frau Emmy Noether."

He smiled. "We called her Herr, not Frau, as a mark of respect," he said. "You are looking at the picture of the last generation of Noether's boys. See? That's me, right there." And he pointed to a slender youth.

"You're one of Noether's boys?"

"Obviously I'm not a boy any longer," he said. "But, yes, I was one of the last. I'm surprised you've heard of us. Usually only other mathematicians know of Noether and her collection of algebraists."

"But I am a mathematician," I said. "Aspiring, at least. I'm a student."

"Ah, what a coincidence! I am a professor." The man twinkled his eyes at me. I noticed they were a deep green, flecked with gold. "Well, then, you should know that Herr Noether's lectures were nearly impossible to follow; she'd just get started and go wherever she wanted to, hardly pausing to answer questions, getting chalk all over her clothes. We'd have to dust her off before we let her leave the room."

"Sounds charming," I said. I laughed. "I'm Katherine." I held out my hand.

He took it and raised it to his lips, half gallantly, half ironically.

"And I'm Karl. What brings you here to this neglected museum of mathematics?" he asked with a flourish of his arm.

"I'm looking for someone," I said.

"Just what I was hoping you'd say," he said. He leaned forward and took my hand back in his—a surprising, intimate gesture. "So tell me," he said, clasping it warmly, "who are you looking for, and where do you come from, and what is your connection to the person you're seeking?"

"Those are unfortunately all questions I seem to lack answers to at the moment."

"Ah, so you're mysterious," he said.

I laughed and blushed and felt—not shy, exactly, but emboldened somehow.

"Let's start smaller then," he said. "What do you do at the university?"

"I don't do anything here," I said. "I'm on break from the University of Bonn, where I'm a visiting scholar in the mathematics department. I'm from America, originally."

"America!" he exclaimed. And then switching to perfect English, "Shall we get some tea, perhaps, some coffee? And you can tell me what I can do to help you with your search?"

"I'm afraid I have an appointment with Professor Mueller very soon."

"Ah. How about dinner?"

Normally I would be wary at the attention of a stranger. But for some reason, coming from Karl, it didn't feel threatening, or even particularly pushy, just friendly and flirtatious, and I found him charming, and attractive.

"I'm having dinner with my friend Henry. I could meet you tomorrow, though."

"Tomorrow, then," he said. "Shall we meet here, in front of the photos of Noether and her boys, at half past five tomorrow?"

"Yes. I'll be here."

"And now you must let me escort you to Professor Mueller's office and give you a small tour along the way," Karl said, offering me his arm. Though I was pressed for time he insisted on taking me on the scenic route to Professor Mueller's office, telling me not to worry, and stopping at various landmarks to tell me the personal histories of how and when famous mathematical and scientific discoveries were made in that exact place, and of proofs written from the trenches of war, and unfinished theorems scribbled down on deathbeds. And finally, we were back at Professor Mueller's office.

"My own office is just down the hall," he said, gesturing in that direction. "Drop by any time." And then, "Ah!" as a man emerged. "Professor Mueller. I've delivered your next appointment. Enjoy!" And with a wave and a flourish, he was off.

Professor Mueller was entirely business, possessing none of Karl's charm. "Ah, yes, the Provost told me you'd be coming," he said, briskly. "My secretary is looking for the information he requested for you, and we can have enrollment lists to you in the next few days. Professor Hektor and Professor Meisenbach may be worth asking as well—Hektor was here then, and Meisenbach was a student at the time. Did he have anything to tell you when you met with him?"

"Professor Hektor is on my list," I said. "But not Meisenbach. Is he the Meisenbach of the Schieling-Meisenbach theorem?"

"Yes," said Professor Mueller. "And as for Karl Meisenbach, I just saw you talking with him outside my door!"

"Karl is . . . Karl *Meisenbach*?"

"Indeed he is." Professor Mueller gave me a sharp look. "You may want to ask him if he knew the people you're looking for."

"I didn't realize who he was," I said. "I didn't know he was still here." The truth was I'd never heard that Meisenbach had produced anything after his one famous theorem and I had just assumed he was dead.

"If anyone would know, it'd be him."

"All right," I said. "Thanks for the tip."

"Check in with my secretary in the next couple days for that list from the registrar's office," Mueller continued. "And if you need anything else, please feel free to stop by."

AT DINNER, Henry and I were both glowing with happiness. We'd each accomplished more in that day than we'd hoped. Henry had seen the Grimm archives, had seen their notes and hand drawings. "At this rate I may finish my book sooner than I'd hoped." She rubbed her hands together. "Oh, I'm so glad we came," she said. "I have a good feeling about what you'll find out while you're here."

Chapter 19

The next morning I went for a walk in town. When I returned to the pension, a note was waiting for me from Frank's office. Inside the envelope were two names: Simon Mannheim and Stefan Mintz. There was a note from Frank. These were the names of the two mathematics students with the initials S. M. for the year I was searching for. If either of these was promising, Frank wrote he'd be happy to search correspondence and records for known whereabouts.

At dinner, I showed Karl the list, and he said, "I knew both of them to varying degrees. What would you like to know?"

"I'm not sure, exactly," I said. I laughed. "When we first met, you thought I was trying to be mysterious, but the truth is I am actually just confused."

"Well," Karl said. "Perhaps I can help un-confuse you. It is, as a professor, part of my job description after all."

I smiled. "I haven't told a lot of people this story," I said, "but I inherited a notebook that has the initials S. M. and the words Universität Göttingen, 1935, etched on the inside cover. And I'm looking for the person who wrote it."

"Fascinating," Karl said. "And the link to the math department?"

"The notebook is filled almost entirely with math," I said.

Karl took a deep breath in. "Well, Simon Mannheim left the university sometime in the 1930s to become a novelist," he said. "He still lives near Göttingen, in a town forty minutes away by train. And Stefan Mintz is a professor somewhere in London, last I heard. I can put you in touch with either of them somewhat easily, though I haven't been in contact myself for quite a long time."

"Thank you," I said. "I'd appreciate it."

"What kind of math was in this notebook of yours? Perhaps I can help you decipher the riddle."

"A lot of equations I couldn't place," I said.

"And why are you looking for the author? Why do you suspect it's significant?"

"I don't," I said. "I'm trying to track the owner down for personal reasons, not professional ones."

Karl nodded. "Have you shown the notebook to anyone else?"

"I haven't."

"I'd be happy to take a look."

"Really?" I asked.

"Yes, of course," Karl said. "Perhaps after dinner I could walk you home and have a peek?"

"I don't know," I said, feeling suddenly skittish. Henry was always laughing at how hesitant I was with strangers, how old-fashioned, but I'd learned from experience that a man can switch from harmless to aggressive in the blink of an eye. I hadn't yet learned how to block or turn away that kind of attention effectively and with grace, in the way that Henry seemed to manage. To be honest, I never did.

But I sometimes felt—as I did now, with Karl, that my caution made me look foolish, as if I expected every man to be attracted to me. As if I thought so highly of myself, as if I thought I deserved the attention. I was embarrassed by this, and I regretted also the opportunities I missed out on because of it. Conversations I'd never had. Friendships I'd never developed. Potential mentors I had spurned.

"Actually, come over," I said. "It will be all right."

"Are you sure?" Karl asked.

"Absolutely," I said. "To see the notebook, right?"

It seemed to me that Karl was nervous for the rest of dinner, and I wondered if I'd made a mistake in inviting him over after my initial hesitation: if he'd noticed, if I'd sent the wrong message. But after we'd agreed that he'd come over, he was very quiet, and I grew more and more embarrassed.

When we arrived at the pension, Henry was home. She flew out to the stair landing in her nightgown crying out, "Kat, Kat, you'll never guess what I discovered today!" And then, upon seeing Karl, she stopped short, and said—"Oh!"

We all stood, frozen in the stairwell. Karl and I looking up, Henry with her long black hair coiled up in a loose mass atop her head.

"Henry, I'm so sorry," I said. "I was telling Karl about my notebook, and he thought maybe it would be useful to take a look."

"Oh, of course!" cried Henry, while Karl said at the same moment, "Would it be better if I came another time?"

Henry burst out laughing and said, "Not at all, but I will go back in and get dressed, and then Kat—you ruffian—will have to introduce us properly."

INSIDE, I MADE KARL some tea and brought out raspberry cookies from the pantry that Henry always kept well stocked. Karl still looked a little nervous, but he brightened a bit when Henry came out in silk pajama pants, a cropped blouse, and a bright scarf tied around her head. That was Henry. Decades later, and I still remember what she wore.

I went into my bedroom and pulled my notebook out of the satchel I kept it in. I shook out the bits of loose paper I'd tucked in over the years—various notes to myself, my translation of the list of commands I'd found after the incident with Blake—exhorting courage, and reminding me to be kind.

"Do you know I've never seen the mysterious notebook?" Henry said to Karl when I brought it out.

"Did you want to?" I asked.

"Of course," she said.

"But you never said anything!"

"It always seemed so private," she said. "I didn't want to impose."

But Karl wasn't paying attention. He was staring at the notebook I held, and when I gave it to him, it seemed to me that he took it with trembling hands.

He flipped through it once, twice, very quickly, and then he took two or three deep breaths as if to calm himself down. He opened it and stared at the inside cover for a long moment. He looked up, his eyes filled with tears, and when he spoke, it was in German. "How did you come upon this book?"

"It was given to me by my father," I said. "Do you know who it belonged to?"

"Yes," he said. "I'd know this notebook anywhere. You must tell me who gave it to you, and when, and under what circumstances. I knew the author well, you see—her name was Sophie Meisenbach, and she was my cousin."

My heart lurched. "Your cousin?" I stammered. "The notebook

belonged to a woman?" Sophie Meisenbach. Had I finally found the name of my mother?

Though I was eager to ask Karl to tell me everything about Sophie Meisenbach, I rushed through my own story first, the one Liliane had told my father about the young couple, the baby, the notebook, me. "And so you see," I finished, "that's why I have been searching for the authorship of this notebook. I am trying to discover who I am."

By then Karl was openly weeping. "Sophie and I grew up together in neighboring towns," he said. "Our fathers were brothers, twins actually, so in some ways we were even closer than typical cousins. Her father had married a Jew, so though we were cousins, she was Jewish and I was not."

He looked at his hands and steadied himself. "Sophie was always a better student than me, though I'm not sure our teachers ever gave her the recognition she deserved, while I was routinely praised. But Sophie knew what she was capable of, or at least she wanted to find out her limits, and when I went to university, she decided she wanted to go too."

He met my eye. "I'm very proud of the influence I had," he said. "Her mother was against Sophie going to school, but she was her father's only daughter and his favorite child, and he couldn't say no to her about anything. And so he let her go. She was here in Göttingen for two and a half years."

"Why wasn't she on the list Frank gave me?" I asked.

"She wasn't an official student," Karl said. "Her parents didn't let her enroll. She had two brothers who were attending a university near their hometown, and her parents didn't want them to feel like she was competing with them—though for my money, Sophie's was the better mind, by far. But Sophie would never admit it, and she didn't want to be enrolled or to outshine them, she didn't care—she just wanted to be here, to study, to learn.

"But like I mentioned, she was Jewish. And so a few years in, after Hitler was elected—that monster, that fool—she was forced to return to her family. When the Jews were told to leave Germany, Sophie's family decided to stay. They thought they were safe. They thought it'd blow over, you see. And of course things got worse, and the borders were closed, and we were at war. Nobody really ever believed, you see, I mean, no one understood how far it would go. We all thought they'd be spared. I do know that they tried to escape after some time in hiding, but after they made the attempt, we lost contact with them. They were just gone. We had hoped that meant they had made it out, but we never heard anything conclusively. When they didn't return after the war or send word, we had to assume they didn't survive."

We were all silent. Karl cleared his throat. "What a way to meet," he said. "What a way to discover a long-lost cousin." He offered me a weak smile.

"Oh," I said. "I'm not trying to claim that Sophie Meisenbach was my mother. I only know that somehow the notebook was found with me."

"Whereas there is no question at all in my mind, my dear, that you are Sophie's child," Karl said. "There is the story, of course, and the matter of the notebook and your talent for math. But there's more. I noticed right away that there was something familiar about you—something about the shape of your face, and your mouth, I'm not sure exactly what. Something in me recognized you. And it cannot be denied, it all fits together. When Sophie fled, she was known to have been involved with a Chinaman. And she was pregnant. It was quite a scandal."

I felt a prickle of shame at the way he said the words *Chinaman* and *scandal*, but Henry said, "That's amazing! How wonderful." And then, seeing my face, "Oh, poor Kat, it's a lot to take in."

"It is," Karl agreed. "Perhaps that's enough for one night. Katherine, may I take this notebook with me tonight to look over for the next couple days?"

"I don't know, that notebook is very dear to me," I said. "I know it sounds silly, but it's the one thing I've had all my life, and it would make me very nervous to part with it."

"I understand," Karl said. "I promise to take good care of it. It is dear to me as well, you know. I have some photographs of Sophie and a handful of letters she wrote to me. I would be happy to turn them over to you, as insurance, if you would like to take a look. I've kept them safe all these years."

"Okay," I said. I cleared my throat. "Yes, I'd like to see them very much."

Karl rose and tucked the notebook into his inner jacket pocket. I felt a twinge of anxiety watching it be taken into someone else's possession, but I batted that away.

"May I ask one last thing?" I said.

"Go ahead."

"The Chinaman. What was his name?"

"Cao," Karl said, immediately. "Here, let me write it down for you." And he pulled a pen out of his pocket and scribbled "Cao Xi Ling" on a piece of paper.

when we talked about these things about what it must feel like for you—it was like listening to stories . . ." And now her tears overflowed. "We'll adopt you, Kat. You can be my sister. We can spend holidays together and squabble over who gets to shower first. My parents would probably like you better anyway." And now we were both laughing. "I just want to give you what I have."

THE NEXT MORNING a small bundle arrived wrapped in paper and tied with a white string. The moment I saw Sophie's letters, I knew she had been the owner of my notebook: the handwriting I'd spent my life studying was identical, the same swirling *S*'s, the same flourishes on the *M*'s. There were two photographs as well—Karl had attached a note saying that the first was of Sophie at five or six years old with her family, which included two older brothers named Franz and Albert, and her parents—Walter and Anne. Sophie was wearing a white dress with frills around the neck, and an enormous bow atop her light-colored hair. Her eyes were also light, and she was sitting up very straight with her hands folded between her parents, who were also seated—and her brothers, Franz and Albert, were wearing dark suits and standing on either side. They were posed in front of a painted backdrop of bookshelves, and everyone was looking at the camera except Sophie, who—for all the primness of her posture—was looking intently to the side, at something out of the frame.

The second photograph was much more relaxed. It was taken in front of the math building on campus, and it was of Sophie and about ten young men, including Karl. Her hair had darkened since she was a child, and now she stood at the center, wearing a long dress with one foot kicking out. Her face was laughing, her gaze direct. The men stood around her with their hands in their pockets, looking challengingly at the camera. I wondered what Karl had seen in me that reminded him of her: I studied her wide-set eyes, her soft, expressive mouth, and the halo of dark hair surrounding her face. I could not find a resemblance.

There were sixteen letters in all to Karl, and they were friendly and jovial, and had mostly been written in the two years he'd been at Göttingen before her. She sent news of her parents and her brothers, and a girl who, Sophie intimated, may have had a budding romance with Karl—but the purpose of the letters, it seemed, was to ask about his studies, as she always closed the same way, exclaiming, "Send me your lecture notes, please!" with the *please* underlined three times. "You don't want me falling behind!"

I WENT TO UPDATE FRANK on my progress the next day and asked if he could find all the known addresses of Sophie Meisenbach and Cao Xi Ling. Frank said that because Sophie hadn't been officially enrolled at the university, they would not have records of that nature, but that he would reach out to a city official he knew, who might be able to help. Cao Xi Ling, if I gave him some time, he would definitely be able to track down. I didn't tell him who these people were to me, or the nature of my search, and he didn't ask. I did tell him about meeting Karl.

"Between us," he said, "I would watch out for Karl Meisenbach."

"How come?"

"If it was up to me, I would have fired him a long time ago."

"Wow," I said. "Can you tell me why?"

"Do you know anything about our history here?"

"Only the math."

"Some universities fought the Nazis, some put up with them, but not Göttingen. Göttingen embraced them. We were a *braun Stadt*—a brown city, where so many of our youth wore the brown shirts of the SA. Many faculty members stood by their Jewish colleagues, of course—but you can believe me when I say their students did not, and certainly not the people of this town.

"I tell you in confidence: if it was up to me, I would fire Meisenbach. He was a student when all this happened. Noether was his mentor. Do you think he would still be here if he had stood up for her, if he had defended her and his other Jewish professors? Well, he didn't. Instead he took a position that only existed because they were gone."

"Well, that wasn't exactly his fault," I said, after a moment. "You can't blame him for everything that happened."

"Then who do you blame?" Frank asked. "Everyone in this town would say that they were against the Nazis. Everyone would claim their families were part of the resistance. Do you think, given what happened, that could possibly be true? I often think that it would have been better if this place had been bombed during the war. I wish it had been."

"What do you mean?"

"Everyone who remains benefited from the exiles and murders of Jews, don't you see? We all did, we citizens of this country, whether we wrung our hands and regretted what was happening or openly celebrated when they were cast out of their jobs. We took whatever came our way and pretended it was ours to have by right.

"My father would tell you he was opposed to the Nazis, and that he spoke out against them until it became dangerous to do so. But what kind of courage is that? My father would say he stayed quiet in order to survive, that everyone who opposed them openly is dead. He was a film theorist, a scholar. He would never tell you this, never, but before I was born, he made propaganda films for the Nazi Party, and his only excuse is they asked him to, and he felt he couldn't say no." Frank laughed, angrily. "But his name is on the film, and that will be true forever, no matter what he—or I—can say of it now." He scowled at his hands. "A Jewish girl taught me how to read. Ask my father now about the Nazis and he'll tell you he hid two young nurses in our attic for the duration of the war, and afterward they went to Palestine, where they live to this day. They'll never return here, and if they did, who would welcome them? My father thinks hiding them makes him a hero, despite his job, despite his name on a Nazi propaganda film. The families of those two girls, dead. Millions dead, and he thinks he's a hero. Better he had died," he said. "Better he had been killed." There was real bitterness in his voice.

"Wow," I said. "Maybe those girls disagree."

He shrugged. "Maybe they do and maybe they don't. I grew up with nurses and tutors, and beautiful things in our house. Gold candlesticks. Expensive paintings. Those girls lived in our attic. I grew up rich with stolen wealth, and we never returned it."

"My father was a soldier in the war," I told him. "When I was a child, I tried to imagine the terrible things he might have done. He would never talk about it. I wondered what secrets he carried inside him. It didn't make me afraid of him, though; it made me—afraid *for* him."

"The government in Bonn and most German residents do not support extending the statute of limitations on war crimes," Frank said. "I do not think that as a country we are reckoning with our history. I do not think we're facing up to what we did."

"War criminals are one thing," I said. "But Karl Meisenbach never harmed anyone. How can you really justify firing everyone who was here during the war? That seems to me just to be an accident of timing. Anyway, that kind of policy would upend society. It would ruin people's lives."

Frank smiled. "The tyranny of history," he said, "is that it's always too late for justice, the price is always too high."

"But you can't punish everyone," I said. "Especially people who didn't commit any actual crimes. When would it stop? What about Professor Behr? What about you? According to you, shouldn't both of you be fired as well?"

I thought I'd offend him, that I'd gone too far. Instead, he laughed. "Exactly," he said. "My point exactly."

I left that conversation profoundly unnerved. It made me realize that something about the city of Göttingen—how pristine and untouched it remained—felt sinister in a way that Bonn, rebuilding, did not. And I realized with a jolt how at every mention of what had happened to the Jews I felt a chill in my veins, like the blood I had recently learned ran through them had gone cold.

I WENT TO SEE KARL that same afternoon, and I took him the letters and photographs he'd sent over, but he pushed them back into my hands and said, "Keep them, they're yours."

"Thank you," I said. "And if you're done looking over the notebook, could I have it back? I thought of something I wanted to take a look at." This was a lie, but I didn't know how to politely say I missed it and wanted it back in my possession.

"Really?" Karl said. "May I ask what you're looking for?" He paused. "I'm afraid I left the notebook at home, but I will be sure to bring it in tomorrow. Either way, perhaps I can be of assistance."

"Oh, it's probably nothing. I'd rather not say until I am sure," I said.

"Well, I hope it is something," he said. "That would be so exciting."

I sat in his office for another hour and a half, while Karl told me more about Sophie. His family had stayed with her family every summer. He'd been an only child, and her brothers had been like brothers to him, but Sophie, he said, had been special.

He'd been five when she was born and met her at her name day party, when she was eight days old. Her father had named her Sophie, which meant wisdom, though her mother, Anne, had preferred a more flowery name, or a more practical one. Sophie was quiet and thoughtful and carried a notebook with her everywhere she went, even as a child, drawing and making up poems. Her father doted on her, but her mother said, What good was cleverness in a girl when it ruined her mind for the practical details of life? And Sophie—it had to be admitted—was not particularly well suited for the practical details of life. She burned her baking and made a mess of her cooking. She did not seem to care for fashion or boys.

But Karl understood the key to his cousin: he talked to her and showed her things, and in return she showed him her notebooks. Whenever he visited, they'd go for a walk in the woods or sit by the lake talking and talking, and drawing with sticks. Karl taught her what he knew of math, which Sophie had a passion for, and as time went on, Karl began to teach her not only addition and subtraction, but the theory behind numbers, and how to use symbols to stand for them and the relationships between them: how numbers were symbols of symbols. Sophie loved these talks and couldn't get enough of them. And when Karl went to Göttingen, she wanted more than anything else to follow.

When she was fifteen, Sophie's brothers came down with the mumps, one after the other in a week and a half, and her parents decided to send her away—not to France to live with her grandmother as they'd originally intended, but with a governess to Göttingen. Sophie had told Karl the trick of getting what she wanted from her parents. If she sounded too anxious about wanting to do something, no matter how harmless, they would hesitate—wondering, worried, doubting. But if she asked for the same thing in a neutral, reasonable tone of voice, as if she didn't care which way it went, one or the next, they'd capitulate without really considering. In this case, it had worked.

It was with a sense of adventure and relief that Sophie left home. She loved her brothers dearly, and was sorry they were ill, but during her first few weeks away, she hardly thought of them. Because Göttingen was where Sophie first met Emmy Noether. In Noether's classes, the students gathered around her, asking questions that Noether fielded with cheerful willingness, effortlessly manipulating formulae, showing the generalizations that arose from their calculations—*here is the rule demonstrated by these different examples.* This was the game Sophie had learned from Karl, a private language unto themselves, and now she discovered that here were others who could not just speak it fluently, but actually *play* inside it.

Emmy Noether was not beautiful, in her trousers and her cheeks smudged with dust, the lines deep in her face, and yet she held the attention of these men as Sophie had been told only the most beautiful women could ever do. What Noether's mind could draw forth, from itself and from the minds of others! She engaged them wholly, led them through mazes and tunnels and traps, all of them eager at her heels—she gathered them together and then she released them to wander on their own, dazed and giddy with revelation.

Emmy moved among these men without self-consciousness. Without constraint or fear. Later, Sophie told Karl it seemed to her the deepest kind of freedom: Emmy's benevolent, blinking ignorance of what people thought of her in either direction. She did not care. To Sophie it seemed liked a miracle: to not even struggle against the crippling self-consciousness she so often felt, but to simply set it aside! Sophie wanted to learn that power. And it was in those first weeks at Göttingen, watching Emmy Noether, that Sophie decided that she did not wish to aspire to loveliness, but to a different kind of grace.

"Sophie wanted to be a mathematician, and was well on her way to becoming a formidable one. As are you." Karl smiled. "Blood always tells," he said. And then, "Are you sure you don't want to tell me what you think might be in the notebook?"

I felt a flush of shame at my earlier lie. "I really don't feel like I can," I said.

He nodded. I felt I'd displeased him, but he said, "Anything else you'd like to know?"

"Everything, I guess," I said. "Whatever you can tell me."

And so he described Sophie's house to me and drew a beautiful and detailed sketch for me from memory: he said the house had been large and yellow, two stories with six gabled windows facing front, built in the traditional German style. He drew the interior, pointing out where each room had been, including Sophie's and the two guest rooms he and his family had occupied whenever they visited. He drew the living room with its bookshelves reaching all the way to the ceiling, the gleaming grand piano that Sophie's father had given her mother upon their marriage: the one extravagance he was known for. He told me how beautifully Sophie's mother had played it. He told me about a lake that the cousins swam in together nearby, and about picnics and long summer days, and all the beautiful things that had been in their house. Beneath the drawing he scrawled out their address.

At the end of our conversation, Karl said I could keep the drawings he'd made. I had more questions to ask, but at some point, I sensed a constraint in the way he was talking to me that hadn't been there before. It made me feel awkward and confused; I didn't know why his manner would have cooled. I tried to charm him back into the way he'd been when we first met, until I realized that he seemed to be waiting for me to leave.

WHEN I GOT BACK to my pension, I felt inexplicably unsettled. The owners had strictly forbidden long-distance calling, but I called Peter's office from my bedroom, collect.

"Yes?" he answered the phone. His voice was cold.

"Not even hello?" I asked.

"Katherine, you don't call for weeks, not even to say that you arrived in Göttingen safely, and then you call me collect and you're going to complain about how I answer the phone?"

"I'm sorry," I said. "I forgot to call when I got here."

There was a pause. A crackly sigh. "Katherine, I'm at the office. I'm trying to get some work done. What do you need?"

"I just wanted to hear your voice," I said. "I miss you."

"Well," Peter said flatly, "then you should have stayed here."

"Why are you acting like this?" I asked. "Why are you being so cold?" And we went on and on like this for a while until Peter reminded me that this call was collect, and would cost him a fortune, and I said, "Fine, let's hang up." Then he asked for my number and said he'd call back, but I told him no, not to bother. It was an exhausting, stupid conversation, and at the end of it, I had told Peter that if he was so unhappy with us, maybe we should break up, and he—to my shock—had agreed.

I avoided Henry that night and went to bed before she came home, and first thing the next morning I snuck out of our pension and left her a note saying I'd be back late, after dinner. I went to the train station and boarded a train to Sophie's hometown of Gurz, which was a four-hour ride away. I felt weighed down by sadness, but through that sadness, I also felt a thrill of excitement to be traveling by myself, at the thought that no one in the world would know where I was, not Henry, not Karl, who hadn't been to Gurz since Sophie's family had left.

I fell asleep with my head against the window, watching the trees roll by, and I slept deeply until we finally arrived in Gurz around noon. Standing on the platform, I ate the sandwich I had packed. Everyone who passed by turned to look at me and stare. I finished eating my sandwich, took out an old map that I'd marked with the location of Sophie's house, and feeling very conspicuous, began the walk, which Karl had described as being a leisurely half hour out of town and into farmland.

I walked for a long time on the main road out. After an hour, I turned around. The sun was now firmly fixed in the center of the sky, and the books I'd brought weighed heavy on my shoulder. I had only passed three streets on my way out, and though they'd had the wrong names, I thought I would go back and look again.

I walked up and down those three streets with the wrong names—the first was a line of small houses that went on and on. None of them could be Sophie's, I thought—they were too small and close together, some of them gated, with people sitting on their porches or working in their gardens. As I passed one, a dog rushed down from the backyard at me, barking. I saw someone push back a curtain from inside the house, but no door opened, no voice called the dog back. It stood in my way barking and not letting me pass until I decided I had come far enough, the house was not on this street, and I backed away while the dog chased me, rushing at my legs until I stopped and stood still, at which point he stopped and retreated. It went on like that for a while until we were at the main road again, and then the dog was suddenly friendly, wagging his tail and grinning companionably as he followed me on.

The next street I turned on was empty save for one house at the end that was grand and all brick, but nothing like the house Karl had described or drawn for me. As I stood staring up at it, a man came out of the door and walked down toward me. The dog beside me growled at him. "Oh hush," I said irritably. All I needed was for that man to think the dog was mine.

"Guten Tag," said the man, who looked to be in his mid- to late forties, and I responded in German, asking him if he'd known any Meisenbachs who'd lived in town.

"No," he said. "There are no Meisenbachs here."

"Yes, I know they aren't here anymore," I said. "I'm looking for the house they used to live in, before the war."

The man shrugged. "There was never any such family in this town," he said.

The third street I came to had no houses on it whatsoever but led to a large and beautiful lake edged by a flock of birds that lifted into the air as the dog and I approached. He went wild, sprinting after them from one side to the next like a madman. I stood and watched how they rose in one motion, fashioning their bodies into little arrows as they soared.

I sat on a large rock with a flat top, perfect for sitting on, and wondered where Sophie's house was, and if it still stood, and how I could find it. I wondered what I would do if I did find it, who would be living in it now, how I could explain why I'd come. How peaceful it looked all around me. How happy even the dog was now, lying beside me, his tongue lolling out. The birds were still circling overhead, launching themselves onto the water. The sky was cloudless, and the trees on the other side of the lake waved gently at me. It looked like the kind of place generations of a family could come to, year after year.

After a while I rose reluctantly and started on my way back to town. I wanted to get on the next train back to Göttingen, but I felt compelled to ask at the station, and then at the bank, and then at the grocery store, what had happened to the Meisenbachs. I was met with the same blank look, even from those who were old enough to remember. "The Meisenbachs? There was never any such family here."

"The Jewish family," I said, overcome by a creeping sense of déjà vu at the feeling of being in the wrong place, in a parallel reality perhaps, of things not being as they should be, of the facts not lining up.

"There were never any Jews here," the woman at the grocery store said, smiling at me with pity, like the poor foreigner that I was, lost and in over my depth, trying to communicate in my stilted German.

"But what about before the war," I said.

She shrugged. "The Jews lived more in the big cities, not here—never anything like that here," she said, and she looked at me, squinting a bit, and I felt uneasy. I felt no menace or danger coming from her, but a general feeling of distrust mixed in with a reluctant impulse to be friendly.

"What about Brandt Street?" I asked. "Can you tell me where that is, or was?"

She looked at me blankly. "Brandt Street?" she said. "There's no such place here."

"Is this the town of Gurz?" I said, wondering if I had gotten off at the wrong station.

"Yes," she said, smiling exasperatedly now, nodding at the other customers in the shop.

"Is there perhaps another town named Gurz?" I said. "Nearby?"

And now she shook her head with finality, as if she'd finally confirmed an initial poor opinion of me, and said, "This is the only one." She turned her back to me and began to stack cans of peas onto the shelf behind her.

I caught the next train back. As I sat on the train and watched the streets of Gurz roll away, I recalled a memory I had long suppressed. Once, when I was a child, I woke up after a midmorning nap and my mother was not in the house. I ran from room to room, a sick feeling like stones in my stomach. I opened every door, I looked under the bed and in the cabinets, anywhere my mother might fit—as if she was hidden there. I'd read a story about a fox who went out to work every day but really hid under the bed, and I was struck by the terrifying thought that perhaps my mother labored under a similar curse.

And after I had searched the whole house twice and still she had not returned, I tucked myself into a cabinet and waited in the dark, leaning against the cupboard, folded into the small, dank space, waiting. When I heard the door open, I stayed put. I heard her walking from room to room. I heard her steps quicken. I heard her calling my name. Still, I stayed. And then the door opened and my mother was kneeling, peering in at me, on her face the unmistakable and miraculous expression of worry and relief.

I didn't crawl out, but stayed there, my head folded into my arms, until my mother reached in and pulled me out. She didn't ask what I was doing there, or why I had hidden, and I didn't ask where she had gone.

I WAS SUDDENLY EAGER to be back in Göttingen, to see Henry, to ask her to tell me what she had found out about folktales. I wanted to stand in the kitchen of our apartment and cook a meal together. I wanted to lean my head against her shoulder and feel the solidity of her—dear Henry, always so sure.

Before we'd left for Göttingen, she'd shown me some pictures of Bonn that had been taken before the war. Near the university where I now lived, there'd once been a park filled with statues. In the photo, it had been filled with people: children running about among the fountains, a pair of lovers in silhouette kissing against a tree. There was another set of photos taken the following year. Everything was gone. No people, no statues, no gates. The bushes, the flowers, and the trees were now charred black lines against the ground. The buildings framing the garden had been obliterated—entire twelve-story apartment buildings, grand and beautiful, missing, gone, as if they had never existed.

CHAPTER 21

A MAN AND A WOMAN HAVE A BOY. THEY HAVE ANother boy. They have a girl. Aunts and uncles and cousins come through their house, and the days fill with voices, music, and laughter.

There are household pets—two dogs, a rabbit, a snake, and a toad. There are days and days of dinners and jokes, there are nights filled with stars. A war comes in the early years, but the battles are elsewhere, and the boys are barely walking. The father is not called away, and so as terrible the toll on the country and their less-fortunate neighbors, the family itself is untouched. The boys grow up. The girl goes to university. Her brothers get married and have children of their own. Look at them. The parents, their girl, two boys and their families.

There is growing unrest in the world, but for a long time the family is shielded. For a long time it remains untouched. There are rallies and disagreements, but they seem far away. The family believes it is safe. Then there's a shift, and the language of politics grows barbs, but in their house, the family believes in the goodness of people, in the stability of things, and they wait for the moment to pass. Life goes on. In the elections, the wrong man wins. A clown and a bully. A bigot. The changes come fast, the changes come slow, the changes come to their town. They come to their door.

Now. Subtract the father's job. Subtract the girl from university. Subtract the university from the girl.

She is home now, with her brothers and their wives and children. They have gathered in this house their parents built, the house they grew up in. Look at them, standing so somber in the living room, surrounded by candlelight. Nobody in this tableau knows what will come next, but there is fear. Now. Subtract the books standing upright on the shelves. They are the first to go. Then subtract the candlesticks and the jewelry. Subtract the piano from the living room, subtract the mother's favorite songs. Then subtract the mother, bent with worry. Subtract the father. Subtract the boys. Subtract their wives and children. Subtract the beds they slept in, the linens and their clothing. Subtract their woolen slippers, their mismatched mittens, the paintings on the walls. Subtract the walls. Subtract the memory of this family's voices. Subtract the memory of their lives. Just turn them into dust. Do it all at once. Subtract them from this earth.

Chapter 22

I got sick immediately upon returning from Gurz. It was the kind of illness that strikes all of your body at once, needing no time to ramp up and leaving no chance to struggle against it. I stepped out onto the train platform and nearly fell over with dizziness. I staggered back to the pension and crawled into my bed, pushing aside Henry's worried exclamations, and answering only—when she asked how my excursion had gone—"Later."

I asked her to deliver Karl a note, apologizing for not stopping by like I'd promised, and letting him know as soon as I was on my feet I'd come by to see him. For the next week, I lay in bed, hot with fever, restless and aching, and oppressed by a feeling of misery such as I'd never felt before. My throat hurt and it was hard to breathe: I'd had bad colds before, but this illness took hold of my nasal passageways and my throat and coated my lungs in a thick mucus that I could barely cough up, and when I did, I had to tip myself over my bed to cough with one hand to my chest and one to my mouth, everything sticky and gelled inside me, refusing expulsion.

Henry tiptoed in and out of my room, but I turned away from her and moaned for her to leave me be. Still, I gratefully drank the water and ate the warm broth she left by my bedside. But when I closed my eyes, I saw the long and lovely roads of Gurz, the pretty houses, the shining lake. And underneath all that loveliness was an undercurrent of menace: the ground beneath hid terrible secrets, the smiling faces were murderers. I tossed and turned, dreaming I walked up and down the streets of Gurz, as Sophie's voice and the voices of her family called from every house I passed. When I knocked frantically at each door, someone new and yellow haired and perfectly pleasant arrived to greet me. Behind them, voices wailed and pleaded with me to find and free them, but the person at the door blinked at me in a friendly manner as if they didn't hear them, as if they heard nothing unusual at all.

I elbowed my way in, disturbing the furniture, breaking open doors, searching for the source of those voices, and always each house was empty, and always each owner, unperturbed by my agitation, cheerfully wished me luck on my way out. As I searched house after beautiful house, up and down those streets, I began to wonder if I was insane.

I said, "I want my mother," and woke myself up with my voice.

There was a scuffling in the room next door, and the sound brought me back to myself, to my bed, to my room. Henry came in.

"Did you say something?" she said, touching my forehead anxiously. "Did you call for me?"

"I just need to rest," I said. "Please leave me alone."

Afterward, into the emptiness that remained, I said again—quietly, "I want my mother." And I didn't know who or what I meant.

AFTER MY ILLNESS PASSED, I was filled with a restless, nervous energy to leave Göttingen as soon as possible. Gurz had planted a sinking sense of doom in me, which I still felt, its long roots winnowing down.

"I'm going back to Bonn," I told Henry as soon as I was on my feet. "I promised Professor Behr I wouldn't be away too long."

I went as soon as I could to take my leave of Karl and collect my notebook.

"Did you not get it?" Karl said. "I sent it back to your pension."

"When?" I asked, the sense of dread I'd carried since my trip to Gurz mushrooming inside me.

"Weeks ago, after you stopped by to inquire about it," he said. "I sent it by messenger the next day, it seemed urgent."

"I never got it," I gasped. "I didn't know to look out for it."

"And I just assumed you received it," he said. "Oh no."

"Who took it over to the pension? Who accepted it?"

"My errand boy," Karl said. "I'll ask him what happened as soon as I get home this evening. Perhaps somehow he still has it."

"Thank you," I said, and I walked out of his office and straight home, trembling. When I asked the owner of the pension if any package had come, he shook his head. Henry was out, so I had to wait all day and evening until she came home to find me sitting on the sofa in front of the door, wringing my hands.

"What's wrong?" she said.

"Henry, have you gotten any packages for me since we've been in Göttingen?" I asked.

"No," she said. "All the mail that came for you went straight to you."

I started to cry. "It's lost," I wailed. "He lost it. He said he sent it over, but it never came."

Henry sat down next to me and took my hands in hers. "Steady now," she said. "Tell me what happened and we will figure this out."

So I told her the whole story and she exclaimed that it was all too bad, but that she was certain we could sort it out and figure out where the notebook had landed.

Karl himself came the very next morning, to say that his messenger had confirmed he'd delivered the notebook. Karl talked to the owner of our pension who lived downstairs, who again insisted he had not received it.

"I want to talk to your errand boy," I said.

"Yes, of course," Karl agreed. "I was just going to suggest that myself."

So we walked back to Karl's house—a beautiful townhome in the middle of the city center. The boy's was named Martin, and he was twelve or thirteen years old. He looked terrified when I questioned him, cringing as if he thought I might hit him.

"I came to ask about a notebook Herr Meisenbach asked you to deliver last week," I said.

"I delivered it, I swear," he said. "To the exact address that Herr Meisenbach directed me to."

"This one?" I said, showing him my address.

"Yes, that one," he said. "I went Tuesday morning and delivered it first thing, as soon as Herr Meisenbach told me to."

I was grim. "Could you walk us there?" I asked. "To the precise house you delivered it to? And see if you recognize the person who received it?"

Martin looked at Karl, who nodded at him. "Do as the lady asks," he said.

And so Martin led us back toward my neighborhood, glancing back at us over his shoulder the whole way.

"I trust this boy completely," Karl said. "He's been my messenger boy for over a year now; I share him with Professor Hass, and he has never made a mistake up until now."

"But what's the explanation then?" I asked. "Why would the pension owners lie?"

We had reached our street but not our house when Martin stopped. "This house," he declared. "This is the house." The house number was 12, where mine was 21. He'd reversed the numbers.

My heart leapt. "Did you deliver my notebook here?" I asked.

He nodded.

"You fool!" Karl burst out. "This is the wrong house!"

"It's okay," I said. "Surely whoever took the delivery would have saved it, once they realized it wasn't for them."

Karl nodded. "Well, let us ask." He knocked on the door.

A plump middle-aged woman answered the door. We asked if she or anyone in the household had received a delivery of a notebook the week before.

"No," she said. "Not here."

"No one in your household?" I asked. "No small brown leather notebook?"

"No," she said. "I'd be the only one who was here during the day."

I looked at the boy. "Who did you deliver the notebook to?" I asked.

"I delivered it to a young man," he said.

"No young man lives here," the woman said.

"Someone else, maybe?" Karl asked the boy. "Perhaps you have your deliveries confused?"

The boy was rubbing his hand over his face, looking nervous. "Yes, maybe," the boy said. "Maybe I delivered it to a young girl."

The woman put her hands on her hips. "No one lives here but me and my husband," she said. "We haven't any children, and we haven't any servants, so if you delivered anything here, it would have been to me or to him, and I would have known about it."

Martin burst into loud, noisy sobs.

My heart sank.

"Martin," Karl said sternly. "Tell us the truth. What did you do with Katherine's notebook?"

The boy drew his sleeve across his face. "I just stopped for a second," he said. "On my way to deliver the notebook. Just a second to have a chat with the fellows. And I put my bag down on the street, within eyesight the whole time, I swear. And then I went on my way, but when I got to the house, the notebook wasn't in the bag anymore. Please don't fire me, Herr Meisenbach," the boy said, weeping. "We need the money. My parents will murder me if I lose this job."

"Ah, it's just a notebook," the woman from the doorway said. "Go easy on him, sir."

"It wasn't my notebook," Karl said grimly. "Katherine, what will you have us do?"

My hands were shaking. My legs were shaking. All of me was shaking. "Take us to the place where you lost the notebook," I said to Martin. "Where you stopped to chat."

"I went back," Martin said. "I looked and looked, up and down everywhere I'd been, but it wasn't anywhere."

"Take us anyway," I said.

We spent a long day walking up and down streets, stepping into stores and asking strangers if they'd seen a little brown notebook filled with equations. We went to the city lost and found. We looked in more than one garbage can. At a certain point, Karl said there was no more to be done, but I made him go over every street several more times and take me to the garbage heap so we could personally ask the garbage man to look out for the notebook.

At the end of it, I cried, "How could you let it out of your hands, how could you give it to someone else to deliver; didn't you know how important it was?"

"I'm sorry," he said. "Maybe it will turn up yet." He started to speak, stopped, and held his hand over his eyes, overcome with emotion. I felt guilty, but I couldn't forgive him.

"You shouldn't have let it out of your possession," I said. But what I really meant was I should never have let it out of my own possession. I should never have handed over the most valuable thing I owned.

We went out for dinner afterward, as there was nothing left to do, and ate wurst and beer in defeated, prickly silence. "I went to Gurz," I told him after we were finished eating. "The day Martin lost the notebook. That's why I didn't come by. I looked for Sophie's house and couldn't find it. When I asked the people who live there now, they said that no such house existed. That her family was never there."

Karl shrugged. "Perhaps they don't remember," he said. "Or prefer not to. As for the house, it is gone. I could have told you that much. Why didn't you tell me you were going?"

"I don't know," I said.

"It was quite an ugly scene when Sophie's family finally left," Karl said. "And Sophie and her father weren't able to leave when the rest of the family did."

"Why? What happened?"

"Well, the biggest problem is they left too late. When the government was encouraging Jews to leave, they stayed put, thinking everything would blow over. And then borders started closing, and it got harder and harder to leave, and they knew they had to make it out while there was still time. Sophie's parents wanted to go to Bulgaria or Sweden, because they had friends in both of those countries who were willing to help them. But Sophie kept saying that Shanghai was the only place that allowed Jews to enter without an entry visa, and that the family should go there. Even the United States had turned away a boat full of Jewish children. But the family thought this was outrageous: What would they do in China? And there was a war there, too. So they argued and waited, and things grew worse.

"They were protected for a while because as I'd said, Sophie's father was not Jewish. But soon the time came when they were no longer protected, and then it was too late to leave. The war started, and there was no longer any choice but to go into hiding with the help of one of their neighbors. And they hid for several years.

"Then the neighbor who'd been helping them died, and they had no safe way to acquire food or coal or any of the things they needed to survive. So that settled it, and at that late and dangerous date, they decided to see if they could make it to Bulgaria. But now Sophie was very sick—she was vomiting blood every day, and it seemed like she might die. They couldn't take her to a doctor, and it was clear she couldn't travel.

"So the rest of her family left without her, because the situation was that dire, but my uncle Walter stayed behind with her, promising to attempt an escape when she was better. And they hid for months, and my family helped as best as we could, bringing them food and money and fuel, and Sophie did slowly get better. It seemed that maybe they could hide out until the war was over, but then her father was caught by the SS, and taken away, and never seen again."

"Why was he taken away if he wasn't Jewish?" I asked.

Karl let out a short, bitter laugh. "For harboring Jews," he said. "For not turning them in, for hiding with them. The truth is, by then the Nazis didn't need an excuse. They could take you away for sneezing the wrong way, and if they came for you, you were gone." He took a breath. "Well, you know how that would have ended. My father never got over it—the loss of his twin." He looked away from me. "He blamed Sophie, you know. It turned out the reason she was sick, the reason she couldn't leave when they had the chance, was that she was pregnant with you."

I felt his words as if they had exploded in my chest. "So then what happened next?" I managed. "Where did she go?"

Karl blinked. "Well, we couldn't take her in. She knew that. We were being watched as it was. She was less sick by then, and obviously pregnant. She sent us a note telling us she didn't want to put us in danger, that she was leaving with Cao to go after the rest of her family, to make her escape. I never got to see her again. I never got to say good-bye. And we never heard anything again until you showed up."

"I see," I said. My hands were trembling. I took a breath. "And you don't have anything else that was hers, other than the letters and photos you already gave me?"

"You have everything," he said. "Most of the family valuables were sold or disposed of long ago. I only kept Sophie's letters because we'd been close."

"I'm glad you did," I said. "What else did you have of her family's before it was disposed of?"

"Nothing of value," Karl said. "The government had already taken most everything of worth. So there's no money or anything like that, I'm afraid."

My face flushed. "I didn't mean money."

"Yes, well," Karl said. "You never know."

I didn't have any response to that, and took my leave soon after. Two days later I left Göttingen, sick at heart.

Chapter 23

When I arrived back in Bonn, the air was cloudy with smoke and the stinging sharpness of tear gas. Police thronged the sidewalks, and scores of students marched in the roads. I heard glass shattering nearby and could sense the crowd of people undulating, pressing against the lines of police as they shouted and surged forward. And yet, nothing felt out of control, only on the brink of something about to happen. "Move along!" a policeman shouted at those of us who were emerging from the train station, waving us ahead, so that we moved parallel to the crowd, away from the station. And so I walked alongside one side of the police, and the protesting students walked along the other.

The mood in the air was somehow both exhilarating and dangerous, like some dark festival, and when I asked a fellow traveler walking beside me if he knew what had happened, he said it had started as a protest of the German Emergency Acts legislation, which would allow the government to restrict civil rights in the case of an emergency. But the protest had grown to include the war in Vietnam, police brutality, and oppressive governments everywhere. Now the students were holding a candlelight vigil for the victim of an assassination attempt, and for a student who'd been killed a year before in another protest against a visit from the shah of Iran. The crowd was moving toward the Capitol, where thousands of students were already gathered, holding hands and waving candles and singing and shouting.

Later, people who had been in Bonn in the late sixties would talk about the protests as a terrifying, electric time, when it felt as if anything could happen—so much shouting in the air, so much violence breaking through the surface. I felt it, too, but after Göttingen and Gurz, I preferred the crowd and its buzzing danger, welcomed it in fact, and as I entered my apartment, it felt like I'd come home, and I fell into my bed as if I had escaped some dark fate by returning.

In the following days, I met up with my friends Maz and Otto and Leena and Renate, who were astonished I'd returned alone. Maz and Otto had paired up while I was gone, and they'd assumed that Henry and I were also lovers. "Is she all right?" they wanted to know. "Why are you back without her? Did you fight?" I assured them that she was fine, that I'd left on good terms. I tried to hide how anxious and unsteady I felt after my trip. I didn't tell them anything of note that had happened, not even when Renate told me about a trip she'd just returned from to Poland where she'd met a woman who'd rescued hundreds of Jewish babies by learning the plumbers' trade and smuggling them out of their houses. She'd been caught by the authorities and had both her legs broken and been sentenced to death, but then had miraculously escaped prison with the help of an old admirer just to go back to it again. I listened hungrily to Renate's stories but found myself holding back and not knowing quite why. I felt restless, as if my trip to Göttingen had shaken something loose, a dissatisfaction, a dormant anger. I felt it as a raging in my blood.

Thus began my season of being another kind of person in the world, when I became more body than mind. On the streets, the student protests continued, expanding to other injustices in the world. I joined them, but hardly paid attention to what they were shouting. Instead, I walked up and down the streets of Bonn, merging in and out of the constant crowds, partially alone, partially embraced in a throng of strangers. I felt my muscles working as I walked, I felt my body's hunger and its every ache. In those days I felt electric. I looked at everyone, I noticed everyone looking at me.

I was aware of the other bodies around me as sacks of warmth and bone and muscle. So many mouths, yelling. So many arms and legs and torsos pressed together, chanting, shouting, pushing forward. I shouted with them. I pressed my body against their bodies, until I had shouted my throat raw, until my body was hot with the heat of the crowd, and all I heard was the wave of voices bearing mine up so that it was no longer distinguishable. Then I broke away and pushed through the bodies and into an open street. I walked farther and farther from the crowd and kept walking. I wanted to go dancing, so I went dancing. I drank until I was dizzy. I let strange men walk me home at night and did not ask their names as I led them up the stairs. I wanted to be reckless and waste myself on life. I wanted their lips on my body, their breath on my breath. Not closeness, it wasn't closeness I was seeking, but contact, and it felt like oblivion.

One day someone gave me LSD on a sugar cube, and I put it on my tongue. It was my first time trying drugs, and as soon as the sugar began to melt I felt a surge of excitement course through my body. It frightened me, and I spit the lump of sugar out on the sidewalk. I excused myself from the party and walked home. I sat in my bed and wondered—*what am I doing?*

Outside, a storm came. The lightning lit up my room. The thunder followed. I lay down in my bed and thought of my mother. I wondered if she thought of me when storms came, as I always thought of her. The rain began to pound upon my window, insistent with questions. What was the temperature of lightning? What was the velocity of light? Numbers blinked in and out, glowing like fairy lights. What was the distance of the earth to the sun? The logarithmic constant of *e*? I thought I could see the underlying structure of the universe pulsing beneath everything. I felt untethered from the earth, like I was flying. I felt as if I'd died.

I don't know what brought me out of this state, or how I eventually came back to myself, just that when I did, I felt different—as if two parts of myself had broken apart and then come together and adhered incompletely. I rose from my bed and discovered that in the last few weeks I'd lost so much weight that my bones showed through my skin, and that my skin itself had thinned and turned sheer as a pair of stockings, so that I could see blue veins running up and down my arms and hands. I didn't feel weak, but as if I had been reduced to my essential core self, as if everything excess had been trimmed away.

When I went to my office at the university, there was a letter waiting for me from Charles Lee. "Of course I remember you," it began. "And I have thought of you often. I read your note with great interest that only grew the more I read. I think you have stumbled upon a solution! As for the trouble you say you run into with regards to randomness, I wonder if it might help to take a look at the Kobalesky formula." He ended, "Wishing you the best of luck, and awaiting further news with eagerness."

This note was just what I had needed, a jolt to get me back to work. All of a sudden the things that had troubled me didn't seem so insurmountable. I thought I could see a way forward. Revisiting the

Mohanty problem was like drinking a clean draught of water after a long illness: refreshing and energizing. My paper raced as it grew. It was a matter of getting it down fast enough: after climbing and climbing, I was finally running downhill.

It was a thrilling but frightening time—I was so close to accomplishing what I'd longed for, and the closer I got, the more afraid I became. I had joked to Henry that the worse my personal life was, the better my work, and ever since, I'd become afraid that this was true, as well as its inverse—if my work was going well, some catastrophe must be in store in my life. I became increasingly superstitious, afraid to cross the street lest I get hit by a car and die before I was able to finish, afraid to leave my apartment for fear that I would be hit by some unforeseen obstacle that would stop me in my tracks.

Chapter 24

PETER ARRIVED JUST A COUPLE WEEKS LATER WITHOUT warning, without a note or explanation. One moment I was sitting at the desk, the door to the hallway and all my windows flung open for air. And then I looked up, and he was standing in the doorway, watching me. He cleared his throat. He smiled.

I felt a pain in my chest.

"Hi," he said. "Hi, Katherine." And I noticed the timbre of his voice, the roughness of it, and how it was not quite deep, and how that made him seem younger than he was, like a schoolboy still. He looked the same as always, rumpled and handsome.

"What are you doing here?" I asked.

"I've been calling you for the last three months," he said. "I wanted to apologize, but my calls never went through," he continued. "When I called the Bonn operator, your number had been disconnected."

"Oh," I said. "I'm sorry about that. My phone was disconnected when I went to Göttingen, and when I got back, my number had been changed. I didn't know you'd try to call me."

He was wearing a blue shirt that I'd bought him, and even from across the room I could smell his Peter-smell. "Of course I tried to call you," he said. "I've missed you."

"I've missed you, too," I said, but I felt tentative about saying anything more. People always talk about thoughts and feelings rushing through their minds in moments of intense emotion, but it's always been the opposite for me. When I feel I've been put on the spot, I shut down, I lose track of my thoughts, I lose track of my feelings. I looked at Peter and felt stupefied.

"You've changed," he said. "Lost weight, maybe. I don't know, you seem different."

"I guess I am." I fidgeted in my chair.

"Listen," he said, still standing in the doorway. "I am so sorry for our last fight. And I'm sorry for not coming to visit you sooner. When you left, I was so angry at you, and hurt, but then these last few months I've just missed you and realized how horrible I was when you first got here when you were trying so hard to be sweet, and I guess all my anger just went away."

I smiled in spite of myself. "Are you saying you came here to tell me that you forgive me?"

"No! Sorry, I began badly." He stepped toward me, and stopped. He ran his hands through his hair, and sighed. "What I wanted to say is that after I stopped being angry I got very sad, and I've been sad ever since." He lifted his shoulders and dropped them. "I'm sad that I hurt you, I'm sad that you left, I'm sad that you've been here without me, and that I took so long to come."

"Oh, Peter," I said. I felt like I had to say something back. I got up and walked over to him. I reached out and touched his arm. "I'm sorry too. I'm glad you're here."

A smile spread across his face.

I let him take me in his arms, and then I took him home with me.

THE NEXT MORNING I woke up sweaty and tangled up in blankets under Peter's arms and leg. I breathed in the smell of him. I'd been surprised by how strange it had felt to be in my apartment with him, like he didn't quite fit in, like he wasn't exactly the person I remembered, or I wasn't exactly the person I remembered being with him.

I'd been certain sleeping with him would jostle us back into place, but I wasn't sure it had. I'd felt self-conscious, assessing our every move instead of surrendering myself to the moment. I wondered now if Peter had felt the same constraint, but he smiled and pulled me closer as I tried to wiggle free.

"Listen," he said. "I wanted to talk about next year."

"Next year?" I said.

"Yes. Are you planning to stay another year?"

"I was," I said slowly. "I've been getting a lot done lately, and I like it here." I shrugged. "And I feel like I should take the support while I can."

He nodded. "So I was thinking this morning while you were sleeping that maybe I'd take the year off," he said. "I could take a sabbatical."

"To do research?" I asked.

"To be with you," he said. He kissed the side of my face from behind. "If that sounds good to you."

"Of course it does," I said. "But I don't want to rush into anything."

"I want to support you," he said. "I want to make sure you have everything you need to succeed."

I smiled. "I have so many things to tell you. And I've missed talking to you about work. I'm so excited: I think I've almost figured out the Mohanty problem."

"Oh?" Peter said.

"Yeah, want to see what I've done?"

He tightened his arms around me. "Not just yet," he said. "First I have other important matters to attend to." And he pulled me over onto him, and we made love again.

For the next few days I neglected my work. Instead, I focused on Peter and enjoying his presence in Germany. I didn't tell him what I'd discovered in Göttingen—not just because that's where we'd had our big fight, or because of the sense of constraint I still felt, but because I wanted—at long last—to have fun. We took a cruise upon the Rhine. We drank beer, we ate hot dogs, we went to classical music concerts, and we looked at apartments together that we might share. I introduced him to my friends. "He's so sexy," Renate said, and Otto and Maz nodded their assent. It made me strangely proud, that they thought he was handsome, that he had their approval.

At the end of the week, however, I told Peter I had to settle down and focus. "I'm so close with this paper that I'm getting paranoid," I said. "And I haven't been putting the time in that I need. First I went to Göttingen, and now I've been completely distracted by you. Happily distracted, I'll add. But I shouldn't procrastinate. Do you think I could show you the progress that I've made?"

"Sure," he said. There was a funny smile on his face, like he had a secret that he was very proud of. "Actually, let me show you something first," he said. "I've been waiting for the right time to tell you this, but this came in the mail yesterday." And he reached into his satchel and pulled out a magazine. He handed it to me. It was the *Annals of Mathematics*. "Open it," he said. He was beaming.

I opened it and shook out the pages, expecting something to fall out.

"No, I mean, open it to the table of contents. Look what's in it."

So I did. And that's when I saw my name, and the title of "The Mohanty Problem" next to it.

I looked up at Peter. "What's this?" I asked slowly.

"I finished your proof using the notes you left behind and our conversations," Peter said. "And I sent it in to *Annals* in your name, and after they had a chance to review, they accepted it, ecstatically. I've just been waiting for this to come out so I could surprise you. I had them rush deliver it."

"Are you kidding me?" I said. "Please tell me this is some kind of elaborate prank."

"Not a prank," he said.

"When did you finish the proof?"

"Two months ago. Once I got going, I thought it'd be quick, but it took me much longer."

"I feel faint," I said. "I think I'm going to pass out." I sat down on the bed. "How did you do it?" I asked.

"Once you figure out you can use the Kobalesky formula, it's all just coasting from there."

So Lee had been right. "I just started working with it two weeks ago," I said.

"Then you were pretty much all the way there," Peter said. "It's just one more step and you're done."

I made a noise between a laugh and a whimper. Mostly I wanted to stab myself. It was my fault, I thought, for getting distracted. It was my fault for waiting so long. Peter had beaten me, but he'd also cheated—he'd used the framework I'd already developed, but not yet published. That was against the rules.

Peter knelt beside me. "Well, aren't you going to say something?" he said.

"I'm trying to understand why you would do something like this," I said.

"I wanted to do something really big for you, and I knew how much you cared about this problem. I wanted to solve it for you. Once I started working on it, I realized how interesting it was in itself, and how brilliant your initial approach was, and then I wanted to work on it for its own sake."

"Peter." It was difficult to speak. "Do you not see how degrading that is? You poached my problem."

"I didn't poach anything! I gave you full credit," Peter said. "I wanted to do something for you. I thought you'd be happy."

A hot, itching sensation was working its way through my body. "Why didn't you just call me and tell me how to fix it? Why did you have to take it over for yourself?"

"I thought it'd be romantic," he said.

"Let me get this straight," I said. "You thought it would be romantic to use my notes without asking me, poach my idea, and then give it back to me as a gift?"

Peter was staring at me with a sort of stunned expression on his face. "Well when you put it that way, it sounds pretty bad," he said. "I swear, I wasn't trying to take anything from you. Look, you're on there as sole author."

"It's not about the credit," I gasped. "If you respected me at all, you would understand."

"That isn't a fair statement, and it isn't true, either," he said carefully. "I do respect you. I wanted to help you."

My heart was pounding. The blood was rushing into my veins. I thought I might be having a heart attack. "All I've ever had is this one thing," I said. "This one talent."

We looked at each other. Peter held up his hands. "I obviously misjudged the situation. I'm sorry. But can't we have a rational conversation about this?"

"I am having a rational conversation about this," I said. I took a breath. "Just tell me this. When you finished my proof for me, was it because you were afraid I wouldn't be able to do it on my own? Or because you were afraid I could?"

"Katherine, stop," he said. "You're getting carried away. I wasn't afraid of either of those things. I was trying to do something for you. I get it, I did the wrong thing. But can we focus on the fact that I was trying to show you I love you?"

"I think I might kill you," I said quietly. "I really think that I might."

He smiled.

"I'm not joking," I said. "I need you to go."

He let out an exasperated breath. "I don't know how to talk to you when you get this way."

"Then please get out of my apartment. Just leave."

Chapter 25

HERE WAS THE PROBLEM: I WAS AMBITIOUS. I WANTED a career. I wanted accolades and validation. More than anything, I wanted to do something that mattered. At a time when it was unseemly for a woman to want these things (is it really so accepted now?), I wanted them desperately. I went after them openly. And when the paper Peter had submitted in my name was published, I got them all. I received a steady stream of notes and telegrams of congratulations. People started hinting at inevitable job offers, of fellowships and invitations to spend time at various think tanks and research institutions. Rob and Leo sent a telegram expressing their admiration. "Come back soon," they said. "Our plants miss you." Lee sent a short, exclamatory note full of excitement and encouragement. I had finally made it, just as I'd promised myself I would all those years ago when Blake stole my homework and I vowed to establish myself so firmly that I would be known, and I'd never be doubted in that way again.

Here was the problem: Peter Hall had submitted a paper in my name. Everything I'd gained from that was built on shaky ground.

Here was another problem: I still loved Peter Hall.

Chapter 26

ALAN TURING WAS A WAR HERO WHO IS OFTEN CALLED the inventor of the computer, and sometimes the father of modern computer science. Some would say that without him, we would never have cracked the German code, and the Allies would never have won the war. But after the war was over, a terrible thing happened to him. His house was broken into, and when he called the police to report it, the policeman who came to investigate discovered he'd been with a male lover at the time of the robbery. This was illegal in England at the time.

So because Turing had called the authorities to report a crime that had been committed against him, he ended up being prosecuted and convicted for homosexual acts under the same law that had sent Oscar Wilde to prison. Turing, however, was given a choice of which punishment to take. He could go to prison, or he could be injected with hormones that would chemically castrate him. He chose the injections. He returned home a free man. Soon after, he committed suicide.

I think it was the choice that killed Turing in the end. The bad law, of course, and the society that made it—but I think perhaps he could have survived the censure, the imprisonment, the castration, if only they hadn't made him participate. I think making him choose, making him complicit, was what ultimately destroyed him.

IN THE END it wasn't a rational decision. It wasn't even a good one. I wish I could say I made it for the right reasons. I wish I could say I thought it all the way through, and I did it for myself, not for Peter. But I have to admit I did it for Peter's sake. To create a problem so large that even he couldn't solve it. To show him something I couldn't explain—how serious what he'd done had been, and also no matter how bad that had been, I could still do worse to myself.

I called the editor of the *Annals of Mathematics* and asked him to withdraw my name as author of my paper. I offered no explanation. I just gave it up. It was self-destructive, and I knew it, but I felt like it was the only choice I had left, other than going along with what Peter had done. And anyway, sometimes it feels good to let go of everything you've been working toward. Sometimes it feels good to raze everything all the way down to the ground.

Even then, I didn't get what I asked for. The editor called Peter and, afterward, didn't take my name off at all but added Peter's name as coauthor. So there was no triumphant moment, no spectacular conflagration, no moral victory. There was only the damage between Peter and me, and the speculation that the addition of his name to the paper stoked, and the subsequent damage to my reputation, unavoidable after all.

THEY CALLED IT A STUNT, a lovers' quarrel, dirty laundry aired in public. The invitations that had been rolling in, the hints at job offers, quietly disappeared. None were formally withdrawn, but when I inquired, the response was silence. And the second year of my fellowship at the University of Bonn was not renewed.

I felt as if I'd seen this coming all along, like every other possible outcome of my life had been a fantasy. All I felt was quiet after all my rage.

"I know you didn't mean to hurt me," I told Peter. "I know you were trying to give me something, not take something away. But I can't be with you anymore."

I guess I must have known he wouldn't fight with me this time, that I had won a battle I'd never wanted to win. He nodded. That was it. I was the one who told him to go, but it broke my heart when he went.

Chapter 27

FOR A LONG TIME I FELT LOW TO THE GROUND, LIKE I had grown heavy, or the force of gravity had increased, and was pulling me down. For a long time I found it hard to get out of bed, to look my friends in the eye, to speak, to laugh, to eat. Breathing, just breathing, seemed difficult and pained.

My friends did not know what to do with me.

"I think what he did was very romantic," Leena said. "I wish someone would do something like that for me."

"Yeah," agreed Maz. "If I were smart enough to do something like that, I definitely would."

Renate said, "I think you need to examine why this happened to you. Perhaps you have some kind of energy that draws this sort of circumstance and needs to be cleansed."

Only Henry, dear Henry, understood. She called long distance from Göttingen. "You were absolutely right to do what you did," she said. "And brave."

She was the only one to whom I could confess my doubts. “He didn’t mean to hurt me,” I said. “In some ways it was very generous what he did.”

“Well, that’s the problem,” Henry said. “Imagine what he could do if he was trying to hurt you.”

“I’m embarrassed,” I said. “I’m ashamed. Renate thinks I draw this sort of disaster on myself.”

“Renate,” Henry said, deliberately, “is a fool.”

Henry’s moral support aside, I was alone as I’d ever been, with nothing to work on, and no ideas for what to do next. My life felt swept barren, empty, like a desert burned clean.

When I was a little girl I used to think if I were granted three wishes, one would be to be old already, so that I would know everything that had happened and know it turned out all right. If I had three wishes now, one would be to go back to who I was as a little girl and tell her: all will be fine. Whatever moments of darkness you face, you will pass through them like clouds—believe this, hold it close to you like a light.

I DON’T KNOW when I would have emerged from this particular cloud if Henry hadn’t come for me. She called from Göttingen and said, “Katherine, you’ve been sad long enough, now it’s time to move on,” and, “I’m coming.”

“I’m going to tell you a secret,” she said when she arrived and took in my unwashed hair and messy apartment. “But only if you promise not to tell.”

“What?” I said, and I sat on my bed and looked up at her. For the first time in a long time, I felt a glimmer of hope, of interest.

Henry sat next to me and patted my head. “Promise first,” she said.

"I promise."

"Well," she said. "Back in San Francisco when my family didn't have money, I sometimes worked as a maid for rich ladies."

I was so surprised I let out a short bark of laughter. Then I looked at her face. "But you're the most glamorous person I know!" I said.

She dimpled. "I'm a master of illusion," she said. "But I'm also, it's a little-known fact, a master of *cleaning*."

I laughed for real this time, and for the first time in weeks. It sounded rusty coming out, but Henry smiled encouragingly.

"The thing is," she said, "sometimes I feel like I have this secret power that no one has ever witnessed, that no one has ever seen. And I've always wanted to show it off to someone who both needs it and would appreciate it." She paused significantly, and then said with great drama, "Katherine, will you be that person?"

I laughed again. "Yes," I said, nodding. "Yes, please, I will."

"Okay," Henry said. "You stay right here," and she patted my head and went to the closet and started pulling out my mop and my broom.

Watching her I felt—how can I describe it?—a bubble of hope, just that, a tiny bubble of hope. The rest of me felt hollowed out, and scraped tender, like any part of me could break at any moment.

"Are you watching?" Henry asked. She was so cheerful, so gentle.

I nodded.

"Okay," she said. "I want you to note how I start first with the broom in this corner by your window here, and how I'm going to place this washcloth and the dustpan and the mop all up against the wall. Now I'm going to sweep, sweep, sweep across the room at a diagonal, and when I reach this other corner I'm going to sweep, sweep, sweep across in this direction." She glided across the room.

"Note how fluidly I move my arms, note how there is no wasted movement," she said. "When I am done with this room, I will end up right where the dustpan is, and I will flick the dust into the pan just so, leave it here, and take up the mop." Thus she narrated each of her actions until the floor was swept and mopped, and every surface was tidied and wiped down.

"Now my dear, I think it's time for you to take a bath, and I will change your sheets and make your bed for you," she said. "Do you want me to organize that jumble of papers on your desk?"

I nodded.

"Good girl," Henry said. She swatted me on my behind as I got off my bed. "Be sure to wash behind your ears," she said, and winked.

Chapter 28

THE DAY BEFORE HENRY WAS SUPPOSED TO RETURN TO Göttingen, she said, "Kat, I have something to tell you." Her eyes met mine, and she blushed. Then she said in an odd, shy voice, "I meant to tell you right away, but it was never the right time—and anyway I don't know why I'm suddenly so shy about it, but Karl and I have fallen in love."

"Karl?" I sputtered. "Karl Meisenbach?"

Henry said, "Yes, Karl." She started laughing.

"Good God, Henry. Love? Really?"

She covered her mouth with her hand, but her shoulders shook with laughter. "Yes," she burst out. "I don't know how it happened, I don't know why, but, Kat, I can't help it."

"Oh, Henry," I managed. "I don't know what to say."

I didn't like Karl Meisenbach, was the thing. Not just because he'd lost my notebook, but because of some shift that had happened between us even before it was lost, after my conversation with Frank.

"I'm going to marry him, Kat." She saw the look on my face and smiled self-consciously. "He's not what you would have imagined for me, is he?"

"Not in a million years."

Henry laughed. "You know, I've been thinking how glad I am we decided to go to Göttingen together, or I would never have met him."

"Are you happy?" I asked.

Henry looked at me. She squared her shoulders. "Yes," she said. "I am."

What was there to say after that? I was riddled with doubts, but they were my doubts, not Henry's, and anyway, I had a terrible track record in terms of knowing which men to trust.

"If you're happy, I'm happy too," I said.

I ACCOMPANIED HENRY back to Göttingen, where she planned to marry Karl in a month's time. I stayed with her in the same pension as before and joined her and Karl for dinner every evening. I watched how solicitous he was to her, how careful he was of her comfort. It was good to see, but I felt a pang of jealousy. I thought, *He will treat her gently.*

In the daytime, we went shopping for her wedding clothes and lingerie, and my heart ached for what I wouldn't have with Peter. One day, I went to the university to visit Frank. I felt somewhat awkward, because I'd left Göttingen without saying good-bye and never followed up. Now I wondered if Professor Behr had told him anything about what had happened with my paper—that I'd been denied a second year of fellowship. But Frank was as warm and cheerful as the first time I'd met him.

"Katherine!" he said, shaking my hand. "It's been far too long." And then he said, "Ah, this reminds me—I found those addresses you'd asked for, but by the time I sent them over to the pension you'd been staying at, I was told you'd already left."

I blushed deeply. "I'm so sorry," I said. "I know I should have taken my leave."

Frank waved his hand. "No, no!" he said. "I meant to forward them to you in Bonn, so the fault is mine. But let me find them while I have you here." He began digging around.

"You found the addresses for Sophie and Cao?" I asked.

"That's right," Frank said, moving piles of papers on top of each other, and then riffling through each page. "I just need to remember where I put them. They'll turn up every week or so, and then I tell myself ah! I must remember to send them to Katherine in Bonn, and then they disappear again."

I watched him go through the entire contents of his desk, and then the surface above his filing cabinet, and then his face lit up. He lifted up his coffee mug, and under it were various sheets of paper. He went through each one and finally said, "Voilà!" And handed me the stack.

There was Sophie's family's address in the town of Gurz of the house I had not been able to find, and the location of her boardinghouse in Göttingen, which had been paid for by her father. He had also acquired Cao's addresses: the first in a residence hall, records for which showed all his bills had been paid on time through a scholarship from the Chinese government, and the second was a private boardinghouse quite close to where I was staying.

I thanked Frank for his help and left in search of whatever I could find out.

I WENT to Cao Xi Ling's boardinghouse and knocked on the door, but no one was there. The house itself was a lovely old stone cottage, probably hundreds of years old. I circled it a few times, and then—too agitated to wait, set off in search of the boardinghouse Sophie had stayed at during her time in Göttingen.

When I knocked on that door, a man answered right away. He was short and plump with a halo of curly white hair framing his face, and he asked in a brisk way when he opened the door what I wanted.

"I'm looking for information about a woman who lived here about thirty years ago," I said. "Her name was Sophie Meisenbach."

The man shook his head and said he was afraid he couldn't help me. This house had belonged to his late sister, who had passed away two years ago. There was nothing he could tell me about any of the people his sister had boarded. I thanked him, deflated, and walked back to Cao Xi Ling's house, which was only ten minutes away. *Close enough to meet quite regularly*, I thought, as I made the walk.

This time a woman who looked to be about forty years old answered the door when I knocked. "May I help you?" she asked.

I told her I was curious about the house and its history, and that specifically I was looking for information about a Chinese mathematics student who had once boarded there.

"The previous owners were my parents, this is my house now, and the Chinese student you speak of was our boarder for several years," she said.

"Was this his name?" I asked, showing her the paper on which Karl had written down Cao's name. "I don't know how it's pronounced, I'm afraid."

"Ah, yes," the woman said. "He spelled his name the Chinese way, so his last name goes first, Cao, which is pronounced *Cow*. And then his given name was Shee Ling."

"Shee Ling," I repeated after her.

"And my name," the woman said, holding out her hand, "is Franzi."

"Franzi," I said, shaking her hand. "Thank you so much. I'm Katherine. If you have some time, do you think you'd be willing to answer some questions for me?"

"Of course," she responded right away. She led me into her parlor and had me sit on a rather uncomfortable ornate old couch. It was a strange thought to think perhaps Xi Ling had sat on this very same couch, maybe next to Sophie.

"I was just twelve years old when Xi Ling came to board at my house," Franzi began. "He was very gentle and very beautiful. I liked to look at him!" She laughed. "His German was not good, and we laughed at it. When he spoke, he moved his hands like birds.

"My mother taught him how to cook, and he liked to do it, but he stood—just so, not like a woman, but a man." Franzi laughed again. "And every morning at sunrise, he went into our courtyard and exercised. On weekends my brothers and I woke early and snuck downstairs to watch him. It was supposed to be fighting, my brothers told me, but it looked like dance." And Franzi raised her hands into the air as if to show me, took a breath, and let them fall.

"It says in these records that he lived here until 1951," I said. "Can you tell me where he went?"

"Oh, no, he left much earlier than that," she said. "Almost ten years earlier, in 1943. He said he was returning to China."

"But it says here his room was paid for through 1951," I said. "Was he in touch during that time?"

"No." Franzi shook her head. "His housing was covered by a scholarship from the government of China. It paid the university and the university paid us. After Xi Ling had been gone a while, my father told the scholarship office he was no longer here, hoping to figure out what had happened. But that led nowhere. And then a year had passed, and another year, and we kept telling the university that he was no longer here, but they said he or his next of kin would have to sign paperwork withdrawing him from the program. We could not track them down, and it was all too hard, so we just took his rent for nearly a decade until one day the payments stopped." She shrugged. "My parents felt bad, but what was there to do?"

"There was no forwarding address for his family in China?" I asked.

"None we were ever able to find."

"Did he leave anything else behind?"

"No," Franzi said slowly. "He owned very little—when he left, I remember he packed nearly everything into a small rucksack he carried on his back. He left behind his textbooks, and his bedding, but that was it." She paused. "He did leave behind a copy of something he was working on for school," she said. "I think it was an accident, because I found it wedged between his desk and the wall when I was cleaning his room, some years later. And I kept it, oh, I don't know—out of fondness I guess. I'd long given up the thought that he'd return. Do you read mathematics? I never could."

I answered that I did.

"Well, let me get it for you then," she said. "Perhaps you can explain it to me."

She returned with a sheaf of yellowing papers. The handwriting on them was quite beautiful, very different from the German style—each letter formed with careful and elegant precision, and every line of each page filled with notations and formulae, exclamation points and underlines. As I began to flip through the pages, a sense of unease took hold of me. The argument seemed familiar, like an echo of something I'd read before. And then spliced in with those papers were other papers, written in a handwriting I recognized.

"Do you know if he worked on this alone?" I asked.

"We never talked about his work."

"Did he have friends?" I said. "Men or women, colleagues with whom he spent a lot of time?"

"He had friends, of course," she said. "But he never brought them here."

I nodded. A buzz of excitement and dread was coursing through my body. "Can I borrow this paper, please?" I said. "I can't tell you why, but there's something I need to check."

Franzi leaned forward and looked deeply into my face, not bothering to hide the curiosity plain to read on her own. "May I first ask you a question of my own, my dear? Why the interest in Xi Ling? What are you hoping to discover?"

I looked down and blushed. "I don't know precisely how to answer," I said. "I thought—perhaps this man might be my father."

"You don't know?" she said.

I shook my head. "No," I said. "I never knew my father or my mother."

"Ah," she said, and her eyes filled with tears. "So he didn't make it out?"

The sight of her tears surprised and moved me, so that my own eyes filled. "No," I said. "I don't know what happened to him."

She nodded and wiped her eyes. "You have something of his expression in your face," she said. "Take the papers. They're yours." She reached out and squeezed my arm. "May I tell you what I know about his departure?"

"Please," I said.

"He left with a woman," she said. "I think she must have been your mother."

"Yes," I said. "She was."

She nodded. "So their plan was to go to China by way of Bulgaria. Her family had gone ahead of her, you see—or they'd made the attempt to leave, and they hadn't heard from them again. So their plan was to look for them and figure out where they might have ended up, and then they would get everyone to China, where Xi Ling was convinced they would be safe."

"Bulgaria," I said. "But she ended up in France."

Franzi looked puzzled. "That's the wrong direction. They must have gotten diverted somehow," she said.

"But how would Sophie have gotten out of Germany to France?" I asked. "It was occupied by then. Surely she would have been stopped at the border and arrested immediately."

"Well, she was traveling as me," Franzi said. "I gave her my papers. We cut out my photo and pasted in hers." She grinned. "I never told anyone that before. Not a single soul, not even my family."

I gasped. "But if the Nazis had found out," I said, "wouldn't you have been in trouble?"

"Oh yes." She nodded. "Tortured. Perhaps killed."

"Were you afraid?" I asked.

"Of course," she said. "Every day I was afraid. How was it possible to be otherwise with those butchers running our country?"

"I mean for yourself, to have taken such a risk."

"Oh, that." She shrugged. "Yes. That too."

"I don't know how to thank you," I said. "For them, I mean. And for me."

"Oh, it was without question the best thing I've ever done in my life. The thing I've always been proudest of. I had hoped so much they made it out all right, though of course when there wasn't any word, I guessed they hadn't." She smiled at me. "We mustn't cry," she said, but she was crying. "And anyway, I'm very glad to know that at least you made it out, and that you found me here."

We sat for a while, quietly, drinking our tea and wiping our tears, but then it was time to take my leave. There was still the matter of the manuscript to attend to.

"Keep the papers," she said. "And let me know how it turns out, and please, my dear—promise that you'll keep in touch."

I nodded and promised that I would. With another barrage of thank-yous from me and good-lucks from her, I rushed out of her house and went straight to the library.

I found what I was looking for right away, a thin, folio-style book wrapped in black leather. I opened it with trembling hands. I placed it next to the papers Franzi had given me and went through them page by page, comparing notes. It was just as I'd suspected. The book was the book Karl Meisenbach had made his name with, and the paper was the Schieling-Meisenbach theorem.

Chapter 29

I went to Karl's office immediately, both the book and the papers in my hand.

"What is it, Katherine?" he said, looking up at me from his desk. "Is everything all right? Is Henry okay?"

I found I couldn't speak. It seemed to me suddenly that this was a man who was capable of anything. Perhaps he'd try to kill me if I confronted him, I thought wildly, backing up against his door, my hand on the doorknob.

"For God's sake, Katherine, settle down and out with it. You're beginning to frighten me," Karl said.

"Cao Xi Ling," I said. "Schieling. I never put it together."

"Put what together?" Karl said calmly.

"Sophie Meisenbach," I said. "And Cao Xi Ling. You stole their theorem."

Karl turned very pale and rose from his desk. "That's a dangerous accusation," he said. "You need to be very careful."

"Stay where you are!" I said, waving the book at him. I turned the knob of the door and opened it a little. "You're the one who needs to be careful! I have the pages right here: Sophie's handwriting in the manuscript for the theorem that everyone thinks you wrote. Sit back down or I'm leaving right now to report you."

"You have it wrong, Katherine," he said. "I can explain it to you. Please have a seat, and don't look as if you're going to fly off, or as if I'm some kind of murderer. I'm nothing of the kind, I promise you."

I released the door but left it open. "Against my better judgment," I announced, "I'm sitting down. But please know if you try anything, I'll scream."

"I'll take that into account," he said, dryly. "Thank you for hearing me out." He sat down too. "You're right," he began. "I did not write that paper, and I took credit for it. But I never meant to steal it. Sophie gave it to me, you see, to submit it for her, when she left." His face contorted into a grimace. "I loved Sophie. All my life I loved her. I would never have harmed her."

I sat in my seat, my throat tight.

He drew his hand across his face. "I submitted that paper with Sophie's initials," he said. "But because I had sent the paper in, the journal editor misunderstood and published it with my initials instead. And by then a year had passed, and Sophie was gone, and everyone thought I had written it. And then the way things happened—I didn't want to take credit for it, but I didn't know where Sophie was; I hadn't heard from her and figured she was most likely dead—I meant to write to the journal and issue a retraction, or a correction, but I also felt superstitious about it, as if doing so could tip some scale in one direction or another. It doesn't make sense, I know, but I felt as if explaining the situation to anyone might be dangerous, or worse, unlucky. I thought there was time to wait until I knew what had happened to her, and then it was too late, the time had passed, and I was here, and there was no explanation I could make."

Listening to him, I felt slightly breathless. For a moment I was disoriented. The thing was, part of me understood. Karl had stolen someone else's work and claimed that he had written it after making zero contributions. He'd taken advantage of a mistake, had profited from the death of the real authors. And yet, when Peter had finished my paper for me, what had infuriated me most was my desire to tell no one else, to just take it.

I cleared my throat. "You say Sophie brought you her paper," I said. "Why didn't she submit it herself?"

"Well, of course she couldn't while she was in hiding, and then I suppose she wanted to leave it somewhere safe."

"That makes sense. Can you tell me how she ended up leaving? How did her father get caught?"

"Ah," Karl said. "This is the part of the story I'm not proud of. When her father discovered that she was pregnant, he was furious. He came to our house, to ask me who had done this to her, because I had been in Göttingen with her.

"I should have claimed ignorance. I should have said I didn't know. But I was shocked, too, to hear how far she'd let it go with the Chinaman." He raised his hands and looked at me pleadingly. "So I told her father about Xi Ling. I told him it was a shame and a travesty. I said a lot of things that I ought not to have said.

"I didn't know it then, but Sophie and Xi Ling hadn't seen each other for months at that point. I don't think he knew she was pregnant. But Sophie's father was furious. She had always been his favorite, you understand, and when everyone told him he was spoiling her, he still gave her everything she asked for. And she'd been writing to Xi Ling even after they'd gone into hiding, which would have put them at risk. So he felt betrayed by her and humiliated. And of course there was no news from the family, who he'd sent off ahead of them. When everything came to light, he forbade her from contacting her lover and made her burn her papers—not just their correspondence, but all her work notes as well."

"What?" I said, aghast.

"Yes." Karl nodded. "He made her burn all the work she'd done during her years in Göttingen. He let her keep most of our letters to each other, but if they contained any kind of mathematics in them, he made her burn those, too. He blamed his leniency with her in her early years, he blamed her education and her modern ideas for everything that happened—not just her pregnancy, but her falling in love with a foreigner, the breaking apart and exile of her family." Karl paused and gazed at me thoughtfully.

"She looked like such a delicate creature, your mother," he said. "But she was tough. When she told me what her father had made her do, she didn't cry a single tear. She just handed me what she'd managed to hide and said it wasn't safe anymore with her where she was. And she asked me to try to publish it. And I promised that I would.

"But then her father was found by the SS and taken away. Someone had seen him when he visited our house and reported him. How Sophie evaded capture I cannot fathom. When I went to find her, she was gone. And when I went to find Xi Ling to tell him what had befallen her, he was gone as well.

"And all I know of what happened next, I'm afraid, is the story you told me when we first met."

"What happened to Sophie's family?" I asked.

He shrugged. "All gone," he said. "No one ever came back."

"You said it was my fault she stayed behind," I said, accusingly. "You made it sound like I'd killed her. Like she and her family could have escaped if not for me."

"I didn't," Karl said, sounding genuinely shocked. "You must have misunderstood."

I waved this off impatiently. "So why is Xi Ling's name spelled wrong on the paper?"

"That's not my fault. The title page got lost in the sending. I gave them the title and his name over the telephone, but they didn't ask me to spell it out."

"Where is my notebook? The one that your messenger boy supposedly lost? You have it, don't you?"

"No, Katherine, I don't," Karl said. "I wouldn't have kept it—I knew what it meant to you. That, at least, is the truth."

I wasn't sure I believed him, but what could I do? Every story I knew about a woman, it occurred to me, involved a story of theft. And I knew that everything that happened next was my decision. I would have to tell Henry what I had discovered. I would have to tell the world. That was what was right, from the perspective of justice, from the perspective of truth. And yet my best friend loved this man. It was an impossible conundrum without any kind of elegant solution.

"You have to tell Henry all this," I said. "Before your wedding."

"I can't." Karl's eyes filled with tears. "It would break her heart."

"You need to tell her by tomorrow."

He fell on his knees: he took my hand. "I'm begging you," he said in his office, though his door was open. "I'm on my knees to you."

I was horrified. "Get up," I hissed. "I don't want you on your knees. I just want you to tell the truth."

"I can't lose Henry," he cried. "I love her. She's my whole life. Please don't do this, Katherine," he said. "Please show me some mercy."

"It's not about mercy," I said. But I was sickened by the sight of him on his knees, and I fled.

For the entire next week I waited for Karl to tell Henry. I thought about telling her myself, but soon enough I had waited too long and felt that I couldn't, and I was aware that this was the same excuse Karl had used for why he had never clarified the authorship of the Schieling-Meisenbach theorem. I felt dirty, corrupted by my involvement thus far. When I couldn't stand it anymore, I went back to Karl's office and said, "I've written a letter to Henry." I waved it in his face. "I'm going to tell her. I'm going to tell her tonight. No more excuses. No more waiting. I know it will destroy my friendship with her, but I'm prepared. I can't let this go on."

Perhaps it was the resoluteness in my voice that made Karl forgo the hysterics. This time there was no dropping on his knees, there were no tears. He just said, "Very well. I agree with you, Katherine. I will tell her."

WHEN HENRY CAME HOME that night, I was sitting in the living room, waiting up.

I stood up. "Henry, darling," I said, but she raised her hand to quiet me.

"No," she said. "I know what you want to say. But, please, let me talk first."

"Okay," I said, a little afraid.

"Karl told me everything," she said. "But there's something you don't know."

"Okay," I said, thinking she would present her argument and I would knock it down.

"I'm pregnant with Karl's child."

"What?" I breathed. "How?"

"How do you think?" she retorted.

"How long?" I asked.

"I don't know," she said. "Two months? Three months?" She took a breath. "Do you see how this changes everything? It's all settled. I can't do this without him."

I sank back down again, openmouthed, completely at a loss. Henry sat down beside me. She looked so vulnerable, her hands shielding her belly as if I threatened what she carried there.

"I don't know what to say," I said.

"I love him, Katherine."

"No, you don't," I said, without thinking it through. "You're pregnant. That's okay. We can deal with that."

She shook her head.

I said, "Remember when we first came here, and you said let's give up men? Let's do it. Let's throw men to the wolves, let Karl sink or swim, let's raise your child together. I'll help you. This is our chance."

Henry stood up and turned away from me, shaking her head. "It's too late for that," she said. "I love him. His life is my life now. I can't." And then she said, "Katherine, for the sake of our friendship, for the sake of our love, please don't expose him. I'm going to marry him. I'm going to have his child. Please don't ruin everything for us before it even starts."

"Did he tell you what he did?" I asked. "Do you know what he did to Sophie and Xi Ling? To my mother and father?"

"I do, but they're dead. What can we do about it now?" Henry asked. Her voice was harsh and desperate. "I'm your best friend. And Karl is your cousin, and we're going to have a child together. Promise you'll stand by me and protect me. Be our child's godmother. Please. I love you," she said. "Please help me."

"Did he get you pregnant on purpose?" I asked. "Were you going to get married before you knew?"

"How can you say that?" she cried. "What does it matter? There's no going back from this." And then she burst into deep, racking sobs that tore at my guts. She cried for what seemed like forever, and though I wanted to resist, I was moved, and I sank off the couch to the ground and put my arms around her.

I thought of Sophie, her life's work gathered together in her hands, the father she had loved her whole life standing above her, telling her to burn it, holding her responsible for the weight of misfortune that had befallen her family. I imagined her kneeling in front of the fire, her family already gone, knowing the risk her father had taken in staying behind to care for her.

Sophie had burned her work for him. She had known that she might lose everything and everyone she'd ever loved, and she'd looked at the man she'd always trusted and, on his command, destroyed everything he'd asked her to—all she'd created, all she'd dreamed of, she'd fed into the fire with her own hands.

I found myself whispering to Henry, "Okay, okay, I'll protect you. I will do as you ask. I choose you." But as Henry began to calm herself, I thought of my mother Meiying at fourteen years old, facing the dwarf men soldiers. She had been fearless, her father's favorite child, and still he had not hesitated to sacrifice her when he thought it might save her brothers. And that had broken her: I knew it had. It had made her leave my father and me. It had broken her for love.

Henry sat up and wiped her eyes with her sleeve. "Thank you," she said, resting her head on my shoulder. I didn't respond. "Kat?" she said after a moment. "You won't change your mind, will you? What are you thinking?"

"I'm just thinking what terrible things we do to each other," I said. "What terrible things we do in the name of love."

Chapter 30

I STAYED IN GÖTTINGEN UNTIL HENRY'S WEDDING TO Karl. I thought, perhaps, that she would change her mind. But she went through with it, and I stood beside her and held the flowers for her. The whole time they were exchanging their vows, I couldn't stop thinking of Karl on his knees weeping. I wished I could scrub the memory from my mind.

After, Henry said, "We're really family now."

"Yes," I said, and meant it, but I also knew that once I left, we would never be close again.

THE DAY I LEFT GERMANY, the streets were covered in snow—a mathematician's dreamscape, everything smoothed over and rendered in outline, transformed into an abstraction of itself. Instead of Massachusetts, I went home to Michigan, where I told my father what had happened with Peter, as well as with Henry and Karl.

"I'm thinking of dropping out of my PhD program," I admitted.

"How close are you to finishing?" my father asked.

"I just have to defend my thesis," I said. "But at this point no one even believes it's actually mine."

My father let out a sigh and looked out the window. "Sometimes I think of your third-grade teacher, Mrs. Linen," he said. "And regret that I mishandled her."

"Because you didn't back her up enough? Well, if it makes you happy to hear, you were right," I told my father. "I should never have gone to graduate school."

"I never said that."

"You said I'd never get a job over a man."

"I never said that, either!"

"Yes, you did," I insisted. "When I told you I was going to apply."

"No," my father said. "I wanted you to know that you'd have difficulty. That the odds were stacked against you."

"You thought I hadn't noticed?"

"No," my father said. "I'm sure you had. Katherine, the problem with you is you never let anyone finish what they're trying to tell you. You're too defensive, too eager to insist that you know best."

"That's right," I said. "I'm a know-it-all, I'm a show-off. I get it."

"No!" my father said. He raised his hand. "Stop it! Enough. What I was trying to tell you just now is I wish I'd pulled you out of Mrs. Linen's class and found you a teacher who encouraged you more. And what I was trying to say about graduate school, and what you still won't let me finish saying, is this: I wanted you to know that I knew you'd have difficulty. That it'd be hard to get a job. And that when the time came, I'd be behind you all the way. I wanted to tell you not to worry about money, that I could support you if you needed. But all you wanted to hear was that it'd be easy. You wanted me to say you'd never have problems. That your talent would knock down all the doors. You were only willing to listen if you thought I would say what you wanted to hear.

"Katherine," my father continued. "I'm your father. I am here to help, and always will be. Even if you've discovered this Karl fellow, and found out Sophie and Xi Ling are your parents, it doesn't change who we are to each other."

I nodded, eyes full. For once, he'd told me just what I needed to hear. I didn't know what to say in response, but after that conversation, I had to acknowledge I'd been wrong about a lot of things. I had been overly defensive, always spoiling for a fight. I know now that this came from a sense of my own vulnerability, being made to feel all my life that I didn't belong, that anything could be taken away. All my life I'd been forced to fight my way through, and I no longer knew how to stop.

I went for a walk around our old neighborhood, past the pond, along the creek, and to the library. It was closed, but lit from the inside, and I walked around it, marveling at how small it was. For my entire childhood it had loomed so large, but it was really just a little building, somewhat dingy, a bit run-down.

I walked home and let myself into the garage. I parked myself in front of the old radio, and just the sight of it comforted my loneliness somewhat. I wiped off the dust that was clogging it with a cloth, and then I wiped down the chair in front of it and sat down. I put on the earphones and took a breath. What would I say? I thought about Peter. I thought about Henry and Karl. I put the headset down. I got up. I walked away.

WHEN IT WAS TIME, I went back to graduate school to defend my thesis. The whole time, I could hardly breathe. Peter was still chair of my committee, but we hadn't spoken since Germany. Afterward each of my professors stood up and shook my hand. Peter was the last to do so, waiting until the others had left.

"Katherine," he said, and his eyes were full of unshed tears—I shook my head and pulled my hand away.

"Please don't," I said. I had seen how happy Karl and Henry were together, despite everything. I had thought to myself that what Peter had done wasn't nearly as bad. If Henry could still love Karl, why couldn't I have Peter? But Peter had done what he'd done to me, not to somebody else. I couldn't look in his eyes. "I can't talk to you," I said. I forced myself to walk away.

PETER ONCE TOLD ME a story that went like this:

Once there was a great artist who was very famous and very old, and at the height of his renown, he fell in love with a young woman who toyed with his affections. This famous artist wooed her in the most public way, sending her expensive gifts, making her extravagant promises—until one of his disciples confronted him one day and asked, Why, at the height of your renown, do you risk everything by making a fool of yourself? Do you not know you've become a laughingstock? That you've put your reputation at risk?

The famous artist smiled, and said, "Who am I not to be made a fool of for love?"

How nice it would be if we could all be the artist! To love and be loved with abandon. And yet what an imbalance exists in that story. How blind it is to how careful women must be: how for us, the stakes have always been higher. I wouldn't have minded risking everything, if Peter had also been risking just half of what I would have been required to risk. Actually, I could have been satisfied if he'd just understood what I was risking, and that I also wanted to be the artist in the story, and why.

I was not able to find a teaching job after graduate school, as my father had predicted, but neither was my situation as dire as either of us had feared. Rob and Leo invited me to join them to work at their lab. Leo had married and was expecting his first child by then, and this gave me a momentary pang. So much had happened while I was away—in just two short years their lives had moved forward in ways mine had not, and I couldn't help remembering my gentle flirtation with Leo and wondering *what if.* It seemed obvious to me then that Leo was the kind of man who would make someone happy, and I wondered if from the beginning I'd made the wrong choices. I wondered, too, if the problem was me, if I was the kind of woman who couldn't make someone else happy.

Aside from these musings, I worked with both Rob and Leo quite happily on applications from my work, such as how to use prime numbers to build an encryption system that even now is being used to protect data in—for instance—every credit card transaction that takes place. The very unpredictability and unknowability of primes is what makes this system work. The irony is, if the Riemann hypothesis were to be solved, then the code of the primes could finally be cracked, whereupon the system Rob and Leo and I built would become useless, and all that data compromised.

Still, the research was interesting, useful, and lucrative, and after some years of productive work of this kind, Charles Lee invited me to teach at his university. That lectureship led to my first tenure-track job. From there I published, I advised students, and my reputation grew and grew. Charles Lee and I became lifelong collaborators and friends. Franzi, too, in Göttingen—I never saw her again in person, but we corresponded for years, by long and frequent letters and by telephone, and we became quite close.

At some point I turned away from number theory and the study of primes to work on dynamical systems, which as it turned out, was useful in attacking any number of problems in almost every other field of mathematics. And not just mathematics, but physics, biology, chemistry, cosmology, and computer science. Still, I never forgot my first love—numbers, and I eagerly followed every new assault on the Riemann hypothesis with interest. And with the years, though Fermat's last theorem and the Poincaré conjecture both fell, the Riemann hypothesis remained intact and only grew in stature.

FOR SOME YEARS following my return from Germany, I searched for records of Sophie's family with my father's and—to my surprise—Linda's help. After a suspicious, uncharitable moment when I thought she was helping search for my birth parents to lessen the bond between my father and me, I finally began to see Linda for who she was: possessive and protective of my father, yes, but also someone who had stayed loyal to a man with a complicated history. She had learned to make him happy and, maybe more importantly, had allowed him to make her happy too.

Together, the three of us searched for the truth of what had happened to Sophie and her family. I could not find any records of her or her father, but what little we could find on the rest of her family revealed that they had died before the end of the war. The confirmations, each time they came for her mother, her siblings, her aunts and uncles, nieces and nephews, were hard to bear, old history as it was. Each death, with so few details, was still a blow.

After many years of silence, I heard from Karl in the late 1980s asking if I would be willing to take a new test that would be able to confirm whether or not we were related by blood. I said yes, and had a blood sample drawn and sent to a laboratory somewhere in Germany. Some weeks later, the results told us what—for many years—I'd already taken as fact. Karl Meisenbach was my cousin, and Sophie and Xi Ling were my parents. It came together as easily as a puzzle, as cleanly as a proof.

I thought perhaps the confirmation would put me more closely in touch with Karl and Henry, and that maybe I'd finally get to meet their child, but after that brief contact, they remained as unresponsive as before. I was baffled both by Karl's sudden request and his subsequent remoteness after I complied, but by then I had long given up on trying to stay close to him or Henry.

That year, I visited China for the first time, and I made my way to the only address I had ever found for Xi Ling, which was not an address at all, just "Hubei Province, China." Everyone said it'd be impossible to find any records, but I asked around anyway. I learned some rudimentary Chinese in preparation for the trip, and Charles Lee put me in touch with a guide and a translator there, who accompanied me for the first two weeks. I traveled the last on my own. Everywhere I went, someone had heard of someone who had gone to Germany to study math, and I was taken to see a dozen Xi Lings, but every lead was a dead end.

The whole time I was there, I kept thinking about my mother Meiying. I had searched for her, too, but to no avail. My father hadn't known a single detail about where she might have come from. She had refused to tell him—he'd never even known her last name before she took his. In China, I saw her everywhere. In the faces of the girls who ran barefoot down the streets, in the faces of the graceful women dressed in beautiful clothes. I saw her even in the faces of the grannies squatting, selling produce on the side of the road.

Toward the end of my stay, while I was visiting the famed mountain of Wudang, I saw a boy practicing kung fu in front of a temple. Facing the sun, he moved with breathtaking grace, and I thought of Franzi hiding behind a curtain, watching Xi Ling as he went through the motions of his daily practice. I wondered what my life might have been like if I had grown up here, in China, if I would have learned to move like that—if that might have become my passion, instead of math.

Near Wutai, I met an old Buddhist monk with long white hair, who had been to the West when he was a little boy and spoke some English. He spent an evening drinking with me in the filthiest hotel I'd ever seen and invited me to go on a hike with him up a high, steep mountain.

He asked what kind of work I did, and when I told him I was a mathematician, he nodded wisely. He wanted to talk about time, and how everyone thinks it goes forward—and possibly backward, but how in his practice time isn't linear at all, but goes in all directions, always. And not just flat along a plane, back and forth—but round and round. Circling and circling. Everything is happening at once, he said, and has happened or will happen.

I told him about wormholes and physics, and parts of the universe that seem far apart but are actually touching, and particles that aren't touching, but are somehow so connected that if you do something to one on one side of the universe, the other will respond from all the way across.

He told me about reincarnation, how past lives affect this one, how we've met everyone at least once before: how anyone could have been our mother. How anyone could have been our child. How our enemy in this life will be our lover in another. After all, isn't it the people we've loved most who have wounded us most deeply? By now, he said, we have lived a thousand lives already, all of us—by the end of the world, we'll already have been everyone else.

He was taking me, he said, to a mountain peak that was considered to be the seat of one of the major bodhisattvas, a place where time and space collapsed. He was speaking in the language of his religion, but it sounded like math to me. Multiple lives, like multiple universes: time as a thing that could be manipulated along with space. The monk said the place we were going to was a place where people went to have a vision, and that it was the vision that was the destination, not the physical place.

He had made it sound like we could make the hike in a day, but in fact it took us several. I was unprepared, and when we summited, I was haggard and dirty and half starved. We had rationed bits of dried vegetables the monk carried in his satchel, we had scavenged for roots, we had begged meals and lodgings from passersby. When I complained of exhaustion or hunger or thirst, the monk laughed at me and said it would ensure a better vision.

"Here you are!" the monk said, when we reached the destination, which was not the destination, but the place where I would have my vision of another place that was the seat of a bodhisattva.

There was a stone statue of a beautiful man with long earlobes, dressed in a flowing gown. "This is the bodhisattva Kwan-Yin," he said.

"Kwan-Yin who hears all human suffering? Isn't Kwan-Yin a woman?"

"Kwan-Yin is both," he said. "Both man and woman. Here she is a man."

I looked at the statue and felt as if indeed space and time were collapsing: my mother's story. Gödel's theorem: truth and untruth.

"What do I do?" I asked.

"First you bow," the monk said. "Then you bathe the statue with the water. And then you have a drink." And so I watched him and did as he did.

"Now," he said, "you sit and meditate. You wait for your vision."

"For how long?" I asked.

"As long as it takes," he said.

And so I sat. I should have asked him how to meditate, but I didn't. I sat with my legs crossed and my eyes closed on top of the mountain and waited for my vision. I tried to clear my mind, but it was full of thoughts. I thought of my mother who had been sold by her father to protect her brothers, somewhere in this country. I wondered what had happened to them, and if I had been one of them in another life. I wondered if I had been her mother, her father, the Japanese soldier who had taken her. I thought of my father who'd tried to give her something to hold on to, and broken her trust, instead. I wondered if in some parallel universe they were together, and happy. If in some other world Sophie and Xi Ling still lived. I thought of Peter Hall and wondered if in another life we'd married and had children. If there was a universe where everyone got to be happy.

I sat for a long time, thinking, waiting for an answer, or a vision, or a visitation, and while none of these arrived, as I sat, I sensed the trees regarding me, as my mother had shown me they could, the day before she left. And not just the trees, but the mountains, and not just the mountains, but the sky. I felt my mind reach out to greet them. When I finally rose, I felt different. I felt changed. I looked for the old monk, but he had left me there. He had disappeared. Still, I felt calm without his guidance and ready to make the hike back down alone.

Chapter 31

IN THE END, I KEPT MY WORD TO HENRY AND ALLOWED Karl to keep the Schieling-Meisenbach theorem: I never breathed a word of the story to anyone. They had two more children, who grew up and had children of their own. But I was right when I left Germany to think that Henry and I would never be close again. There was a necessary distance between us that I regretted, especially since I never had children, and hers happened to be—along with Karl—my only known living relatives.

When I was a child, I used to search for symmetries in nature: now that I'm old, I find myself in the habit of recognizing it everywhere in my life. I spent a great deal of my younger years chasing down the mystery of where and whom I came from, and in my later years, I've spent a great deal of time contemplating just whom and what I'll leave behind. This question of lineage that preoccupied me for so much of my life turns out in the end to be a question of whom I claim as my own, and who claims me.

There are the claims of scholarship: the ones who formed your mind, the ones whose minds you formed. In math the students who studied directly under Emmy Noether are called her children. Those who studied underneath them are her grandchildren. In this regard I am wealthy—I have many mothers and fathers, and many children—and I claim kinship with Charles Lee, with Ramanujan, with Gauss and Hilbert and Riemann and Emmy Noether and more.

Of the claims of blood, I cannot say too much. In my life there has been Karl, and his children whom I have never met, but whom I love because of Henry. When I think of him, I feel only sadness and wonder what good are the claims of blood if they allow you to stand aside while your kin are murdered—what good if you take credit for what should have been theirs?

And then there are the claims of love. The love of those who bore you. The love of those who raised you. The love you find, the love that breaks you. The love you carry from afar. Against these I am helpless: I surrender. To my two sets of parents, to the nun who saved me, to Henry, even, and the memory of Peter Hall, yes, I say—who I am now came from you and will return to you. I am yours.

THREE YEARS AGO KARL DIED, and though we had not spoken in decades, Henry called and asked me to come to her in Germany after his funeral. And so of course I went. The town was much the same as before: beautiful and placid, a pleasant and unassuming place that had once been a paradise for mathematics. Henry was gaunt but elegant as ever, draped in deep black silk, face still radiant through her grief, alive with expression and wit. Still, she was an old woman now, her hair gone gray, her skin thin as tissue paper. I touched my own face self-consciously knowing how much I, too, had aged. I remembered again that train trip to Göttingen—let's never get married, Henry had said. But she'd been the one to get married. She'd been the one to have children. And I'd been the one to have the dazzling—by any measure—career. Both our lives, it occurred to me, had come with their own disappointments, their own specific kinds of loneliness.

What had I hoped for going to her? Friendship, maybe. To exclaim at how differently things had turned out than we'd thought. To see her children, perhaps. What I got instead was dinner at a restaurant, just the two of us, and a box of papers, which she asked me not to look at until I was home.

"What's in it?" I asked.

"I don't know," she said, and her voice was weary—a door closed against me. "But Karl said you would know what to do with what's in there."

"Okay," I said. And then, "Henry, shall I stay for an extra few days? We could catch up properly. I could meet your children."

But Henry shook her head. "I'm tired, Kat," she said. "I'm just not up for it right now."

"I could help," I said. I smiled. "I could clean your house for you."

"No," Henry said. "But thank you."

I nodded, trying not to let it show how much her refusal had hurt me.

The mathematician Charles Fefferman once said that mathematics is like playing chess with the devil. You don't know the rules, you don't know the game—and your only advantage is that you can take back an infinite number of moves, while the devil can take back none. I wished I had an infinite number of moves with Henry to figure things out—to find the words to speak, the key that would unlock again the friendship between us.

There were so many things I wanted to say to her: a lifetime of things. I thought of the stories we'd swapped on the train on that first fateful trip to Göttingen, and how I'd told her my mother's stories about the tenth muse, and Kwan-Yin. Somehow, I'd always thought those were the two options available to me. The tenth muse gave up everything to claim her own voice. Kwan-Yin gave up everything on behalf of everyone else. In my life, I had almost always chosen the path of the tenth muse—my work, my own vision, had always been my priority. But with Henry, I had always put her first. I had tended to her wishes, her suffering, above all other considerations. Even now, I felt compelled to do as she wished.

Once, I had said to her, "I choose you." As if by choosing her, I could not choose myself, too. I wished I could tell her that perhaps it didn't have to be just one or the other—perhaps we had more choices than that, and the world had tricked us out of seeing them.

But Henry's face was blank, her jaw tense. She did not want to talk with me. The choice, for her, was made.

"All right," I said. "I'll go home." And I took the long flight back, full of disappointment.

INSIDE THE BOX were Karl's notes: pages and pages of beautiful, impeccable math, going back years. And beneath his notes was a small leather notebook, Sophie's notebook—the one Karl had claimed he had lost. I lifted it out of the pile of papers, hands trembling. How could this be? Had the whole search, the scene with Martin—all been a manufactured ruse? I had mourned the loss of this notebook like it was a person, but finding it now did not fill me with gladness, as I'd always imagined—but a sort of wounded bewilderment that grew when I found underneath it pages and pages of notes written in Sophie's hand. Notes that Karl had told me long ago didn't exist.

They were unfinished, but when I started reading them, it was clear to me that they were the beginning of a staggering piece of work. I realized with growing excitement that she was making use of the Schieling-Meisenbach theorem to set up an ingenious attack on the Riemann hypothesis, which—whether successful or not—would be the furthest anyone had gotten to solving it yet.

Underneath these notes, at the very bottom of the box was one lone letter, written on a piece of paper whose shape suggested it'd been torn out of Sophie's notebook, dated November 1943.

Dear Karl, it began, *Xi Ling and I have been walking so long I've lost count of the days. Just imagine, me losing count! But the days are short, and the nights so cold and dark, and the mountains go on and on, and the border seems so far away. Please pray for our safe passage. If you have word from my mother or brothers, tell them this: that I wrote and said I am coming to find them.*

Today, the sun stayed behind the clouds, and the frost on the ground stayed crisp and white and did not melt from the ground. It was a hard day, but when it seemed we could not go on, we saw a hut in the distance, at the top of the mountain we have been ascending. We were afraid to approach it, afraid to be caught, but this time there was no choice but to risk it. When we finally reached it, we saw that the hut was in fact a lovely stone cottage, unlocked and empty, standing stout and welcoming in the bitter wind. And behind the cottage was a field of pumpkins all glazed over with frost.

Xi Ling went out to find wood. How loyal he is. How tireless. You are wrong about him. He will never leave me. I know this. When he returned, he returned with one of the pumpkins, much too large for us—an extravagance of pumpkin, he said—and he threw it into the fire that he built, and as it bubbled, the whole night went dark around us.

We sat and waited, so hungry—and when we finally ate, the earthy rich taste of the pumpkin was almost too much to bear. But tonight we have eaten something hot and will sleep by the warmth of a fire.

Even now, the baby kicks, always active, as if to hurry us on our way. But I think she is pleased by tonight's arrangements. We will leave this cottage in the morning. I will leave this letter addressed to you on the table and trust you will receive it: we feel certain that this was left unlocked for travelers such as us, a safe harbor for those who journey on.

Be well, my dear cousin. Be good and safe.

Sophie

I SAT FOR A LONG TIME after reading this note. So Karl had always had this in his possession. All these years, when it would have meant so much to me, he'd kept it hidden. Everything he'd told me had been a lie. Still, why had he left this to me now? Would he have done so if that test he'd asked me to take so many years ago hadn't confirmed that we were cousins? And were the contents of this box supposed to serve as a confession or a defense? The one thing I knew was that if I'd exposed Karl years ago, I would never have seen the contents of this box: this was an acknowledgment of that, a reward for my silence, my complicity.

I wondered now why he had never published his results, these papers he'd apparently written and stored. I'd always assumed he hadn't the talent, but it was clear now that he did—and that he'd worked on a wide range of subjects. I thought of what he'd said all those years ago, "Blood always tells."

He'd been a real mathematician who'd never published a single one of his works. And neither had Henry—for all her glittering talent, she had abandoned her research as far as I knew, and she'd never finished a book. Would that have been different, I wondered, if I had exposed Karl all those years ago? Would it have freed them both? I thought of Peter, and the Mohanty problem, and how if I'd taken his gift, if I'd taken that proof and said nothing—it would have broken something inside me—it would have poisoned my relationship to my work.

Still, every time I saw Peter at a conference, as I did once or twice in each decade of my life, I wondered: If I had just been braver or wiser, if I'd had the imagination for it, could we have found some way to be together? He went on to marry someone else, a few years after Germany—a lovely, gracious woman, quite bright, by all accounts, a professor of art history who filled their house with beautiful things and interesting people, a born hostess. And together they had two children. My treacherous heart! It broke every time I saw him—clamored for him, turned in on itself in grief for him. That part never changed, but as I grew older, I also grew better able to bear it. An ache that I stopped fighting, a wound I carry to this day.

All the same, there were consolations. I applied my imagination and my energy in other directions, where I was able to make my mark. I am recognized now as one of the pioneers of dynamical systems and was one of the first to use it to solve problems in other fields like game theory and topology. At the celebrations I'm invited to talk at these days, the introductions of my life and work grow ever grander, and two years ago, an entire conference was named after me. These days I'm casually referred to quite often as a "genius," and my name is invariably included in those "best of" lists that rank mathematicians by order of influence. And while I haven't quite risen to the heights I once dreamed of, I can't complain. My work has been used in fields as disparate as probability theory, thermodynamics, and most recently, artificial intelligence—my work remains at the frontier of new things.

But this return to the Riemann hypothesis by way of the

Schieling-Meisenbach theorem is something else altogether. It is personal. This is the problem that brought Sophie and Xi Ling together, and in some ways split me and Peter apart—even as our contribution links us together in name, forever. The connection it claims between the distribution of prime numbers and the zeta function is so stunning as to be seen as miraculous, as improbable and astounding as life. This hypothesis, which has baffled mathematicians for over 150 years and lit up my youth with all its mystique, feels within striking distance again.

I wonder if this was what had kept Karl enthralled and kept him from publishing any more work. The hope that with these notes he would one day complete Sophie and Xi Ling's work and be able to claim—potentially—the Riemann hypothesis himself. He must have known when he had Henry send me the box that I would not expose him, that my choice was made irrevocably, long ago. Not for him, but for Henry, who had come and cleaned my apartment when I was so low I thought I'd sink into the ground. Who'd said she'd adopt me, that her family would be my family, that she wanted to give me whatever she had.

I have spent the last three years putting the pieces of Xi Ling and Sophie's final proof together and will spend the rest of my life chasing the answer. Whether I finish or not, when I die, I will send Karl's notes to a colleague who will recognize them for what they are—I do not want to withhold them from the mathematical world. But if he's scooped in the meantime, well, that's how it goes.

AS FOR THIS PROOF I am working on now, I've come to think of it as my twin, conceived of by the same parents and carried across the same mountains. If I could, I'd travel in time to the night Sophie wrote her letter to Karl. I'd find her and Xi Ling in their stone cabin at the peak of the mountain they'd climbed and would later cross—the wind blowing around them and Xi Ling looking for wood. No candles, no light between them, just me, unborn, and the steel trap of hunger opening and closing their stomachs, hope clawing at their hearts, and love. I would keep them there forever, I would keep them there until the end of war.

But history has happened, and there is no such thing as safe forever. Perhaps there is no such thing as the end of war. Sophie and Xi Ling will leave their cottage in the morning. There are so many things they do not know. So much suffering and uncertainty ahead. And there's nothing I can do, no burden I can take except for what's left of their work. I will finish what I can: I will make it my life's work, and gladly—but otherwise I must leave them here, grateful, at least, that they have found for this night some sort of shelter.

I cannot give back what was taken from Sophie or Xi Ling. I cannot restore them to life. But perhaps I can carry their final proof a little longer and try to give it a life. Perhaps I can complete this part of their journey. And if I succeed, their proof, like all mathematical truths, will live forever.

As I work through the proof, tracing the twists and turns of their logic, I often think of Peter. I see now what dedication it must have taken on his part to tackle the Mohanty problem for me—not mere commitment, but what painstaking love—to enter so wholly the architecture of my mind, to follow so carefully its rhythms. I can admit now how much I owe him for all that he taught me, and how he encouraged me, and how even that terrible betrayal he made out of love. I wish I could have told him I realized this before he died. I wish he could have known.

Sometimes I think of the problem he gave me in grad school, before we were lovers, when we were still just teacher and student. There's a girl and a boy living on opposite sides of a lake. There's a ferryman who can go back and forth, carrying a box on which you can put any lock. He'll take anything over locked in the box, but anything else he will steal. The boy has a lock and the key to his lock, and the girl has a lock and the key to her lock. How can the boy get her a ring?

The solution is this: the boy puts the ring in the box, and then locks it shut with his lock. The ferryman takes it across. When it arrives, the girl puts her lock on the box, next to the boy's, and sends the ferryman back. The box at this point is locked twice, and when it reaches the shore, the boy takes out his key and unlocks his lock, leaving only the girl's. Then the ferryman makes his trip across the lake, back to the girl. She takes out her key and unlocks her own lock. And now the box is completely unlocked, and the girl opens it, and takes out the ring.

And so we've brought the boy and the girl together at last, but what they do next will be up to them. Because though we've found the solution, here is the lesson: in the end, we can only unlock our own locks, we have only the gift of ourselves.

NOVEMBER 1943

THEY ARE WALKING, JUST THE TWO OF THEM: SOPHIE and Xi Ling, Schieling and Meisenbach. It seems to Sophie they have always been walking and will never stop. After months of sickness, she has finally stopped vomiting, but she is always hungry and cold, her legs are tight and her stomach is heavy and sore. She can see in the bones of her lover's face what a toll this journey has taken on him. When she runs her fingers along the bones of her own face, she can feel their sharpness under her skin. They have been reduced to the essentials, to so little, and now they are walking what she hopes will be the final leg of this journey, if only they can cross over to safety.

Xi Ling carries on his back the culmination of their work together. Each night while she lies on her side and tries to sleep, he stays awake and shuffles through their papers, muttering to himself, scratching out formulae that sometimes he whispers into her ear as she lies in the dark, wishing he would lay himself against her and wrap her in his warmth. But she does not interrupt him. There is an urgency to his whispering: she knows he is racing against time. They feel it always, running against them. Sophie sighs. She has not contributed to their work in months. Her mind is foggy, her body taken over by the needs of the life she carries in her belly: heavy, rounded, as full as the earth. She runs her hands over the swell of it: the one part of her not left emaciated—the one part of her that is not, really, herself.

In her pocket is a notebook, just one small notebook that fits in the palm of her hand. All around them are mountains, beautiful to look at and treacherous to cross. Beside her is the man she loves, who has pledged never to leave her, his child stirring in her belly. In her mouth is a sour taste, tinged with blood. The world, she knows, is coming apart around her. Everything in Sophie's mind comes down to this: these mountains, this man, this promise of a life that will come, regardless. *Let her be all right*, she thinks. *This child of mine.* It is her only thought. *I would gladly trade in everything. Anything that is mine to give I would give, willingly, with gratitude.* She is not creating life, this much she understands. She is the vessel: life is creating itself inside her, using her, making itself out of her.

What wouldn't she steal, who wouldn't she murder, what wouldn't she do for this child? She would die right now, this moment, give up meeting this bit of life that has so hungrily devoured and distorted her body. What wouldn't she give? She clenches her fists. *Let her live*, she thinks. *Let me safely deliver this child into her life.*

Author's Note

I am indebted to a number of texts, including, in particular: *The Music of the Primes: Searching to Solve the Greatest Mystery in Mathematics* by Marcus du Sautoy, *Birth of a Theorem* by Cédric Villani, *Prime Obsession* by John Derbyshire, *Emmy Noether, 1882–1935* by Auguste Dick, *Hilbert* by Constance Reid, *Men of Mathematics* by E. T. Bell, *A Mathematician's Apology* by G. H. Hardy, *Geons, Black Holes, and Quantum Foam: A Life in Physics* by John Archibald Wheeler with Kenneth Ford, *The Apprenticeship of a Mathematician* by André Weil, *The Man Who Knew Infinity* by Robert Kanigel, *The Honors Class: Hilbert's Problems and Their Solvers* by Ben Yandell, "The Sexual Politics of Genius" by Moon Duchin, "The Pursuit of Beauty" by Alec Wilkinson, *Asian Americans in Michigan*, edited by Sook Wilkinson and Victor Jew, *Higher Education for Women in Postwar America, 1945–1965* by Linda Eisenmann, and *Keep the Damned Women Out* by Nancy Weiss Malkiel.

I am also indebted to the Institute for Advanced Study in Princeton for the use of its archives, and the library at the University of Göttingen, where I was able to read letters and notebooks relating to (and written by) Emmy Noether, Albert Einstein, David Hilbert, Abraham Flexner, Oswald Veblen, and Hermann Weyl.

The historical figures mentioned in *The Tenth Muse* are almost entirely made up of mathematicians and scientists. The stories of Emmy Noether, Sophie Germain, Sofia Kovalevskaya, Maria Mayer, Hypatia, Srinivasa Ramanujan, Alan Turing, and David Hilbert and his program in Göttingen make brief appearances in this book. Also mentioned are Jocelyn Burnell, Chien-Shiung Wu, Rosalind Franklin, Lise Meitner, Albert Einstein, Felix Klein, Alexander Grothendieck, Charles Fefferman, Kurt Gödel, G. H. Hardy, Carl Friedrich Gauss, Richard Courant, Henri Poincaré, Niels Bohr, Ludwig Boltzmann, Janos Bolyai, Leonard Euler, Otto Hahn, Werner Heisenberg, Andrey Kolmogorov, Edmund Landau, Adrien-Marie Legendre, Nikolai Lobackevsky, Edward Lorenz, Hermann Minkowski, Friedrich Nietzsche, Atle Selberg, Stephen Smale, Lawrence Summers, Hermann Weyl, and Ludwig Wittgenstein.

I make use of a number of real equations and formulas:

In the 1700s Carl Friedrich Gauss shocked his elementary school teacher by solving the sum of numbers between 1 and 100 in a matter of minutes (some say seconds). Like Katherine, he recognized a pattern—that if he split the group in half—the numbers from 1 to 50 and 51 to 100, and added them together from opposite sides, he'd get $1 + 100 = 101$, $2 + 99 = 101$, and so on and so forth until $50 + 51 = 101$. Since there'd be fifty such pairings, $50 \times 101 = 5050$. Thanks to Gauss we even have a shortcut to this shortcut in the guise of a formula for calculating such sums: $S = \frac{n(n+1)}{2}$. So the sum S of Gauss's elementary school problem up to 100 is: $S = \frac{100(100+1)}{2} = 5050$, and if you remember Katherine's much simplified problem, the sum of the numbers 1 through 9 is $\frac{9(9+1)}{2} = 45$.

The Boltzmann equation and the zeta function, also mentioned in this novel, are real, as is the Riemann hypothesis, which was first proposed by Bernhard Riemann in 1859. In 1900 David Hilbert included it in his list of twenty-three problems to define the future of mathematics at the International Congress of Mathematicians, and it remains unsolved to this day. In fact, the Clay Institute is offering $1 million to the person who solves it first. The Schieling-Meisenbach theorem is pure fiction, as are the Mohanty problem and the Kobalesky formula, and so—alas—will be of no help at all in the search for a final proof of the Riemann hypothesis.

Acknowledgments

I am grateful to so many people without whom this book would not exist. To Karen Uhlenbeck, meeting you was a great stroke of good luck. Thank you for your time and generosity, and above all your warmth and kindness, and for whispering the name of the Riemann hypothesis into my ear.

To Amanda Folsom, thank you for your perspective and insight, and for explaining some math to me in a moment of critical need. To Ben Recht, for gamely answering my preposterous questions with the same patience and generosity as when you were my favorite math TA in college, thank you.

Thank you to Pablo Londero for explaining Hawking radiation to me, and to Freeman Dyson for telling me about chaos theory and Mary Cartwright, and to all the people who talked to me about math and science over the years: this book is infused with the spirit of those conversations. To Debbie Endo and Keith Endo for your heroic last-minute reads and consultations about some of the times depicted in this book, I thank you. Thanks also to Michael Lynch, James Walsh, and Michelle Cahr for so kindly and quickly responding to my questions. Any errors or crimes against mathematics or history that may remain are unintentional and mine alone. Thanks to Jen Gann at *The Cut*, for publishing a tiny piece of mine containing a nod to a line from this book.

To Jin Auh, thank you for reading this book five million times! You are equal parts ferocity and grace, and I am so grateful for you. To Jessica Friedman, thank you. To Andrew Wylie, Alexandra Christie, Alba Ziegler-Bailey, Sarah Chalfant, Jessica Bullock, and everyone at the Wylie Agency, you guys are the best of the best.

To Megan Lynch, I am always amazed by your keen eye and killer instinct. Thank you for making this story so much better, and for ushering another one of my books into the world. To Daniel Halpern, Sara Birmingham, Laurie McGee, Miriam Parker, Meghan Deans, Ashlyn Edwards, Allison Saltzman, Suet Chong, Nyamekye Waliyaya, Kristin Bowers, Caitlin Mulrooney-Lyski, and David Palmer, I am so deeply grateful. Long live Team Ecco! Thank you to Joan Wong for the beautiful cover. Heartfelt thanks to my UK editor, Clare Smith, at Little, Brown.

Everlasting gratitude to my brilliant readers and beloved friends—thank you for reading the earliest scratchings of what became this book, and for selflessly reading drafts in the midst of your own busy schedules to drag me across the finish line: Autumn Watts, Ben Warner, Dwayne Betts, Helen Oyeyemi, Kimberly (Panshee!) Capinpin, Lauren Alleyne, Matthew Salesses, Pilar Gómez-Ibáñez, Rita Zoey Chin, and Seth Endo, thank you. Where would I be without you? (To shamelessly misquote Whitman: We were together. I forget the rest.)

To the Institute of Advanced Study: you are a dream made real. Thank you for the months I spent happily buried in your archives. Thanks especially to Robbert Dijkgraaf and Stephen Adler for the inspiration and wisdom, and for bringing me there, and to Sebastian Currier for his friendship. Erica Mosner, your help in the archives was absolutely essential, and your kindness and radiance of spirit still warm my soul. To Anthony Adler—thank you! To Piet Hut: I thank you in particular for the beautiful memory of the afternoon when we sat in the shade and you showed me how to look at the trees and the buildings, and how they were regarding me back in return.

Thank you to Thomas Richter, for your tour of Göttingen and your spectacular generosity. Thanks also to Bernhard Hackstette, Samuel Patterson, Susanne Ude-Koeller, Doris Hayne, Roswitha Brinkmann, and Esther von Richthofen. To Helmut Rohlfing, thank you for letting me hold the letters of Emmy Noether, Carl Gauss, and Albert Einstein in my hands.

I am forever grateful for the support of the National Endowment for the Arts, the Frederick Lewis Allen Room at the New York Public Library (and especially Melanie Locay), the Jerome Foundation, the MacDowell Colony, Yaddo, UCross, VCCA, and Civitella Rainieri (O you beautiful castle on a hill!). Dana Prescott, your warm encouragement and our poetry exchange have meant so much to me. To MEC, thank you for letting me write in your office, where I got so much done. I am grateful to the memory of Lee Hall, whose encouragement and faith warmed these pages.

Thanks also to Sam Grogg and Adelphi University for the research support to write this book, and to Peter West and Judith Baumel for encouraging me to take the time. Thanks to my students there and elsewhere for your hunger and ambition, and for reminding me that stories are always being born anew.

To Clare Wu, Frances Cowhig, and Faye Chiao, thank you for running away with me on our writing retreats. To Steph Opitz, Michael Lowenthal, Christine Hyung-Oak Lee, Sharon Guskin, Alex Chee, Meakin Armstrong, and Téa Obreht, your friendship and faith mean the world to me. Thank you to Mingmar Lama and Judy Brown-Steele.

To Lena Mushkina-Livshiz, Michael Livshiz, and Toma Livshiz, thank you for your enthusiasm and warmth, and your spirited conversations. I love being part of your family.

To my whole family, thank you. To my father, Moon Jung Chung, who infused my life with his love of mathematics, and whose math-riddles and stories are woven throughout this book as they were through my childhood, I thank you, and am grateful every day that you were my dad. To my mama, Sejin Chung, I owe you everything. Thank you forever times infinity. And to all mamas who give so much so that their children can flourish—bless you all, every one. To my beloved grandmother, thank you. Thank you to Heesoo Chung, for being the coolest and best brother in all the land, and my go-to person for questions about radios and building things and rockets and science. To Dawn and Olivia, I am so grateful to have you in my life.

And to David and Ella, agh! What can I say? You make me so happy. You just blast my life through with joy.

Continue reading for an extract from
***Forgotten Country* by Catherine Chung**

'A richly emotional portrait of a family that had me spellbound from page one' Cheryl Strayed, bestselling author of *Wild*

The night before Janie's sister, Hannah, is born, her grandmother tells her a story: Since the Japanese occupation of Korea, their family has lost a daughter in every generation, and Janie is told to keep Hannah safe.

Years later, when Hannah cuts all ties and disappears, Janie goes to find her. It is the start of a journey that will force her to confront her family's painful silence, the truth behind her parents' sudden move to America twenty years earlier, and her own conflicted feelings toward Hannah.

Weaving Korean folklore with a modern narrative of immigration and identity, *Forgotten Country* is a gripping story of a family struggling to find its way out of silence and back to one another.

1.

The year that Hannah disappeared, the first frost came early, killing everything in the garden. It took the cantaloupe and the tomatoes; the leaves of lettuce turned brittle and snapped. Even the kale withered and died. In front, the wine-colored roses froze, powdered gray with the cold, like silk flowers in an attic covered with dust. My father and I had planted the garden over several weekends, and tended it carefully. Then it had overgrown itself, the tomatoes winding themselves up the wall of our house and stretching out to span the distance to the fence. After the frost we'd left it all winter without trimming anything back. Now we stood on the lawn, surveying the ruin, tracking damp patches of ground wherever we stepped.

"We're selling the house," my father said, blowing warm air on his hands.

"That makes sense," I said, but it felt suddenly difficult to breathe. My parents had told me they were going back to Korea, so I'd known selling our house was a possibility, but I hadn't expected it.

"We're going to have to clean this up," my father said, gesturing at the garden.

"It's cold," I said. "Let's go inside."

He nodded. The tendons in his neck were taut. His breath steamed slowly around his face. Everything was inside out, or at least the cold had turned the insides of things visible. The green tomatoes were now gray and translucent, their skins puckered at the stems, still hanging from their frozen vines. "We want you to find Hannah," he said.

"When are you leaving?" I asked.

"As soon as possible," my father said.

"I want to go with you."

My father shook his head. "Find your sister," he said. He had blamed me after the initial panic, when we discovered that Hannah hadn't been abducted or killed, but had simply left without telling us, without leaving us a way to contact her. I was her older sister, living in the same city. He thought I should have seen it coming.

When I moved back home for the summer, my father grilled me about her. He wanted to know everything about the months prior to her departure: what she had looked like, what she had said. What I had noticed: why I hadn't noticed more. He was already sick then, but didn't know it yet. I wonder if Hannah would have been able to pick up and leave like that if she had known.

Inside, we made tea and sat at our kitchen table, waiting for my mother to come down. My father's hands relaxed on the table, his fingers eased into a slight curl around his mug. They looked fragile against the smooth blue ceramic, his veins raised thick and soft. For a moment I wanted to cover his hands with mine, even though they had always looked like that.

Growing up, Hannah and I worried we'd inherit those veins, huge and tinged blue. It was true that my father's body had pulled into itself in the last couple of years so that his bones protruded, but his eyes were still sharp and discerning, and his hands were the same hands that had built this table, the same hands that refused to let anything go.

"I want to go with you when you go to Korea," I said.

My father grimaced. "It's more important that you find Hannah. You need to bring her home."

"I can't do that."

"She's your only sister."

"She's a brat."

My mother's footsteps sounded down the stairs, and together we looked toward the hallway. My father tilted his head and called out, "We're in the kitchen!" He leaned forward and took my hand in his. It was warm. He whispered, "Don't upset her."

One word about Hannah was enough to make my mother dissolve into tears for at least an hour. "Dissolve" was not too strong a word. When my mother wept, the whole world vanished. My father and I ceased to exist, and even Hannah's shadowy figure was obscured. This could happen anywhere, at any time—even in public. At first I wondered how my mother could sustain such anxiety, how one body could hold it all. Then I realized it was a question of density.

There's a theorem in mathematics that says if you take something the size of an onion and cut it into small enough pieces, you can take those pieces and construct something larger than the sun. In those first months after Hannah went missing, we learned to be careful around my mother. We had no past. Everything was off limits. Coming home was entering oblivion—my father was obsessed with my last conversations with Hannah, and my mother resolutely surrounded herself with silence. So when she came padding into the kitchen, I slapped a smile onto my face, same as my father.

To be honest, I never really understood what Hannah had against my parents. Sure they'd made mistakes, but nothing we shouldn't be able to get over. They had tried their best. When Hannah left for college in Chicago, I was already in my junior year at the University of Michigan. My dorm was a forty-five-minute drive from our house, and I came home every other weekend to visit. The summer before Hannah left for school, she broke curfew nearly every night. At first my parents waited up for her. As the summer wore on, they waited until morning to pound on her door. How she slept through all that pounding, I'll never know. I woke up after two seconds of it. I'd jump into the shower to drown out the noise. Besides, I knew what came next. After several minutes my father would call, "I'm coming in!" and pick her lock open with a toothpick. Then my parents would stand over Hannah's defiantly sleeping body, prodding her shoulders to wake her up. And Hannah would turn, scowling, hugging her pillow over her head.

"Let me sleep," she murmured. "Go away."